CHRISTOPHER BRAM is the author of two other novels, *Hold Tight*, available in a Plume edition, and *Surprising Myself*. He is also a film critic whose reviews have been published in national publications. His story "Aphrodisiac" became the cornerstone piece in a short story collection of the same name. He makes his home in New York City.

D1379065

ALSO BY
CHRISTOPHER BRAM

Hold Tight

Surprising Myself

IN MEMORY OF ANGEL CLARE

A NOVEL BY

Christopher Bram

A PLUME BOOK

PLUME

Published by the Penguin Group

Penguin Books USA Inc., 375 Hudson Street, New York, New York 10014, U.S.A.
Penguin Books Ltd, 27 Wrights Lane, London W8 5TZ, England
Penguin Books Australia Ltd, Ringwood, Victoria, Australia
Penguin Books Canada Ltd, 2801 John Street, Markham, Ontario, Canada L3R 1B4
Penguin Books (N.Z.) Ltd, 182–190 Wairau Road, Auckland 10, New Zealand

Penguin Books Ltd, Registered Offices: Harmondsworth, Middlesex, England

This is an authorized reprint of a hardcover edition published by
Donald I. Fine, Inc.

First Plume Printing, July, 1990
10 9 8 7 6 5 4 3 2 1

 REGISTERED TRADEMARK—MARCA REGISTRADA

Library of Congress Cataloging-in-Publication Data

Bram, Christopher.
    In memory of Angel Clare : a novel / by Christopher Bram.
       p.   cm.
    "A Plume book."
    "Authorized reprint of a hardcover edition published by Donald
I. Fine, Inc."—T.p. verso.
    ISBN 0-452-26434-0
    I. Title.
PS3552.R281715   1990
813'.54—dc20   89-77097
                                                               CIP

Printed in the United States of America

Set in Trump Mediaeval
Original hardcover design by Irving Perkins Associates

PUBLISHER'S NOTE
This is a work of fiction. Names, characters, places, and incidents are either the
product of the author's imagination or are used fictitiously, and any resemblance to
actual persons, living or dead, events, or locales is entirely coincidental.

BOOKS ARE AVAILABLE AT QUANTITY DISCOUNTS WHEN USED TO PROMOTE PRODUCTS OR
SERVICES. FOR INFORMATION PLEASE WRITE TO PREMIUM MARKETING DIVISION, PENGUIN
BOOKS USA INC., 375 HUDSON STREET, NEW YORK, NEW YORK 10014.

Friends shared their intelligence and experience
with me on this book. I owe special thanks to
Mary Gentile, Henri Cole, Robert Marshall,
John Niespolo, Nancy Nowak and George Coleman.
I thank Eric Ashworth for encouraging me to
tell this story, and Draper Shreeve for
providing more than words can say.

We are born with the dead:
See, they return, and bring us with them.

—T.S. Eliot, "Little Gidding"

1

MICHAEL stood in the Louvre one afternoon and self-consciously looked at paintings. Thin, with pale skin and curly dark hair, he wore a white shirt buttoned at the collar and the dark blazer he thought made him look European. He had been in Paris two weeks, but going to the Louvre sooner would have implied he needed to go there. Michael liked to skip the introductory stages of things, trusting the basics would come to him later. He would have preferred not going to the Louvre at all, but he had run out of obscure places to visit.

He stood in a hall that felt overcast and gloomy, weak light coming through the skylight overhead, the russet walls and muddy canvases making the space seem darker than it was. A handful of people wandered among the pictures, but the squeak of their shoes and occasional whisper of words did not quite belong to them, like poor sound effects added to a movie after it was shot, or like the repressed, unattached sounds inside a hospital. Michael tried to concentrate on a nude male who lay on the corner of a crowded raft. He kept his distance from the painting.

A live boy stepped into the frame.

The boy looked about Michael's age, although Michael found his peers very young compared to himself. The boy stood with his back to Michael and studied the plum-gray nude. He had to be American. He had a canvas shoulder bag and a guidebook, and wore jeans and an oxford cloth shirt. The seat of his jeans had pale spots rubbed away at the base of each cheek, like the gleams that suggest roundness in a painting of an apple. The boy looked like an advertisement for American homosexuality. Michael was annoyed to find him attractive. He had not come here for that.

The boy turned his head, as if to see where the next painting was, and Michael saw a blue eye dart into the corner of the lid and lashes. Michael turned away and faced a picture on the opposite wall: several women and a horse were being slaughtered for a despondent sultan.

He had fallen twice during his two months in Europe. He had wanted to the first time—a friendly Dutch sales-man met between trains in Rotterdam—but had felt so terrible afterward he decided to go back to renouncing sex. The second time had been an accident, at least on his part if not that of the German waiter who had offered him a bed for the night. He felt less bad that time, but still feared such behavior was inappropriate on this trip, con-sidering whose money brought him here.

Michael drifted toward the next room and thought he might look up the "Mona Lisa." There was nothing to look at on the way out but a large, drab painting hung on a temporary wall by the doorway. He stopped and pretended to examine it. Glancing back, he saw the American still loitering beneath the cloudy skylight, making no effort to catch up with Michael.

The wide canvas showed a painter painting, a bearded man with a Peter Pan collar working beside a chubby woman whose arms were folded around her nakedness. A small child stood between them, not looking at the naked woman but at the picture the man painted, which wasn't the woman but a landscape. Stranger still, the space around them was crowded with people in coats and stovepipe hats, a few gazing at the artist and woman but most just sitting there, as if waiting for a train. Michael could not decide if the painting was a philosophical statement about representation and reality, a precursor of surrealism, or a piece of kitsch.

"Courbet. 'The Painter in His Studio.'"

Michael turned. The American stood beside him, peeking at Michael, then back at the painting. He was half a head shorter than Michael and needed a haircut. His lips remained slightly bowed apart when he closed his mouth.

"It's boring," said Michael, the quickest response for suggesting he was intelligent and nobody's fool.

The boy shrugged and smiled. "It's nothing great as art," he admitted. "It's the people that make it interesting."

Michael eased his hands into his pockets to show he was willing to listen.

"That's Gustave Courbet." The boy pointed at the paint-

1 1

er. "Of course. And the woman's his mistress. The little boy's their illegitimate son. The others are Courbet's friends. I think Theophile Gautier's in there somewhere."

He sounded like he knew a lot, but Michael knew more about life itself, which was the important thing.

"And that's Baudelaire." The boy jabbed his finger toward a young man with a shaved head who sat cross-legged on a table. "The poet. *Fleurs du mal?*"

"I know who Baudelaire is." Although he usually confused him with Rimbaud.

The boy was too enraptured with his learning to be stopped by Michael's tone. He spouted some French, then translated it when Michael looked blank. "'Search for my heart no longer. The beasts have eaten it.' It's the only French I know, but I haven't gotten to use it yet." The boy laughed at himself. "See that patch of color beside him? That's where Courbet had Baudelaire's mistress. But Baudelaire didn't want her to be immortalized with him, so he had Courbet paint her out."

"That proves it's a bad painting." Michael declared. "The artist letting his subjects tell him what to do? And it's sexist." Always a handy judgment. "No, it's dull, kitschy, compromised art. Repulsive."

The boy drew a quick breath, as if to argue, then released the breath in a sigh. "I like it," he said, nodded at Michael, and walked away.

Michael was sincerely indignant over the fate of Baudelaire's mistress, but he had condemned the painting only to make intelligent conversation. He had not intended to chase the boy off. He thought a moment, then followed the boy into a room with windows and sunlight.

The boy stood before another painting. He tensed his

shoulders when Michael stopped beside him; he kept his eyes locked on the canvas.

The brass nameplate said, "Ingres." Michael's first impulse was to reopen conversation by saying the name aloud, but he was never certain what to do with the extra consonants. So he said, "Do you have plans for dinner tonight?"

The boy looked at him, surprised.

Michael was surprised, too. He had spoken so rarely during the past weeks his speech had lost touch with his thoughts. But it might be good to have company his last night in Paris. He made a slight smile, to prove he was in earnest. He considered apologizing for Courbet—it must be the boy's favorite painting—but that was best forgotten.

"Yes," said the boy. "I mean—no, I don't have any plans. Did you want to have dinner together?" The boy was suddenly very nervous and interested.

"Just a thought." Michael didn't want to sound desperate. "It's still early. We could go somewhere for drinks or coffee first. Unless you wanted to stay here a little longer."

"Almost closing time. This is my third visit in three days and I've already seen everything twice." The boy laughed at himself again—he really was a boy. "Coffee sounds great. Oh, I'm Tim. Tim Hart." His hand was soft and cold.

"Michael Sousza," said Michael, wondering if this was a mistake.

They left the museum on the side facing the Tuileries. It was late afternoon, and the warm September light stretched the shadows of trees, people, and pebbles across the sandy paths. Green, papery leaves were dusted with bronze; the city traffic sounded very far away. Michael thought about taking Tim up toward the Orangerie to show him what he had discovered a week ago: a terrace in the park where men arranged themselves along the balustrades and benches and eyed each other. Michael had walked through there every day since he stumbled upon it, never talking to anyone, never learning if the men were free or for sale, simply keeping in touch with his knowledge that this spot existed. He wanted to show Tim he knew about things that weren't in books or museums, but decided against it. The boy might think Michael was suggesting they go to bed together.

"Let's go over to the Left Bank," he suggested. "I know a few places near my hotel."

Tim was staying on the Left Bank too, but in a student hostel where he shared a room with five strangers. He stated the fact wistfully, as if explaining why they couldn't go back to his place. As if he already thought Michael had asked him out for that.

The thought felt different when it came from the other person.

"I'm on the Rue Dauphine," said Michael. "Do you mind if we swing by my room? I'd like to wash up first."

"Not at all!"

They walked toward the river and Tim began to talk eagerly about Europe: London, Munich, Florence, Rome. Loved Italy, hated France. The French were so aloof.

"They don't seem bad to me," said Michael. "But then, I live in New York."

"New York? Ah," went Tim, as if that explained something. He was from Illinois and was a junior at Ann Arbor, where he studied art history, of course. He was still young enough that his life could be summed up by his college and major.

They started across a bridge; the Seine looked like it was roofed with bridges. The water below streamed with pleats of green and bronze. Notre Dame stood way off to the left, bone white and square above the pastel trees. The afternoon light settled like old varnish on the buildings crowded together at the end of the bridge.

Tim suddenly stopped. He slowly turned around and took everything in, then leaned against the verdigrised railing and took in Michael.

"You know? I was terribly disappointed with Paris. Until now. It really is a beautiful city."

Michael nodded. The boy looked too soft, padded all around with baby fat. He was younger than anyone Michael had ever slept with, although that was really just one person. "How old are you, Tim?"

"Twenty," he said, as if it were a point of pride. "And you?"

"Twenty-three." Michael resumed walking, embarrassed to have brought up something so literal as age.

Tim was immediately beside him. "I guess New Yorkers age quickly. Emotionally, I mean. You're still quite attractive, you know."

Tim was with him only for sex, Michael decided. If they went back to Michael's room and did it, that would be the end of this. Michael would want to be alone when they were through, and maybe Tim would too. Michael preferred company at dinner tonight to company in bed, although what he really wanted was both.

They reached the other side of the river and the city closed in around them. The sidewalk was very narrow and Michael had to walk in front of Tim. He looked back at him to say, "I'm really thirsty right now. Let's just go straight to a café."

"You don't need to go by your room?" Tim sounded disappointed. "I've never been inside a Paris hotel." He looked annoyed, then confused. "Well, all right." He began to swat the canvas bag at his side.

"We'll have a drink and then go have a nice dinner somewhere."

"Not too nice," Tim muttered. "I'm low on cash."

"Didn't I tell you? I'm buying." Michael hadn't thought of that until now, but he hoped it might work as effectively as sex in keeping Tim with him. He wished he were back in New York, among older friends with whom he didn't have to play games.

Tim still hadn't given him an answer when they reached a corner and stood side by side again. Tim looked like he was about to say something. Finally, he stared at Michael and said, "Are you gay?"

Michael was stunned, the question was so unnecessary, so uncool. He began to smile, but the smile felt condescending, so he suppressed it. "Of course," he said, as kindly as possible. "Aren't you?"

The boy nodded. "Okay. Stupid question, but I had to be sure. If not, I was going to be a nervous wreck all night. Okay then. I have to ask the next question. Is there a *chance* you're interested in me the same way I'm interested in you?"

Michael was touched by the boy's openness, touched and worried for him. "Yes," he said calmly. "But let's spend some time together first. Then see how we feel about each other after dinner."

"Okay. Fair enough." Relieved, the boy burst out laughing. "You must think I'm a real geek," he said, without shame. "I'd never come right out and ask that back home. But here, what've I got to lose if I make an ass of myself? I'll never see the other person again."

"Don't let it bother you," Michael mumbled, and looked for the way to the Boulevard St. Germain. He was glad he had been spared the obnoxious, vulnerable stage Tim was still going through.

After a few blocks, Michael found what he was looking for: the Café de Flore. They took a place in the acre of round tables out front and Tim ordered a beer, Michael a cognac. All around them, well-dressed adults and casually dressed students chattered away in French, columns of smelly blue smoke rising from their plump cigarettes. What was left of the day fell in yellow scraps through the trees along the curb.

Tim gulped his beer, looked very serious and said, "Is it because of AIDS?"

"Is what?" said Michael sharply, then regained himself.

"Your wanting to know me first? I can tell you right off, I haven't been promiscuous. As I'm sure you can tell.'

Michael made a slight shrug, which he tried to clarify with a philosophical wave of his hand.

"I've only done it with six guys and it's always been safe. Lucky for me, the things I like best are all safe." Tim spoke as if the people around them wouldn't understand English; Michael wasn't so sure.

"I was scared to do anything for the longest time because of AIDS. But I realize now I was just using it as another excuse not to take the leap. It's all so abstract to me. I know it's not a hoax, but that's what it feels like sometimes. Living in New York, you probably think about it differently. It's probably old hat to you by now."

There were so many things to say, Michael was tempted to say nothing. But if he were silent, Tim might think *Michael* had it. So Michael said, "You learn to live with it."

Instead of pressing further, Tim said, "I only came out six months ago. Started doing things, I mean. I've been telling people I'm gay ever since I was eighteen."

Luckily, Tim was young and needed to talk about himself. High-school crushes, glimpses of magazines, the novels read in the library, then the conversation after dinner with Mom and Dad: he went into it at length without fearing it might be "old hat" to Michael. Actually, it was all so innocent, so unlike the experience of Michael and everyone he knew it seemed sweetly foreign. Tim had discovered he was gay without any blood being shed, without even dirtying his hands. And then took two years to actually do anything. It was funny hearing the story told backward like that.

Michael finished one cognac, then another, sank down further in his chair and listened. Tim's parents sounded quite liberal and educated, Evanston a more enlightened place than Phillipsburg, New Jersey, but Michael did not feel envious. He could feel affectionate toward the boy from his superior position of experience. He wanted to tell Tim a little about that experience, as a way of preparing the boy for the pain ahead of him. But not yet.

Shifting his legs beneath the table that was little bigger than a dinner plate, Michael brushed his foot against something. That something brushed back, then pressed a knee against Michael's knee. Michael caught the knee between his knees, and lightly squeezed it.

Tim smiled. "You sure you don't want to eat a late dinner?"

"It's so nice here," said Michael. "Why spoil it?" But he held the knob of knee between his thighs and smiled back at Tim. For once in his life, he was the older man, the mentor, the seducer, although Tim didn't require seducing. Michael glanced at the stack of two saucers on the table and wondered if he was drunk. He hadn't eaten anything all day.

"What do you do?" And Tim giggled. "For a living, I mean."

"I'm a male stripper."

Tim giggled again. "I mean really."

"I'm a filmmaker."

"Really?" Tim paused, as if this too might be a tease. "Oh, like experimental shorts. Video or 16 millimeter? I guess nobody does Super 8 anymore."

So the boy knew about film as well as art and literature. Sublimation, Michael thought, those two years between knowing and doing. But he could put Tim in his place. "I did those in the beginning, yes. But feature films now. Well, one feature anyway." Michael heard himself and liked the picture he presented. "Just a low-budget horror film. But one has to start somewhere."

"Yeah? Wow. I had no idea. What's it called? Maybe I saw it."

"*Disco of the Damned.*"

Tim laughed, of course.

"The title was the producer's doing. He said dumb titles are the best sell in that market. We wanted to call it *Nightshade*."

"You know, I think I read about that somewhere," said Tim, surprised by the thought. "Honest. Something about it being better than it sounded?"

Michael became excited. "Jack Arcalli wrote about it in *Film Comment*. In the front section. Jack was a good friend of Clarence's."

"No. I don't read *Film Comment*. But somewhere. Who's Clarence?"

"Clarence Laird. He was the director."

"You didn't direct it?"

Had Michael intended to give that impression? "No. I kind of codirected. Actually, I was more the screenwriter." Which had some truth to it.

"Still. That's really something. Even a cheapo horror film. Some good people got started that way. Are you and Clarence working on something else now?"

"A few possibilities. Nothing definite." But saying that, Michael remembered there were no possibilities now, no future plans, no future. He released Tim's knee and snapped his fingers at the waiter for another cognac. "What's London like?"

He pretended to listen while Tim talked about museums and plays. He let the glow of alcohol in his stomach and face fill up the sudden space inside him.

The sensation of drinking while it was still light, combined with the parade of people on the sidewalk, made him feel as if he were already back in New York. Then he thought he saw Peter Griffith. Michael looked again. He saw a balding man with a red beard who looked very much like Peter. The man stood out on the sidewalk, looking through the smoky air and gesticulating hands of the café, as if at Michael. A stocky woman with iron-gray hair stood with her back to the café and furiously whispered in the man's ear. She glanced over her shoulder, quickly looked away, and tried to haul the man down the street.

"Livy!" Michael shouted, and jumped up. "Livy! Peter!" He stumbled around feet and chairs, hurrying out to the street.

Livy Griffith slowly turned around and faced him. She set her teeth in a grin, crow's feet spreading over her tanned face. Peter smiled more naturally and opened his arms to Michael.

"Hey, hey. Small world," he said with his Carolina drawl, and hugged Michael hello. "We knew you were over here. Never dreamed we'd run into you."

"Michael," said Livy flatly when he hugged her, gingerly patting him on the back.

He stepped away, looked at both of them, then at the street. "You're in Paris," he said. "That's wonderful."

Peter wiggled his eyebrows. "Just for a few days. We fly home tomorrow. I'm doing the poster for a French film they're distributing in America, and they thought I should see the thing here. Little junket to make up for what they're paying me."

"I wish I'd known you were here!" Michael cried. "I've been here two weeks and don't know a soul. We could've seen Paris together."

Peter gave Livy a sidelong glance and Livy said, "Oh, you see plenty of us in New York, Michael. We wouldn't want to spoil your fun." She nodded at the tables beneath the café awning. "And it looks like you know at least *one* soul here."

Michael saw Tim watching them, face propped on his fist, knuckles covering his mouth.

"Just an American tourist I met today. Come over and join us and I'll buy you a drink." He grinned at Tim, gestured at Peter and Livy to follow him, and headed back toward the table, overjoyed to be playing host to the Griffiths.

But when he reached the table, only Peter was with him. Livy stood out on the sidewalk, studying her wristwatch.

"Livy can't join us?"

Peter gritted his teeth inside his beard. "Neither of us can, Michael. We're having dinner with some business people tonight and were on our way back to the hotel to change."

"Aw," Michael groaned. "I wanted to take us all out to dinner." He noticed Tim frowning.

"That's very kind of you." Peter glanced out at Livy. "If we had the time, we would've taken *you* out. But I'm afraid the pursuit of lucre comes first."

"I understand," said Michael, deeply disappointed, faintly hurt. "Oh, this is Tim," he remembered to say. "Tim's an art student. Peter Griffith, the painter." He could at least show Tim the kind of important friends he had.

"More an illustrator nowadays," said Peter, shaking the boy's hand.

"Peter did the poster for the film I was telling you about."

"*Disco of the Damned?*" said Tim.

Peter snorted and shook his head. "Or whatever that

fool producer ended up calling it. Yes, I did that. As a favor for a very close friend of mine. And Michael's," he added. He looked at Michael for a moment, then laid his hand on Michael's shoulder. "So how you doing?" he said softly. "You having a good time on your trip?"

"Of course." But Peter was someone who understood. "There's good days and bad days. It's strangest when I go to places he used to talk about."

"He loved this place, you know."

"I know." But Michael had come alone to the Café de Flore so many times he had forgotten. Would Peter and Livy think ill of him for bringing somebody else here?

"You should enjoy yourself," Peter told him. "You deserve it. He'd want you to enjoy yourself. Youth, freedom, and a bit of money in Paris," he sighed. "I must say I envy you." He gave Michael's shoulder a squeeze and released it. "I better be going. Livy's going to chide me for my long Southern goodbyes. I'm sure we'll see you back in New York. Nice meeting you," he told Tim. "All right then. Bye now." He bowed sideways as he stepped back and didn't turn away completely until he was halfway to the street.

"Have a nice dinner!" Michael called out and waved goodbye to Livy.

Livy lifted her hand and smiled, then took Peter by the arm and hurried him off, her long dark skirt beating around their legs.

Michael remained standing, feeling confused, sad, and oddly content. It was as though he were pleased by the sorrow revived in him by Peter's sympathy. Sorrow felt more genuine than all his petty doubts and anxieties.

Tim looked bucktoothed and younger than ever after

Peter and Livy. He seemed to be thinking something out.

Michael sat down. "What a coincidence! Those are two of my very best friends." Which was an exaggeration, but meeting anyone in a foreign place elevated them in importance. "Don't let Peter fool you. He's still a very good painter. The poster he did for us was as good as anything you see in SoHo."

"I was afraid at first they were friends of your parents. But they're your friends?" Tim hesitated. "They didn't seem very friendly. Especially the woman."

"No?" The thought had crossed Michael's mind too, but he didn't trust it. "They had to be somewhere," he insisted. "You have to know them. And Livy's that way. She plays the oboe."

"The guy you two were talking about? That was Clarence?"

"Clarence Laird, yes."

"He was your boyfriend?"

The question startled Michael. His conversation with Peter had given him away. He tried being very still and stoical. He nodded his head.

"I know it's none of my business, but—"

It did not feel right to tell Tim about Clarence. It was too intimate and important a fact to waste on a stranger. And yet, Michael felt a sudden urge to be wasteful with everything he had been saving.

"He's dead now?" said Tim.

"Yes."

"Oh God. I'm sorry. I really am. That's really awful." Tim contorted his face over it, grimaced and blinked, embarrassed at having asked something he did not know how to respond to. Then he said, "AIDS," in a voice so reverent there wasn't room for it to sound like a question.

Michael nodded, finding it perfectly natural the boy already knew.

"I'm sorry. Damn. When?"

"Last October."

"Almost a year then."

He sounded faintly relieved, as if that were a long time ago. Time had stood so still since then that Michael could not believe it was almost a year.

But the look Tim gave him remained full of embarrassed wonder and awe. He looked at Michael as if Michael were more real than anything he had ever seen. It was a strangely flattering look. He reached out and touched Michael on the arm, sadly, boldly, as if to prove he weren't afraid of touching him.

"I don't have it," said Michael. "Not even the antibodies."

Tim let go, flustered to have his thought read. "That's good. That must be a big relief to you." He held his hand in midair a moment, then returned it to his lap.

"He was thirty-eight," Michael announced. "Everything was coming together for him. For us. Careerwise. But we were everything to each other. 'Boyfriend' wasn't the right word for either of us. We were together three years, you see."

Michael began calmly, wanting the boy to think about Clarence and not him. But as he continued he found himself touching emotions he had kept packed down since he left New York. Sadness came back to him changed, more physical than he remembered it being. The rich, warm sorrow that had begun when Peter Griffith touched his shoulder grew until Michael could feel it in his eyes.

"He was a wonderful person," Michael declared. "He was the first man I ever loved. He was handsome, wise, and talented. We were going to go to Europe when we finished our movie. We were so close. His death is the most important thing that'll ever happen to me . . ."

He was crying now and couldn't continue. He lowered his head, trying to keep the tears from running down his face, but his eyes only filled more quickly. He couldn't breathe without sobbing, so he tried not to breathe. When he finally took a breath, it felt so good to sob and blubber he couldn't stop. He let himself cry, enjoying the sensation of grief washing away everything.

Then it was over. He tried shuddering up another wave of tears, but he was dry. He looked up and found Tim's face next to his, pale and staring, the boy's arm wrapped around his shoulders, the other hand gripping Michael's beneath the table. Biting his lower lip, Tim looked sweetly helpless.

"It's all right. It's okay," he whispered. "You'll be okay. Maybe we should—" He hunted around the table, then rummaged in his canvas bag, but all he could offer Michael to blow his nose with was a map of Paris.

Michael smiled politely and shook his head. He sniffed his nose clear and looked around. The people at the nearest tables were silent, their eyes averted.

But instead of feeling ashamed, Michael was proud he had cried in public. And at the Café de Flore. Grief was such a pure, honest emotion.

2

"WE really should have had a drink with him," Peter moaned, "but Livy was adamant. And you know Livy."

Jack Arcalli nodded. He certainly knew Livy and her faintly nervous decisiveness, and he knew Peter too. He suspected Peter had wanted to avoid Michael as much as his wife did, but had been too much the Southern gentleman to admit it to himself.

"She insisted she hadn't come all the way to Paris to be trapped for another evening with Michael. So we made our excuses and snuck off. We had to sit *inside* Deux Magots for fear Michael might see us if we sat out front. We didn't want to hurt his feelings," Peter quickly added. "And it's not that Michael's really so terrible. He's just not very interesting company. None of *us* were at that age. Poor Michael."

"Poor Michael," Jack uncomfortably agreed. "You sure you don't have time for a cup of coffee?"

Jack and Peter stood in the lobby of the Brill Building, where they had run into each other, Peter on his way in to see a distributor, Jack on his way out after a screening. It was late afternoon outside and spokes of light spun through the cool, shadowy lobby each time another lawyer or messenger came through the brass-trimmed revolving door. They had been standing here talking for five minutes.

Peter tapped the portfolio under his arm. "I have to get upstairs and show these sketches. But we really should get together sometime soon."

"We should," said Jack, knowing it might be months before they did. Peter Griffith confused him. Warm and effusive each time they met, grinning in his friendly red beard, Peter seemed to promise friendship yet had never delivered on that promise. Jack didn't know if he misread Peter because Peter was straight, or because he himself was single and had different expectations.

In his usual dutiful manner, Peter still didn't say goodbye. "You're back in the city for good?"

"I only got away for a couple of weeks," said Jack. "The Jersey shore with my mother and aunt."

"You don't look like you got much sun."

Jack gestured at his bulky body and smirked. "This isn't a shape one parades around in a swimsuit."

"You're not the only one," laughed Peter, patting his own paunch and bowing his head to show Jack his pink bald spot. "The joys of pushing the big Four-O."

Peter had in fact a few years to go yet. Jack was thirty-nine but already felt like he was in his fifties. Jack protected himself by thinking ahead. He had felt forty when he was thirty and thirty when he was twenty. He had never felt twenty.

"But Michael seemed in good spirits?" Jack asked.

"Quite happy, yes. I was glad to see he's enjoying his trip. He certainly deserves it."

"He does. Did he say how much longer he's staying over there?"

Peter couldn't remember. When Michael left for Europe a couple of months ago, his plans were wide open. Jack hadn't given any thought to the boy these past weeks and was annoyed to find Michael weighing on his consciousness again.

"Well, I better get upstairs to fight the philistines in sales," said Peter. "But we'll talk. You seeing Laurie and Carla anytime soon?"

"As always."

"Give them my love."

"My love to Livy."

They shook hands and Peter headed for the elevators, looking back at Jack with an apologetic grin, the courteous Southerner to the end.

Walking toward the subway, Jack did not feel like going downtown to his apartment, where nothing waited for him except his cat and the chore of reviewing the movie he just saw. Chatting with Peter made him hungry for a real conversation, which he could have with Laurie. She should be getting home around now. He went down the steps to the uptown train without bothering to call her first. There was no feeling of duty or ceremony between

Jack and Laurie. Today was Monday and he knew she'd be in.

The train was crowded and Jack had to stand on the ride uptown, unable to look over the publicity packet from the screening or pull out the paperback of *The Old Curiosity Shop* that was his subway reading this month. He hung on a bar and found himself swaying beside his reflection in a darkened window. *He* still had a full head of hair, unlike Peter. Ben Slover was losing his hair, too, through politics or life with Danny. But Jack lived alone and kept his hair, although it was full of gray now. The reflection in the window was too weak to show the threads like steel wool in his full black beard or the permanent bags under his eyes, but Jack knew they were there. All of them were growing old, the women more gracefully than the men. It was still odd to remember that Clarence would never be forty. Jack wondered why Peter Griffith's distance bothered him: Peter had been Clarence's friend, not Jack's.

He got off at Ninety-sixth Street, walked down Broadway, then stepped briskly downhill toward the river, to the homey loaf of stone and windows near Riverside Drive. He pressed the button for Laurie and Carla's apartment.

"Who is it?"

"Jack. Just happened to be in the neighborhood."

"Great. Come on up."

She buzzed him in, and Jack entered Clarence's building. Even after a year he still thought of the building as Clarence's. There were days when Jack barely noticed that fact, and days when it was very important to him.

Laurie Frazier was waiting for him in Clarence's door

when the elevator opened. "Perfect timing, Jack-o. Just got home."

She still wore one of the suits with floppy bows she put on when she spent the afternoon at her investment service's parent company. Overdoing the corporate look was Laurie's way of staying ironic about her work. Her short blond hair was still brushed down in its executive mode, but her shoes were off, her feet blurred by nylons. She went up on her toes and Jack bent down when they kissed each other hello. Her grin was lopsided, as if she had something else on her mind.

"Don't let me interrupt anything," said Jack, stepping past her into the long front hallway.

"Nothing to interrupt. I had a feeling you'd show up." She closed the door and followed him down the hall.

Walking by the bathroom, Jack glanced in and saw women's things. Walking by the spare bedroom, he saw a suitcase and green garment bag sitting on the bed.

"Oh." He stopped and stared into the room. "*Michael*'s back?"

"Yup. Buzzed us out of bed yesterday morning." Laurie stepped around him and continued to the kitchen. "Tea? I was just about to put some on."

Jack pictured Michael still sitting in a sidewalk café in Paris. It was a shock to see his things on the bare mattress. He joined Laurie in the large, dark kitchen. "Peter told me they saw him in Paris just last week."

"Well, he flew back on Sunday," Laurie said wearily. "Tea tea or herbal?"

"I'll fix the tea. You finish changing."

Jack wasn't eager to talk about Michael either, and he

knew Laurie hated remaining dressed like that at home. She padded out of the kitchen, already mussing her hair with both hands.

Michael was back. So what? They knew he'd be back sometime. Jack tried telling himself it wasn't important while he glanced over Laurie and Carla's unopened mail on the painted breakfront. He put on water for tea, then rinsed out the teapot and set out two mugs. He looked in the refrigerator to see if they had something sweet for him to nibble.

"Have an apple!" Laurie shouted from the bedroom.

Jack took an apple, although he had wanted something artificial. "Where's Michael now?" he called out.

"Off to Connecticut. To see Ben and Danny."

"Whatever for?"

"Danny told him to come if he got back in time. And he wanted to see some letters Ben took with him." She stopped in the kitchen door on her way to the bathroom, looking more herself in jeans and a bra. "Fine by me. It gives me time to decide how to tell him."

"You still want Michael out."

"Yes," Laurie said firmly. "Back in a jiff," and she went down the hall.

Jack quietly groaned to himself. Waiting for the water to boil, he ate his apple and wandered out into the dining room, the living room, then around the corner into the deep alcove that Laurie used as her office. It was a wonderfully huge apartment, one room opening into another under high ceilings, an apartment you could waltz in. Jack never felt as big and clumsy here as he did in other private spaces. He often regretted not having had the money to buy the place himself. If he had, would *he* want Michael here?

The building had been going co-op when Clarence died. Jack didn't understand all the legal technicalities, but Clarence's right as a tenant to purchase the apartment at an insider's reduced price was retained by his brother in Danville, Virginia. The brother sold that right to Laurie and Carla for a reasonable sum. Jack encouraged them to take the apartment. The women wanted to move out of their shoebox studio after Laurie's recent financial success and were the only ones in their circle who could afford the place. Jack had his selfish reasons for wanting them to buy. This way, he could still come here, still visit a past that might otherwise be sealed off to him.

The past expressed itself chiefly in absences this afternoon. A framed anti-nuke poster hung on the living room wall where there had been a brown photo of a boy in knickerbockers, a French foyer card for *The Conformist*, and the collage Clarence had made himself that featured a famous athlete in jockey shorts standing in a cornfield with Marcel Proust and Charlie Chaplin. Jack had the collage in his kitchen now, but he often missed seeing it here.

The untuned baby grand in the alcove, always layered with art books, storyboards, and cigarette ash, had been replaced with filing cabinets and a desk heaped with newspapers—Laurie's success came when she branched out from tax preparation into socially responsible investing. The great black camelback sofa was gone. Even the ashtrays were gone. Laurie and Carla did not own enough things, or care enough, to redo the apartment and make it completely theirs. But the only real physical evidence of Clarence was a long gouge across the dining room floor left by his rented Steenbeck film editor. And, once again, there was his last boyfriend.

Michael was back, like an obnoxious ghost. Jack found it both sad and ridiculous. The spirit of their talented, contented, gentle friend hung on in the form of an arrogant boy. There had been many boyfriends in the twenty years Jack had known Clarence, although none so young. Yet it was the youngest who was there at the end, then through the end and after, long after his presence made sense. Clarence's brother, a Fundamentalist but a decent man, did not contest the will. All money remaining after the apartment was sold and the debts were paid went to Michael: $37,000. But instead of using the money to start a new life, or going wild with it as some feared, Michael set the money aside and stayed put. He continued to live in the spare bedroom where he slept when Clarence became ill. He never saw anyone except Clarence's friends, not understanding they had been his friends, too, only out of deference to Clarence.

Nobody actively disliked Michael, and they weren't indifferent to his situation. They had been touched at first to see such loyalty to their friend, then worried when Michael's mourning continued. Then they became irritated. Jack often questioned the emotions beneath the irritation. Being bored with Michael was natural enough, but he wondered if they were annoyed and sometimes angry because Michael was behaving in a way they felt they should behave. A friend had died and yet they went on with their lives. Jack went on with his life, too, but, unlike the others, Jack was single. He felt he was more conscious of Clarence's absence than they were, conscious enough to want to look past his irritation with Michael to the sympathy and respect he had for the boy. Jack and Michael had something in common.

Jack was pouring tea when Laurie strolled into the kitchen, the sleeves of her flannel shirt rolled up and the shirttail out. She saw the publicity pack. "Good movie?"

"Wretched. More misunderstood teens. God but I don't want to write another what-does-this-tell-us-about-society review."

"None of the boys took off their pants?"

"No. And they were too cute and insipid for me to care." Jack was annoyed when Laurie teased him about sex; there was always a note of condescension. But he sounded condescending when he teased her about being politically correct on Wall Street. Their friendship included stepping on each other's toes. "Speaking of cute and insipid . . ."

Laurie sighed. "Okay. I don't *want* to throw him out. But it's gone on much too long. And I resent his blind assumption this is still his home. I know you think it's a humongous apartment, Jack. But Michael takes up a lot of psychic space. It was heaven while he was gone. Carla and I discussed it last night. When he gets back from Connecticut, we're going to tell him, nicely, that he has a month to find his own place."

Jack nodded understandingly, then said, "He's going to feel rejected."

"Well? We *are* rejecting him." Laurie frowned. "We know he's been through a terrible experience. We do feel sorry for him. But we can't continue to baby him. How would you like to live with Ego in Arcadia?"

It was Jack's phrase, coined in a fit of irritation. As if

their lives were remotely Arcadian. "I wouldn't," he admitted. "I just wish there were a gentler way."

"I'd hoped that once he got out of his room and had some fun in Europe, he'd be able to go off on his own. But it was embarrassing how happy he was to see me and Carla yesterday. Like we were his mother."

"Have you talked with Livy since they got back?"

She hadn't, so Jack finished telling her what Peter told him.

"He was with a boy?" said Laurie. "Maybe that's what he needs."

"I doubt he's jumping into anything after what he's been through." For some reason, the idea of Michael becoming romantically involved disturbed Jack. "What I'm saying is we can't *all* start snubbing Michael. It could be traumatic for him."

"But Jack! Michael doesn't notice he's being snubbed. I've been cool to him for months and it still hasn't sunk in. He dismisses it as my acting butch, which infuriates me."

Jack understood. He once told Michael off for a racist remark, and the boy treated it as just more dry wit from old Jack the curmudgeon. Remembering the boy's refusal to take him seriously made Jack angry all over again. "If he's too impossible for you and Laurie, maybe Michael *should* live with me."

"Are you serious?"

"It's not fair that you and Carla are stuck with him."

"You don't have enough room in your place to swing a cat, pardon the expression."

"Which should be enough to force anyone to look for an apartment. That and living with me." He wondered why he suggested this. "Tell Michael you need his room for something and I said he could stay with me until he found his own place. That'll sound friendlier than hitting him with a one-month deadline."

"He'll take you up on it, Jack. And then you'll never get rid of him."

"That'll be my problem."

Laurie considered the suggestion, then considered Jack. "It's penance, isn't it?" she said. "For not liking Michael."

Jack hadn't thought that yet, but would have without Laurie. "Probably. You know me."

"And Clarence is in there somewhere."

"Of course."

Laurie groaned and shook her head. "Oh, Jack-o. When you step down from art into real life, you show what a romantic masochist you really are."

It was an old accusation, part of the game of identities they played with each other where Laurie saw Jack as Art and herself as Real Life. That was shorthand for their differences, two poses they had assumed in college but no longer treated as concrete fact. But they did use each other to define themselves. Actually, Jack saw Clarence as Art and Laurie as Morality, with himself caught somewhere in between. He wondered how he would redefine himself now that Clarence was gone.

"The thing is," said Laurie, "we might have to take you up on it. Short of changing the locks, it might be the only way of getting Michael out of here."

"I'm perfectly serious," Jack insisted.

"I believe you. Well, let's run it past Carla when she gets home and see what she thinks." Even Real Life needed to consult a professional counselor, which was what Carla did at LGMH—Lesbian/Gay Mental Health.

They drank more tea and tried to talk about other things: Laurie's disturbing discovery that the high-heeled weasel she dealt with at the brokerage firm was also a lesbian; Jack's last book review in the *Village Voice* and the obnoxious head they'd given it. But Jack had to come back to the important subject.

"When's he due back?"

"Michael? He didn't say. When he finishes reading these important letters of Clarence's, or when Ben and Danny's fights drive him away. Whichever comes first," Laurie muttered. "When did Clarence ever write letters?"

"Very rarely. But he wrote quite a few the first time he went to Europe. Ben said he wanted to use his to do a little memoir, something to make up for that self-serving obituary he wrote for the *Native.* But the letters Ben got were nothing but sexploits. I got the ones about art and places, which are more like Clarence."

"Interesting," said Laurie. "I never knew Clarence could write."

Jack narrowed his eyes at her.

"I mean he was so visual! Don't look at me like that. I swear, Jack. You can be as bad as Michael. Clarence was not without faults. You certainly complained about them enough over the years."

Jack nodded sheepishly. He suspected Laurie had a distorted image of Clarence after years of Jack's criticisms. Because she wasn't close to Clarence, Jack had told her things he otherwise would have kept to himself. "He wasn't stupid. I sometimes think that's the impression you have of him."

"It's not. His movies weren't my style, but I never thought a stupid person made them. Their latent misogyny disturbed me, as you know."

Jack thought the misogyny was all in Laurie's eye, but he did not feel like having that argument today.

A lock clacked in the distance, a door opened, and Carla sang out, "Home!"

"We're in the kitchen!" Laurie called back, adding, "Just Jack. Don't worry."

Carla swung around the corner, wearing jeans and a jean jacket and carrying a briefcase. Her brown hair sat neatly on her head like a cap of owl feathers.

"Why, Jack!" she chirped. "When did you get back?" It was Carla's professional chirp, used at home only when she was tired and wished you weren't there. "Pooty!" she told Laurie, who had stood up to kiss and hug her.

"It's so good to have you home," Laurie sang, and they cuddled for a minute or so. They looked like little girls in each other's arms.

Jack watched and smiled patiently. He thought Laurie and Carla overdid the affection, but there was no irony here. And he assumed they behaved the same way even if no witnesses were present. This was their gestalt, their method for dealing with the complications of living together, just as violent arguments were Ben and Danny's. Jack wondered which mode he would fall into if he ever lived with someone.

"Damn, it's good to be out of the Center today," Carla groaned, sinking into a chair while Laurie started another pot of tea. "You know what your damn friend Ben did before he went off on vacation?"

"He's your friend, too," said Jack.

Carla only grimaced and told another Ben story. Ben Slover worked with her at LGMH, although, as a busy political activist, he tended to use his position as just a base of operations, something that gave him a title and salary while he ran around speaking at rallies, giving interviews on television, and founding new organizations. Carla was supposed to counsel the distressed, while Ben handled the paperwork, but Carla was often stuck with finishing jobs Ben had only started. "So I have no qualms about sticking him with Michael," she told Laurie.

"Oh. Carla"—Laurie became uncharacteristically deferential when she spoke to her partner seriously—"Jack and I have been talking and Jack has a suggestion."

Jack let Laurie do the talking. Carla quietly listened until Laurie finished, then smirked knowingly at Jack. "I thought Michael wasn't your type?"

"Don't be silly." He knew she'd think that. "I have no ulterior motives. I just felt it was time I do my bit to help you and Laurie."

Carla nodded, in the same noncommittal way she probably nodded at clients.

"I don't think of Michael sexually. I don't think of *anyone* sexually anymore, but I know Michael too well to even think of thinking it."

"He's right," said Laurie. "Jack can't stand Michael. And he's not a chickenhawk."

"Neither was Clarence," said Carla.

"Clarence isn't Jack," Laurie argued.

"And there was something else going on with Clarence," Jack pointed out.

Carla's calm, challenging look never wavered, until she

suddenly burst out laughing. Carla had the unaffected laugh of an exuberant child. "I don't know why I should be trying to talk you out of it," she said. "It would certainly make our job easier. Sure. Why not?" But she did not think they should be as completely tenderhearted and dishonest with Michael as Jack proposed. It was time to tell Michael enough was enough and that hiding in his grief was bad for him as well as annoying to others. Maybe they could use the excuse of needing the room as a way of bringing that up, explaining this was something they should have settled long ago. "Whatever. We can't let it drag on like it did before. Damn. I say things like that to clients every day. But it's different when you share a roof with them and you have to live with the consequences. Oh well. I'm Michaeled-out for the day. I just want a quiet evening at home," she cried. "Alone with my Pooty." Carla leaned over and laid her head on Laurie's shoulder.

Jack took that as his cue to leave. He stood up, shook their hands, and kissed each of them on the cheek. Laurie promised him that, whatever they told Michael, they'd do their best not to stick Jack with a worse wreck than the boy already was.

Riding down in the elevator, Jack hoped Michael would turn up his nose at the offer. His apartment really was too small for two difficult people.

Out on the street, the city was beginning to feel like autumn. There was a smell of fall fermenting in the trees that Jack could not remember ever smelling on this street. Then he realized that it wasn't what he smelled but what he didn't smell that was different. His clothes usually reeked of cigarette smoke when he left Clarence's building. No more. He was like a man whose house had disappeared in a bomb blast and would spend the rest of his life suddenly remembering trivial objects and forgotten keepsakes that had vanished in the explosion.

Walking up the hill toward the subway, he pictured the apartment. Remembered instead of seen, vague and mental again, it was easier to remember Clarence living there. Jack suddenly pictured "Angel Clare" racing around the room, pulling down volumes of Raphael, Botticelli, and George Hurrell when words failed him in his passionate attempt to describe the man who had come to fix the telephone. Or the more serious Clare hunched over the rented Steenbeck as if at a sewing machine, so beatifically absorbed in snipping and matching bits of film that he would forget Jack was still there. Then Clarence shakily sitting up on the camelback sofa the afternoon Jack brought the issue of *Film Comment* with his article about him. That had been a September day like today, roughly a year ago.

Jack visited almost every day that month, when Clarence seemed to wax and wane like a moon—even then, Jack tried to protect himself with metaphors. Slim to begin with, Clarence looked like the long bones of himself, bundled in a sweater and sweatpants despite the warm day. His neck seemed longer and his nose more prominent. "I'm turning into Jean Cocteau," he laughed. He laughed several times when Jack read him the article, careful laughs so he wouldn't start coughing. Jack had wanted the piece to be funny while making clear that this cheesy horror film with the embarrassing title was far below the director's abilities. It was the least he could do for Clarence, publicizing his friend without publicizing the illness. Clarence's first fear when he was diagnosed, stronger than his fear of death, was that nobody would hire him to do another movie, a real movie this time, if they thought he might not live long enough to finish it. He sighed when Jack finished—every breath sounded like a sigh though—and thanked him for the fifteen minutes of fame.

"You'll get a whole hour when you do your next film," Jack told him, or something like that.

Clarence smiled at Jack, a smile that looked more cynical than tolerant on his thin face. Then he said that if worse came to worst, looking on the bright side, his friends would never know what a terrible filmmaker he really might be. He seemed genuinely relieved by that idea. "I'll be remembered as all potential and promise. It's almost as good as being a precocious teenager again."

Jack told him he was being silly and had the wrong attitude, but he thought to himself that if *he* were to die that day there would be no mystery about who Jack Arcalli was. That he was all he ever would be. No matter how deeply you love someone, you selfishly use their death to imagine your own.

Clarence apologized for being "spacey," but he hadn't slept well the night before and needed another nap. Jack said no apology was necessary, gently squeezed his bird-like shoulder—a kiss or hug might seem like he was saying goodbye forever—and left, wishing hard the pneumonia would go into complete remission.

Even then, he did not like to think or say, "Clarence has AIDS." The word was loaded with so much moralizing and

43

politics that it reduced Clarence's dying to a statistic, a social trend; it denied him a personal death. Jack might have felt differently if he knew others with the disease, but Jack lived in a small circle and all he knew were acquaintances of acquaintances and what he read in the newspaper. The word also had a sexual aura that made Jack uncomfortable. He knew the disease was not really about sex, that to say AIDS was punishment for sex was like saying the cholera epidemics of the nineteenth century were punishment for the capitalism and free trade that spread them—Laurie's analogy. But Jack still *felt* a connection. That Clarence had AIDS and Jack was spared seemed like the final proof that Clarence had lived a full life and Jack hadn't. He knew it was the most perverse expression of survivor's guilt imaginable.

Was it during that visit or another that Michael stood waiting for him in the door to the spare bedroom on Jack's way out? It was always a shock that skin and bones could look gawky but healthy after seeming so sickly. Michael wore T-shirts with funny sayings and baggy gym shorts when he was home. Jack usually stopped by his room to ask if he needed anything, although Ben came by twice a week to help with the shopping. But this time Michael was waiting for Jack, and he whispered him into his room, importantly, as if he needed to talk about Clarence. Jack had tried several times to get the boy to share his feelings, without success. He sat beside Michael on the bed and felt very sad and sympathetic over what he thought he was going to hear. Instead, Michael read him a poem he had written, a thin complaint without meter about how he hated his father for being fat and working-class and obsessed with status. He wanted to know where to send it for publication. It was as though he didn't know the man in the next room was dying.

He knew now. Or acted like he did. And Michael's family *had* broken off from him, although Michael seemed more pleased than hurt by that. But Jack was furious with Michael for having been so oblivious when Clarence was dying, only to carry on now as if he were the only person on earth who remembered Clarence. Jack had known Clarence almost twenty years; Michael had known him only three. Jack tried to forgive and understand, but it was difficult when he was alone.

3

CONTINUING this blow-by-blow (so to speak)
account of a tramp abroad, Vienna was all
window-shopping, until I sat on a bench one
night outside the Ratshaus—imagine building a
house for rats—looking at my map when a big,
kind, cleanshaven, shorthaired, thirty-ish Aus-
trian kindly asked if I was lost and sat down
beside me to tell me I should visit some of Vienna's many churches. He pointed to them on the
map in my lap, poking at the map until I began to
notice—smart boy—how many churches were
located in the vicinity of my penis. When I did
not scurry off, he offered to give me a personal
tour of the nearby university, which was closed
for the night, if I was curious about Hapsburg

*architecture. He showed me a dark baroque
courtyard where he groped me, a darker neoclas-
sical vestibule where he kissed me, and a well-lit
contemporary toilet where the rest is silence. So
I've finally done it in a toilet, which was anticli-
mactic, so to speak, after the Englishman who
carried his own roll of toilet paper in the Tro-
cadero. Cut to: a smoky coffeehouse later that
evening where an old man whose English was
even worse than mine asked me if I was "a
Christ." He meant Christian of course but he was
so sincere and I so polite that it was almost like
chasing away the postcoitals talking with Jack
in the caf after a night of forgetting the unre-
quiteds for Larry Breaststroke in a horny visit to
you. (Please don't show this letter or the other to
Jack! We don't want to spoil his innocence and I
rather he not even know I was gay until he
knows he is. And he is. I know it.)*

Michael was wondering if he should go to Vienna after
all, when he looked up from the letter and remembered he
sat outside a house near Norwich, Connecticut. But he
really felt as though he were still in Europe, still un-
moored in the world and just passing through. His brief
stop by the apartment yesterday had not been enough to
make him feel he was home.

He had never been to this place and it was as foreign as a
corner of Europe. Michael sat in a redwood chair on a shelf
of lawn terraced a few feet above a country road, the lawn
going back just a few feet before it ended against a rocky

hillside scabbed with lichen and topped by scrub pine. Below, in the orchard on the other side of the road, checkers of shadow played over the long grass and collapsed stone wall. The long shelf of lawn was in the sun, but Michael kept to the shade of a tree at the far end, sweating in his white dress shirt and gray slacks. The house itself stood at the other end of the shelf, built into the hillside and looking very red, restored, and quaint. Ben and Danny were house- and dog-sitting for Ben's sister and brother-in-law. Michael had arrived by train the previous evening and only now was getting to his real purpose in being here.

He riffled through the folder of letters in his lap—a motley assortment of different kinds of paper, all covered with the same perfect handwriting—and looked again at the sawtoothed sheet of notebook paper in his hand. Clarence's letters weren't what he expected. He wasn't sure what he had expected during his lonely week after Paris, when he remembered Ben mentioning the letters and suddenly wanted to see them. Michael had no letters of his own, not even a postcard; Clarence telephoned the few times they were apart. But Ben's letters were all from 1972, long before Clarence knew Michael, before Clarence really became Clarence. He didn't even sound like Clarence here, the Clarence he knew, whose speech was full of unfinished sentences and desperate noises and thoughts he could express only with his hands. These letters had his headlong rush, but they were campy, which Clarence wasn't, and they prattled about sex with a glee that was positively adolescent. Michael wasn't disturbed by the amount of sex Clarence seemed to be having fifteen years ago, although he wondered if Clarence was actually saying he had slept with Ben. What disturbed Michael was that there was no mention of *him*. He was eight years old when these letters were written and such a distant past seemed irrelevant, but he felt strangely hurt that there wasn't even a wish, or place, in Clarence's thoughts for someone like Michael.

There was shouting inside the house: Ben and Danny were fighting again.

"You can't go outside like that! What'll the neighbors say?"

"Listen to the big radical! What neighbors?"

"People drive by on their way home, dammit!"

"You think two old hippies like your sister and brother-in-law are going to care who sees me like this?"

The tall house was implausibly compact, like the exterior of a house in a play, and every word was audible outside. The big white dog continued to doze on her chain by the door, a heap of angel-hair, already accustomed to the noisy fighting. Michael was accustomed to it, too, but he believed there was something flawed and cowardly about Ben and Danny for them to fight like this and still be together. He would never stay with anyone who shouted at him the way they shouted at each other. They had been on their best behavior last night and this morning, overjoyed to have a guest. They had been so sweet and attentive over dinner, teasing each other while they asked Michael about Europe, food, and men, that Michael had become worried they might ask him to join them in bed. Ben and Danny had a reputation for threeways. Now they were back to their old selves.

"Get off my case!" Danny cried. "You're just bored because there's nobody to make speeches at out here!"

"And you're getting at me because you didn't get any summer stock!" Ben snarled.

"I would've if I didn't have to temp and provide this household with *one* decent income!"

"You'll get your turn! What I'm doing right now just happens to be more important than your *occasional* flings with acting."

"Important to your ego, fucker!"

"Fuck off!"

Boots banged down stairs inside the house. The screen door was kicked open and Ben charged out, arms folded tightly across his chest. Jesse, the dog, jumped to her feet and went wild with joy, thinking Ben was here to take her for a walk. "Cool it," Ben told the dog, and stood there, breathing deeply and glaring up at a window. Then he saw Michael at the other end of the lawn, smiled sheepishly, undid his arms, and ambled toward him as if nothing were wrong.

"Well," he said, touching Michael on the arm. "Great to be out of the city, isn't it? Nothing like a little peace and quiet."

Ben Slover was short, which surprised people who had seen him only on the local news or up on a podium. His auburn hair was combed back to show his receding hairline, which was supposed to make up for the seriousness he lost when he shaved off his mustache last year. His upper lip looked very long, mild and flexible after being covered for so long. Clarence had a mustache when Michael first met him.

Standing beside the chair, Ben was reading over Michael's shoulder. "Oh yeah. The good old days. What do you make of all that?"

Michael almost covered the letter before he remembered it had been written to Ben. "Oh. It seems like a very long time ago," he said.

"It was. Back then it took some of us forever to enjoy what we were doing, although it didn't stop us from doing it. Guilt and self-hatred. Your generation was spared all that. But now, we all have something besides ourselves to be scared of."

Michael nodded solemnly. He wondered if it would be tacky to ask Ben if he had slept with Clarence in college.

"I'd be interested in hearing your perspective on those letters when you finish reading them," said Ben. "It's a good thing I brought them with me, even if I never got to writing my memoir of Clare. The best laid plans of mice and Ben." He laughed and touched Michael's arm again. Danny touched because that was just the way he talked to people, but Ben seemed to have to think about touching. "I was going down to the grocery to pick up stuff for tonight. You need anything? Toothpaste? Razor blades? Condoms?"

"Uh, nothing, thank you."

Ben faced the house and shouted, "My reason for living! What do you want for dinner tonight?"

Danny's voice hollered out, "Your balls on a plate!"

Ben turned back to Michael, faked a laugh, and went over to the dog, who sat there looking demented with her pale, ice-blue eyes and her tongue hanging out of her black lips. "How about a walk, Jesse Dog?" Ben unhooked her, snapped on her leash, and she promptly hauled him down the stone steps to the road. Bouncing along to keep up with her, Ben went up the road past Michael and out of sight.

Michael wondered about Ben's mention of condoms,

which could be a harmless joke, then the razor blades. Had he forgotten Michael's state of mind?

The screen door squealed open. Danny came out, carrying a blanket and wearing a broad-brimmed straw hat and bright red bikini briefs.

The sight was obscene, or surreal. The colored underwear called too much attention to itself. The body was smoothly muscled, just enough to look naked, not discreetly dressed in muscles. With straight black hair and hairless olive skin, Danny Padilla looked Puerto Rican, which he was, but he spoke the accentless English of any New York actor. "Ah. Nobody here but us chickens," he said as he tiptoed barefoot over the grass.

"I am not chicken," Michael said curtly.

Danny wasn't either. He was thirty, but being younger than Ben, he sometimes played "the boy," just as he sometimes played the fishwife, the jaded queen, or even the street-smart Puerto Rican.

"No. You're not chicken," Danny replied. "You're an old fart. Loosen up, Mikey. I was just joking." He opened up the blanket and spread it on the grass. "I'm not letting this last gorgeous day go to waste. Screw the neighbors. You should get a little sun yourself, Michael. There's plenty of room on this blanket if you'd like to join me."

"Thank you, no."

Danny shrugged and stretched out on his back, the pale soles of his feet spread apart and his crotch aimed at Michael. He pulled the hat down, peeked at Michael from under the brim, then sat the hat squarely over his face and lay perfectly still. In a few minutes, the curves and crests of his torso were shiny with perspiration.

Michael turned sideways so he wouldn't have to look at

Danny. He undid a few buttons on his shirt so he wouldn't feel overdressed. Connecticut became very quiet and simple again. Michael resumed reading the letter where the ink changed from black to green.

That was my single encounter with Vienna sausage. The rest of my stay was nothing but art and beauty and three glorious nights at the Stadtsoper, which I know you don't want to hear about, but on the night train to Venice yesterday —I'm in Venice now, can't you feel the sunlight and water?—I shared a compartment with a pretty German boy with beautiful blond shoulder-length hair and shallow Tadzio eyes. Too young and shallow for my tastes, really, maybe eighteen or nineteen, but it was three whole days since I got kissed in the vestibule and I was so horny I could feel it in my teeth. When you consider I went twenty-two years without getting kissed anywhere— Anyway, I thought he was too young to offer a cig to, my usual icebreaker and the chief reason why I'm smoking now, so I offered him a cookie, or biscuit as we call them over here, of which I had a whole pack. Cookie led to talk which led to many cigs (he smoked after all) which led to more talk which led to—Nothing yet. But he's staying with friends of his family in Venice and we're rendevousing (sp?) tomorrow morning in San Marco Square, unless something more mature crosses my path in the meantime. Tad's (Tod's) English is quite good but I don't know if it's good enough

*for him to read between my lines. He certainly
should've read it in my eyes . . ."*

Michael skimmed down to the bottom of the page, then
on to the other side, wanting to see how it ended—the boy
never showed up the next day—then jumped back to the
sentences about the meeting on the train. Michael first
met Clarence on a train.

They ate a late dinner, just as they did in the city. Ben
made his version of beef stroganoff, Danny made a salad,
and they criticized each other's method of preparation
while Michael sat at the table and drank iced tea. They
had offered him beer or wine, but Michael no longer
trusted himself with alcohol: it brought his emotions too
close to the surface. Music did that, too, but there was
nothing classical in the boxes of records downstairs in the
living room and the stereo below was playing safe, unfamiliar folk songs. The house had three floors staggered
along the hillside with short flights of stairs between each
level, an antique kind of split-level with low ceilings and
no central hallway on the bedroom floor. To get to the
guest room, you had to walk through Ben and Danny's
room, which was just five steps up from the kitchen. The
cupboards in the kitchen had been painted with flowers
by Ben's sister, like watercolors in an old botany book, and
there were hanging plants and potted ferns everywhere.
  When dinner was served, Ben and Danny immediately
focused their attention on Michael again: Ben wanted to
talk about the letters, Danny wanted to know what
Michael was going to do now that he was back.

"Have you thought about returning to school?" Danny asked.

"What struck me most when I reread Clarence's letters," said Ben, "was his joy over discovering and exploring his gayness."

They often did that to you, forcing you to choose one of them. Michael chose Ben, because talking about a future without Clarence might seem disloyal to his friends, and because med school or any kind of school was no longer a possibility.

"Clarence didn't know he was gay in college?"

"Eventually he did. But I don't think Laird even noticed he had a body until he was twenty-one, he was so wrapped up in music, art, and movies. Our generation had a gift for sublimation, Michael."

"Except for you, you whore," Danny muttered. "Who set up shop in the library tea room."

"It's true," Ben admitted with a certain pride. "I knew what I liked and couldn't understand people like Clarence or Jack Arcalli who took forever in accepting they liked sex with guys. I was a good example to them."

When Michael tried to picture Ben and Jack at the University of Virginia with Clarence, and Laurie, who was there too, he pictured them as adults, only shorter, already knowing everything.

"But once Laird knew, it took him forever to enjoy it. Well, not forever, but a couple of years, which seems like forever when you're that age, and a trip to Europe. He had to go to Europe to be gay. Before then, he might do things but, God, was he depressed afterward."

Michael remembered his own mixed feelings after sex

with the boy in Paris, but that was different. "He did things with you?" he finally asked.

Ben paused, then said, "Sure. Why not? Well, only two, maybe three times. We were just making do with each other. He was in love with some unattainable jock on the swim team, and I had the hots for a campus radical, radical for Virginia anyway. I was probably the first guy Laird ever did it with in a bed. But it wasn't very good sex. It never is between friends. It almost wrecked our friendship, in fact."

Danny sneered. "See, even back then you were bourgeois." He leaned over and smiled at Michael. "For some of us, sex is just a conversation—"

"In a horizontal position," Ben chanted. "Yeah, I know that now, but back then I needed love or fantasy, which are precluded by friendship. Uh, this was long before you, Michael. Clarence and I never did anything after college."

That possibility hadn't crossed Michael's mind and he wondered why Ben felt obligated to say it. Maybe for Danny's sake? He tried out the image of Ben and Clarence in bed and it meant nothing to him, gave him no jab of jealousy or pain that might have given him a sharpened sense of Clarence. Sex as sex seemed utterly unimportant to Michael, and he was scornful of Ben and Danny for dwelling upon it.

"Friendship never stopped me," Danny purred. "It guarantees you have something to talk about afterward."

Ben ignored him. "So those letters are a document of Clarence's sexual awakening, his invention of his identity as a gay man during an age when you had to do it all yourself. Without any support systems or gay community. *I* was Clarence's gay community, which isn't saying much."

"I'll say."

"But even now, even with the support and all, that kind of feverish sexual exploration is still the best way of defining yourself," Ben continued. "Despite the current health situation. People could still connect with each other like that, safely of course. That they're not, proves to me that AIDS is just a part of this new sobriety, which is really a failure of nerve. Gay men are just using it as an excuse to avoid the Dionysian, which is what really scares them. Nobody talks enough about J.O. parties."

Danny rolled his eyes. "When I'm with a bunch of really bad actors, I prefer to keep my clothes on, thank you."

"You went to John and Ted's with the wrong attitude."

"It was like being in the world's slowest porn movie!" Danny insisted. "Like a porn video directed by Robert Wilson." He nudged Michael and said, "Uh uh, my idea of sex is just me and a bed and one or two or three other guys." When Michael didn't respond, he said to Ben, "You wouldn't have gone back if you didn't think you had to set a *good example* for your so-called community. Why can't you just go to ethnic restaurants like other politicians?"

"I am not a politician," Ben declared.

"'If nominated I will not run, if elected I will not . . .' When we get back to New York," he told Michael, "there's somebody I'd like you to meet."

"Who?" said Ben.

"Stephen Greer. The little blond at HB."

"I don't think Michael needs a neurotic, self-involved actor."

Michael caught up with what they were saying and curtly shook his head. "Thank you, but I'm not looking for anyone right now."

"Who said anything about something serious?" said Danny. "I'm just talking about coffee, conversation, and maybe a little Dionysian mutual masturbation."

Michael froze; they didn't understand, neither of them. He hoped Ben might understand and would explain him to Danny, but Clarence's close friend only argued that Stephen Greer was a self-involved dingbat, cute though he may be.

"When *are* you going back?" Ben asked Michael.

Michael said he might go back tomorrow morning, if one of them could run him down to the train station in Mystic.

"No problem," said Ben.

They were driving back on Friday and Michael had hoped they might ask him to stay and ride back with them. But it was just as well they didn't. He had done all he needed to do here, and he had a strong desire to see his and Clarence's movie again, which Jack had on videotape.

They finished dinner and Michael remained at the table while Ben and Danny did the dishes. It was after ten when they finished, but Danny suggested they drive down to New London, to the only gay bar within a hundred miles. Ben said he didn't feel like driving and didn't trust Danny at the wheel after a couple of beers. Danny argued for a half hour until Ben gave in, then told Ben it was too late to go anywhere and what he really wanted to do tonight was read over *The Seagull* again for his audition next week. He went up the short flight of steps to their bedroom.

"I'll join you," Ben told him and went downstairs to turn on the television for Michael. "You see how impossible he's gotten?" he whispered. "These two weeks alone with him have made me realize enough is enough. Seven years is plenty." He told Michael he was welcome to stay up as late as he liked and asked only that he be sure to leave the porch light on for Jesse outside.

Michael tried watching television. He waited to hear a heated argument in the bedroom overhead, but things became very quiet up there. People who still had each other were fools to spend so much time fighting. Michael felt very wise and sad. He slowly realized how sleepy he was now that there was nobody to see him. His body did not seem to know what time it was, was still in transit, still caught somewhere between Europe and here. He decided the best solution was to go to bed himself. He turned off the television and lights and went up to the kitchen.

Without thinking, he passed through Ben and Danny's room on his way to get his toilet kit. They were both awake, sitting up in bed under the covers, Danny reading Chekhov, Ben a newspaper, Danny wearing his reading glasses and a T-shirt, Ben wearing nothing, at least from the waist up. The crinkly hair on Ben's chest looked crunchy.

"Pardon," said Michael, lowering his head and going into the guest room. "Excuse me," he said when he came out with his kit and passed through on his way to the kitchen and bathroom. The layout of the house had not been a problem last night when Michael was too exhausted from his airline flight through time to think of anything besides sleep.

In the bathroom he brushed his teeth, washed his face and armpits, and put his shirt back on, even though he'd be taking it off again when he went to bed. Returning through their room, he carefully looked away from them until he heard Ben say, "You going to bed, Michael? Good night."

"Yes. Good night," said Michael. "Dinner was very good."

"If you get scared by the quiet," said Danny, slyly smiling under his glasses, "or lonely, just remember we're right outside your door."

Ben glanced at Danny, looked at Michael, looked down at his newspaper.

"Good night," Michael repeated, hurried into the room, and closed his door.

He undressed quickly. Luckily, there were no mirrors in the room. He turned off the light, jumped into bed, and hugged a pillow to his chest. He thought he would fall asleep instantly, the rural darkness was so complete, but he kept seeing Ben and Danny reading in bed, then Clarence.

He suddenly remembered Saturday nights with Clarence, when they bought the early edition of the Sunday *Times*, came home, and went to bed with it. The memory felt warm and homey, like Sunday mornings when he was a little kid and climbed into bed with his parents, only Clarence was his lover and Michael was always naked under the blankets. He seemed to have spent his entire life bound up in clothes and loved being nude every chance he got with Clarence, even if it was only while he did the crossword puzzle. Clarence read things aloud or showed Michael the ads for new movies they should see.

Michael asked for suggestions for this word or that in the puzzle, although Clarence was useless with anything unrelated to the arts. Sometimes they made love when they finished; sometimes they only went to sleep, which was nice too because it proved they didn't need sex to be together. That era of Saturday nights at home lasted only the first month or so, but Michael felt it represented their whole life with each other.

Lying alone in the dark, comparing that with this, feeling an empty bed all around him, Michael became very nervous and afraid. The occasional rustle of paper or whisper from the next room hurt him, made him feel more lost than ever, abandoned and alone. There was a wide chink of light beneath the irregular handmade door. He did not want to sleep by himself tonight when he had friends so close.

He got out of bed and stepped to the door. Michael slept in his underwear now, shirt tucked snugly into the briefs, and he adjusted himself to make sure he was covered before he lightly knocked.

"Come in. Come out, rather. We're decent."

He opened the door and stood in the light.

Ben and Danny looked at him, calmly, then with interest.

Michael finally said, "Is it okay if I sleep with you guys tonight?" He did not want to plead for sympathy, but truth was required so they wouldn't misunderstand. "I feel really strange sleeping alone tonight. After reading his letters, I guess."

Ben and Danny looked at each other. Ben shrugged; Danny turned and said, "Sure."

"Let me get a pillow," Michael told them, noticing their

bed had only two. When he came back, Ben was scooting to his side of the bed, Danny to the middle, meaning Michael would be next to Danny. "Don't let me interrupt anything," he told them. "The light won't bother me." He set his pillow beside Danny's and climbed into bed without looking at either of them. He lay on his stomach, turned his face to the wall, burrowed his head into his pillow, and said, "Good night."

Ben cleared his throat and Danny hummed, noises that sounded like part of an earlier conversation. The newspaper rattled, a page in a book was turned, and things seemed to be as they were. Michael felt better. He began to feel drowsy, soothed by the presence of other legs radiating beneath the covers.

It felt more sexual than Michael thought it would be.

He began to remember Tim in Paris and how good he had felt. But these were friends. They knew Michael's other friends, and anything that happened here would get back to the others and make them think Michael had forgotten Clarence. There had been sexual signals ever since Michael arrived, but there were always odd signals from Ben and Danny. They had offered to introduce him to some new guy, but maybe they were only testing Michael's faith. Tim had been so uncertain what was safe and what wasn't they had to negotiate over each thing they did in Michael's hotel room. That wouldn't be necessary with Ben and Danny.

A warm body leaned against him. But Danny was only setting his book and glasses on the night table. There was the moist squeak of a kiss between two men and one of them whispered, "Good night, Michael."

"G'night," he muttered into his pillow.

The light was clicked off. The bed shook as the other bodies settled in. A foot grazed Michael's foot as legs were shifted about. Then the bed was still again.

Everyone lay very still for a long time. Michael heard breathing behind him but couldn't sort out one set of breaths from the other, couldn't decide if they were asleep yet. He lifted his head and rolled over on his side to look.

Unlike the city, there was absolutely no light from the street; the room was so dark it was as though his eyes were still closed. Michael thought he saw two blurred faces floating like spots on his retina.

"Something we can do, Mikey?"

A hand gently took hold of his shoulder and Michael suddenly realized how close Danny's face was to his. The hand held the back of Michael's neck, fingering the wispy, untrimmed down beneath his hair. Michael opened his mouth against another mouth and was kissed.

It was a slow, quiet kiss that left him too much room to think. He held Danny's head with one hand while he tried to decide whose fault this was. They shouldn't be doing this, sliding two tongues in Michael's mouth. What would Ben think? Ben might approve but that wouldn't make this right. Michael pressed his hand against Danny's chest and broke off the kiss. He felt the curve of Danny's chest against his hand. He lay on his back a moment. Then, with a quick flip of his shoulders and hips, Michael slipped his undershirt over his head and his underpants into the foot of the covers, as easily as socks or conscience, and stretched out against the body beside him.

He felt himself kissed, stroked, and held again. Arms embraced him around his shoulders and ass and he was rolled over one body and lay between two, a confusion of hands and legs. Nobody spoke, which was good. He could pretend to forget this was Ben and Danny, pretend he couldn't tell them apart once clothing disappeared, although he distinguished a familiarly older body with soft belly and muscular legs from a body that was all of one piece. And Ben's body was gritty with hair and he jabbed with his tongue when he kissed. Even though Danny started this, Ben seemed to enjoy what was happening. The cock beneath a slight roll of stomach was as hard as Michael's while the other longer one remained slightly flexible. But all identity seemed only cerebral in the dark.

He was kissing a throat and fizzy chest when the bed began to seem less crowded. He hoped Danny was not fetching something peculiar. The light in the kitchen came on and the dark void suddenly gained a wallpapered wall, a dresser, and shadows. Michael glanced down and saw long white legs tangled with darker, stubby ones, but their bodies did not look as different as he had imagined them. They were doing each other with their hands. He kissed the mouth again so that, up close, all he saw of Ben was an enormous blur of eye shifting back and forth as if looking for someone. Michael hoped Danny didn't intend to keep the light on so they could watch themselves.

Ben's hand was slowing down, as if tired. Michael stopped kissing. Ben gestured for him to wait, then twisted around to look at the light from the kitchen.

"Right back," he whispered. "I better see what happened to Danny."

He got up from the bed and stepped over to the light coming up from the kitchen. It really was Ben whose mouth and cock Michael had been touching, Ben Slover who spoke at rallies and bickered with his boyfriend, who gave advice and talked about the past like he was your older brother. Standing in the light and frowning at someone in the kitchen, he looked shorter and bulkier than he had felt in bed. A cock looked inappropriate on him. He started down the steps and disappeared through the doorway that stood at a right angle to the bed. Michael couldn't see the kitchen from where he lay.

He heard Ben whisper, "We were wondering what happened to you."

Danny's voice answered, "Nothing. Just go on without me."

Something inaudible followed, then, "You've been talking about this all along."

"I know. I guess I'm just not in the mood tonight. But you go ahead. All I ask is that he go back to his own bed when you're through."

"But I don't want to do it without you there."

"You seemed to be doing pretty good a minute ago."

Michael wondered if it was his fault, if he'd been giving too much attention to Ben. It was just that Ben's body was the kind he was most familiar with.

"I was doing it just because I thought you wanted me to do it," Ben whispered.

"Forget it. I'm not blaming you. Just go back and finish, please."

But all the vague feelings of wrong Michael had been able to push aside in the dark were back now that he was alone on the bed. He slowly sat up, bringing the knots of his knees against his chest, wrapping his arms around his legs. He didn't think he could continue when Ben returned.

A chair scraped across the floor and was sat on. The

whispering grew inaudible, but Ben seemed to be asking Danny why. There was the repeated mention of another "it."

Danny was suddenly annoyed enough to be heard again. "You think I don't know *that*? Hearing it from you day after day? It's not something I'm afraid of. Jeez, you and I are probably already— It just feels creepy. Don't you feel that? It's the boyfriend of *your* best friend. I don't know. It's not something rational. It's like what I felt when I wore my dead grandfather's coat."

And Michael finally understood.

There was more whispering, and his mind raced ahead with what they had to be saying against him. He had suspected this was wrong all along, but had been too selfish to follow his suspicions or even stop to understand them: he was betraying Clarence.

Going to bed with someone was bad enough. Going to bed with Clarence's friends was like boasting Clarence no longer mattered. That Michael had already recovered from his death. That Michael had never really loved him to begin with.

But he *had* loved him! He still loved him. Nevertheless, he horrified himself with the idea of his own heartlessness, sickened himself with how he must look to the others.

His own body sickened him. He quickly hunted around the bed for his things. The undershirt was on the floor. The briefs were wadded up like a rag beneath the kicked-back covers. He pulled everything on and it wasn't enough.

The stair creaked and Ben reappeared, followed by

Danny. Ben looked sheepish, Danny disgusted and unable to look at Michael. Their nakedness was strange and sexless, like the nakedness of cadavers in a classroom. Michael was sitting on the far side of the bed with his feet on the floor, wanting to run into his room and slam the door.

Ben leaned against the footboard and said, "We apologize, Michael. It wasn't fair of us to get you all worked up and not be able to follow through. It's something between Danny and me. I'm sorry you were caught in the middle."

Danny had grabbed his T-shirt off the bed and hurriedly pulled it on. He tugged it down as far as it would go but he still hung beneath it. "This has nothing to do with you, Michael. I still think you're an attractive guy. I just wasn't in the mood tonight."

"Can you forgive us?" said Ben.

They were being polite, being cowards and not telling Michael what they really thought. Their lies didn't even match. Michael sniffed and said, "There's nothing to forgive. I should never have gotten into bed with you in the first place." He said it accusingly, accusing himself.

Ben glanced at Danny and Danny lowered his head.

"Don't say that," said Ben. "It could've been fun. Under different circumstances. Nothing wrong with friends having fun with each other. It just wasn't in the cards tonight."

Michael closed his eyes and nodded. It hurt that they thought so little of him they wouldn't tell him he was selfish, disloyal, and wrong. They had been doing it too, but Clarence was only their friend while he was Michael's lover, and they had known well enough to stop.

"So don't take it personally," said Ben. "These things

happen. Why, I remember Danny brought a dancer home once and I was the one who didn't feel . . ."

Danny sat on the bed and looked away while Ben talked, ashamed of Ben's lying or Michael's presence or maybe even himself.

"I'd like to do something to make up for our rudeness," Ben offered. "You're still welcome to sleep with us. Just sleep, mind you. If that really *would* make you feel better."

He couldn't actually mean it. He could only want to remind Michael he was the one who had started this when he came in whining about not wanting to sleep alone.

"No thank you," Michael said stiffly. "I should sleep alone."

"Probably better all around," said Ben. "Given the circumstances. Again, I'm sorry it didn't work out. But, no harm done. Right?"

Michael nodded again and stood up. "Good night," he said, for what felt like the hundredth time that night. "See you tomorrow."

Ben stepped forward before Michael could get away. He carefully touched Michael's arm, then gave him a sudden hug. The very feel of skin was obscene. "We'll laugh about this in the morning," he claimed.

"You want me to drive you to the train station tomorrow?" said Danny. Kindly? Or eager to be rid of him? Danny was always more honest than Ben.

"Yes," said Michael. "I do." He stepped around Ben and into the next room, taking care not to slam the door when he closed it behind him.

He found the empty bed in the dark and buried himself

in it. He could not cry. He hated himself too much to feel pity. The empty darkness of this bed and room was where he belonged. Where no one could tell him lies he was tempted to believe. Where there was nothing to break his focus on the absence that was the real center of his life.

4

THEY met on the train between Philadelphia and New York.

Michael Sousza transferred to Columbia his sophomore year, after a year at Haverford College outside Philadelphia. His grades were good, and Michael had wanted to go to Columbia all along, but his father distrusted New York City and insisted Michael spend his first year away from home in a small, protected place. Mr. Sousza was a self-made man, a second-generation Czech who had worked his way up from carpenter to contractor. He was proud he had enough money to send his youngest, brightest son to a good school. He had hoped his son would stay at Haverford once he was there, but gave in when Michael's heart remained set on Columbia.

Perhaps he had anticipated it too long, but Michael was

miserable his first semester in New York. Surrounded by cliques and circles formed the year before, neither the preppie nor New York Jew that everyone else seemed to be, Michael felt utterly alone. The city intimidated him. He did not have the spending money that would've enabled him to go out with the few people he did meet. He spent his evenings in the library or lab and his grades remained good, but he was so unhappy he could not remember why he had burned to live in New York City. He stood outside Earl Hall one damp night in October when there was a gay dance inside, listening to the disco music thumping through the dripping trees, and decided he wasn't so lonely he had to resort to *that*.

He went down to Haverford one weekend in November to visit friends from freshman year, only to find they weren't as friendly as he remembered them. It was just as well. He couldn't transfer back there without giving his father the terrible satisfaction of being right again. Michael caught the train back late Sunday night. The train was packed and he walked all the way to the smoking car before he found an empty seat. An older man reluctantly lifted his Walkman and nylon windbreaker from the seat beside him when Michael approached. Not until Michael had put his bag in the overhead rack and settled in did he bother to look at the man. He instantly felt the man was gay. He dressed gay, wearing black jeans and a white T-shirt although he looked like he was at least thirty. (Clarence, in fact, was thirty-five.) His mustache looked gay: neatly trimmed hairs bordering his mouth. Michael knew what they did with their mouths. Michael was very nervous, terrified the man might try something.

But the man didn't look at Michael, not even at Michael's knees. The Walkman turned in his lap and his shaggy head was wired with the headset. He closed his eyes like someone in church while he listened to the music in his skull. All Michael heard was a tinny orchestra of ants.

Michael decided to be relieved the man was occupied. He took out his chemistry notebook and tried to forget him, although that was difficult with the man leaking music. The long passenger car shuddered once, then seemed to float in space, the darkness outside turning the windows into long black mirrors.

The Walkman clicked to a stop. Michael glanced over while the man flipped the cassette. He assumed it would be disco, but the yellow label on the cassette read: "Humperdinck, Highlights from *Hansel and Gretel*." The man pressed a button and disappeared into his music again.

Michael listened more closely. That was a children's story, but this sounded like opera. Michael was ashamed of how little he knew about music, how working-class he really was, like his family. But knowing the man listened to something called *Hansel and Gretel* changed him in Michael's eyes. It made him seem less gay, less intimidating. Maybe he taught elementary school. He didn't have the cool, predatory look of the gay men Michael saw on the street, but looked rather mild and benevolent, despite the mustache. He had a big cowlike jaw, thin lips, and long, sensitive eyelids. The T-shirt wasn't pumped up with muscles, and there was a slight cushion of tummy above his belt. His eyelids quivered and his nostrils dilated, as if he were deeply moved by something.

Then his eyes opened. "Oh!" He looked at Michael and

pulled the plugs out of his ears; there was a whistle of music. "Do I have this too loud? I'm terribly sorry."

"Uh, no. Not really. Not at all." Michael had looked too much, forgetting the music didn't make him as invisible as he felt. He didn't want the man to think he'd been looking at him, so he added, "*Hansel and Gretel*, isn't it?"

"Huh? Oh. Yes!" said the man, surprised by Michael's interest. "Wonderful piece of music. Grossly underrated." He spoke slowly at first, lazily savoring his words yet also shy about them. "Most people think it's only a children's opera, but ... " He shrugged sheepishly, as if afraid Michael might disagree with him. "Anyway, it's wonderful music for train trips."

"You don't say."

"Absolutely. Like this part here. In the finale." The man eagerly fast-forwarded the tape and listened to it. "Just a sec. The chorus of the gingerbread children," he explained. "Where they ask Gretel to touch their eyes and bring them back to life. Ah. Here it is." The man took his headset and, before Michael could stop him, slipped the whole thing over Michael's head, his fingers brushing Michael's ears. It was much too intimate. The cord remained wrapped once around the man's neck. "Okay. Now listen to this, and slowly turn your head around while you listen."

Michael had no choice except to seat the plugs in his ears and nod. The music came on, filling his head with a slow, sweet current. Then there were children singing, softly, dreamily, the orchestra carrying them along in their trance as if they all floated on their backs in a river. Without knowing what he was supposed to listen for, Michael slowly turned his head as the man instructed, until he saw the skyline of a small city float forward outside in the darkness, then the man looking straight at him.

He was smiling at Michael, his eyes wide open and expectant.

Michael smiled back at him.

The Walkman was turned off and the protective shell of music vanished, along with Michael's smile. The dreary rumble of wheels and the hiss of the ventilators returned.

"Yes?" said the man, taking the headset Michael passed back to him. "It makes even Amtrak interesting. I feel I'm being rude when I use these things, and it's not good the way they turn everything around you into a movie. But it's interesting. The way the music brings out rhythms in things you wouldn't notice otherwise."

"Very interesting," said Michael.

"It's even better with Poulenc, whose music always makes me think of scores for silent movies, only they're movies that existed only in his head. Do you like Poulenc? Or *Pou-lank*, however it's pronounced?"

"I'm not familiar with him. I don't know much classical music," Michael admitted. "I'm not very strong on culture."

"Yeah? Well, I don't really think of it as culture," the man said with a trace of embarrassment. "It's just stuff I happen to like." He actually did talk about music as if it were an innocent passion, with no social clout attached to it, no desire to impress Michael with his sophistication. Which was why Michael had been able to confess his ignorance so easily. "What kind of music *do* you like?"

"Music doesn't really interest me."

"Ah." The man fumbled with the jacket gathered in his

lap and pulled out a pack of Winstons. "Cigarette?" he offered.

Michael was tempted to take one, just to be friendly, so he rebelled against his desire to be friendly and said, "Don't you know smoking's bad for you?"

"Yeah. I know I shouldn't, but—" The man shrugged guiltily, stuck a cigarette in his mouth, and lit it.

Someone who was tryng to pick you up would respect your wishes, wouldn't he? Michael decided the man wasn't interested in him. He was annoyed by the thick smoke.

The man sat and said nothing while he smoked, apparently thinking about someone or something else. But his headset remained around his neck like a collar. He didn't go back to his music, which would've declared their encounter over.

"You visiting New York?" Michael asked. He assumed the man lived elsewhere. He had a faint Southern slur, and no New Yorker would be as openly enthusiastic about anything as this man was about music.

"I live in New York. Just going home after a weekend in D.C. And you?"

Michael explained he was a student at Columbia and the man asked what that was like. They talked about living in New York. The man was from Danville, Virginia, had lived in New York twelve years, worked in a midtown film lab, and lived on the Upper West Side. He never mentioned being gay, but he never mentioned a wife or girlfriend either.

The man seemed to grow bored with their talk, because he suddenly asked, "Seen any good movies lately?" always a sure sign conversation was running down. Michael mentioned a couple of recent titles—bored and lonely, he had seen more movies his first months in New York than he'd seen all year at Haverford. So they talked about movies. Actually, the man did most of the talking, having seen more movies than Michael knew existed, becoming as bashfully animated over movies as he'd been with music. He went on at length about one in particular, a foreign film he said Michael must see the next time it played at a revival house. It was called *The Conformist*, and although the man never made clear what its story was, he went into great detail about its use of camera movement and music. He did not talk about movies like a normal person; Michael was never conscious of anything but the story and how he felt afterward.

They talked movies until the illuminated tip of the Empire State Building slid along the dark house-covered ridge in New Jersey and the train plunged into a tunnel. Beneath the Hudson River, people began to collect their things. Michael collected his thoughts, wondering why he was so nervous that this meeting was ending when he should be pleased to be back in New York, where he could be miserable without being confused. He stood up to get his bag and let the man get out.

"You know," said the man, remaining in his seat, "I just remembered. They're showing that movie I was telling you about. Next week at the Thalia. I see it every time it's shown. If you like, we could see it together."

"Yes!" said Michael. "I mean, it depends. When is it?"

The man didn't know, but offered to give Michael his telephone number so they could arrange something. Michael passed the man his notebook, then a pen, then took them back when the man finished. Michael couldn't remember the number of the pay phone in his dorm, but the man didn't ask for it. The train had come to a stop, and people swept Michael down the aisle before he could say more to the man than goodbye. Not until he was upstairs in the concourse did Michael have a chance to look at his notebook before slipping it into his bag. Neatly written across the top of a page covered with chemical equations was a number that looked like just another equation, except there was a name beside it: Clarence Laird.

(The next day, talking to a friend on the telephone, Clarence moaned, "I'm getting old, Ben. I tried to set up a date with a kid I met on the way back from meeting that would-be producer in Washington. I'm turning into a god-damn chickenhawk, Ben! Thank God, I'll never hear from this kid. I don't even know if he's gay, and I'll bet he doesn't know either." Ben assured him the younger generation were quicker about these things than they had been.)

Michael sometimes thought about naked men, but he didn't think that made him gay. Such homosexual fantasies were a symptom of loneliness, he believed. He'd been having these thoughts since high school, but he'd been lonely since high school. And he had these thoughts only when he was alone. Sometimes particular guys, sometimes just any guy, but he never thought of anyone that way when he was with him, only when he was by himself. There had been a senior dorm counselor at Haverford whom Michael needed to see at least once each day, so he wouldn't think about him naked. In the beginning, there'd been naked women too, but it had been nothing but men since he was sixteen.

What proved to Michael he wasn't gay was his discomfort with gay men. There were openly gay students at Columbia, unlike Haverford, and Michael never thought about them the way he thought about other guys. In fact, the mere presence of an obvious homosexual made Michael forget he ever had such thoughts or, if he remembered, assured him his thoughts had nothing to do with their behavior. It was as though he could have his fantasies only when they were private, completely original, and incapable of being shared. Michael used the word *gay* not for liberal reasons but because *queer* and even *homo* might apply to his fantasies. *Gay* suggested an identity as solid and apart from him as *black*, an identity now shored up by rumors of a disease that struck only gays. Michael never worried about the disease because he wasn't gay.

The night he returned from Philadelphia and all the next day, Michael thought about the man on the train. Not naked, however. He was too nervous for that. He thought about not calling the man, but things left unfinished were harder to forget. He considered throwing away the man's telephone number, but it was written on an important page of notes and Michael hated to mar his notebook by tearing off a corner of paper. And he actually wanted to see this Clarence Laird again. The man was a nice guy, could talk to someone younger without condescension, knew things Michael felt he should learn—cultural things. So what if the man were gay? So what if he made a pass? If he made a pass, if he actually made Michael do things with him, it might cure Michael for good of his morbid thoughts. There had been black moods when Michael worried himself with the idea he had come to New York mainly to find someone to do that to him. Michael was only nineteen. The discovery that his imagination and emotions seemed to have a life of their own sometimes struck him as evidence of insanity.

He telephoned Clarence on Monday night, gave his name—he had never mentioned it on the train—and said he wanted to see that movie, whose title he had forgotten. It was being shown the following Sunday, and Michael spent the rest of the week changing his mind and making it up again until the overcast afternoon when he walked twenty blocks down Broadway to the Thalia.

("Much to my surprise," Clarence told Ben over the phone, "Amtrak Junior called. I think he's the type who expects to be seduced, so he won't feel responsible. But I don't have the energy to play that game these days, not with so much else on my mind. Or the interest. He's way too young. Well, I'm not counting on anything. I was going to the movie anyway.")

The man was waiting for Michael beneath a shabby, small-town movie marquee. Michael was surprised the man was the same height as he was. He'd imagined him to be taller, just because he was older, but they'd been sitting the whole time they met. The man looked disappointingly normal and unphysical, like a college teacher, nothing like the dangerously physical presence Michael had been imagining all week. He had not dressed up for their meeting but must have shaved, because there was still a dab of shaving cream on his left earlobe, like a pearl earring. Exchanging hellos and pleasantries outside the theater, Michael had to fight an impulse to reach out and wipe the man's ear.

"Seeing this with someone who's seeing it for the first time is almost as good as seeing it for the first time yourself," said the man as they stepped inside and sat in the smoking section. He talked about nothing but the movie, telling Michael about the director, how young the director had been when he made it, warning Michael that the movie had an extremely tricky flashback structure.

"I'm sure I'll be able to handle it," Michael said.

The movie began, and Michael was surprised the man had not warned him it had subtitles. He tried to get used to that, tried to concentrate on the movie, but although it seemed as beautiful as the man said it was—the camera moving in weird, noticeable ways—things flashbacked all over the place and Michael became lost, uninvolved enough to be conscious of the man's knee beside his. Their knees brushed, once. Nevertheless, the man looked as utterly absorbed in the movie as he'd been in *Hansel and Gretel* on the train. It was as though they were still on the train, only now the scenery was in front of them.

Ladies with parasols looked on while a gang of boys humiliated a pale boy in a sailor outfit, jeering at him and pulling his pants down. Michael responded to that. Then the boy went off with a uniformed chauffeur, who showed sympathy for the boy, took him to an enormous deserted mansion, lured him to his quarters, and threw him on the bed. *This* was why the man had lured him here, Michael decided. He watched excitedly. The boy seemed to want something to happen. He ran his hands through the man's shoulder-length hair. The movie flashbacked somewhere else, and when it got back to the boy and chauffeur, something must have already happened, because the boy grabbed the pistol the chauffeur had shown him and started firing wildly around the room, killing the chauffeur, then fleeing.

The movie settled down and became easier to follow—a secret agent and his wife in Paris—but Michael watched it in a daze, still haunted by the boy and the chauffeur, until the final scene, when a dark curly-haired young man lay bare-bottomed on a bed in an alley, watched by the secret agent through iron bars.

When the lights came up, the man was sunk back in his chair and grinning at the ceiling. "It never ceases to amaze me," the man murmured. "And I've seen it at least twenty times. You want to come back to earth with a drink somewhere?"

Michael nodded and followed the man out to the street, wondering if they'd seen the same movie. It had affected Michael, but more like a bad dream than a movie, a disturbing dream that might have seemed sexual except that nothing like intercourse had been involved. He pushed aside his confused excitement by dwelling on questions of fact: had the man behind bars already had sex with the naked guy or was he only considering it?

"Anywhere you'd like to go?" the man asked outside. "There's a bar nearby, or, if you'd just like beer, my apartment's only a few blocks from here."

"Beer'd be fine," said Michael, telling himself he accepted the man's invitation only because he couldn't afford to go to a bar.

But the man—Clarence—did not seem especially excited Michael was coming home with him. He resumed talking about the movie, asking Michael what he thought of this or that, genuinely curious about what Michael understood and what had escaped him. He brought up the ambiguous ending himself, but the mystery for him was what it meant, not what had happened. "I've got this friend who's a film critic who thinks it's an anti-gay script that accidentally became homoerotic when they were filming it, that Marcello is supposed to be another evil homosexual. He thinks the director was concentrating so hard on making each shot beautiful he didnt' realize what he was doing. My friend thinks it's all gorgeously photographed claptrap, but that's just Jack. Who doesn't trust anything that can't be put into words."

It was the man's first mention of homosexuality, safely buried inside the mention of a friend who was a film critic. Michael pictured someone like Siskel and Ebert and was impressed. He expected the man to use the movie to talk about homosexuality, to make a pass at Michael, but the man began to talk about the poetics of editing against camera movement, whatever that meant, and sex became just a vague threat again.

The man took him to an enormous, old apartment building over toward the river. There was no doorman. Riding up in the elevator, Michael needed to make conversation.

"You know so much about movies," he told the man, "you should be a director."

The man smiled. "That's what I want to be when I grow up."

Even as a joke, it was odd to hear an adult say that.

The man unlocked a door at the end of a hall and led Michael into a darker hallway. He turned on lights. "And what do you want to be when *you* grow up?"

"My family wants me to be a doctor."

The apartment was so big Michael wondered if the man were rich or maybe famous. But nobody famous would ride Amtrak, and the ill-assorted pieces of old and new furniture did not suggest money. Michael wandered deeper into the apartment while the man went into the kitchen to get beers. In an alcove at the far end of the living room was a wall covered with squares of paper. They were sketches laid out like the panels of a comic book, just the outlines of figures but very clean and precise. The first panels bore words: "Last Week at the A&P" and "A Film by Clarence Laird."

"Just something silly I'm working on," said a voice over Michael's shoulder. "Uh, I was wrong about the beer. There isn't any."

He felt the man standing very close behind him. Michael did not step away or turn around. Without thinking, he relaxed his body when the man embraced him from behind, as if his body were relieved to have something to lean against.

A friendly pair of hands touched Michael's front. Michael put his own hands over them, intending to stop the man before he went too far. But he liked the feel of other knuckles and fingers in his hands.

"Well, enough about movies," whispered Clarence.

It was not yet nine o'clock when Michael left. Unlike the movie, he did not shoot Clarence afterward. He did not really feel like shooting Clarence. It had not been as awful or obscene or even as strange as Michael had imagined. He never wanted to do it again, but it had been interesting to be touched, different to be in bed with another body, exciting to have someone do to him what Michael always had to do for himself, until it was over. Michael walked back uptown to his dorm, immediately took a shower, and sat at his desk to study his chemistry. The phone number in the notebook no longer bothered him now that the business was finished.

Over the next few days, the need to picture naked men did not return. Instead, Michael began to think about being held and rubbed and things they hadn't done that he read about in *The Joy of Gay Sex* the next afternoon in a half-deserted bookstore. Two days later, he telephoned Clarence again. There was an answering machine on the other end and he was too startled to leave a message. He wondered if the man needed a machine because he had so many guys calling him.

He called repeatedly the next day until he finally got Clarence in person. He asked if there was a movie playing somewhere they should see. Clarence said he was busy every night for the next week and never got home until eleven.

"I was going to be down in your neighborhood tonight," said Michael. "What if I dropped by after eleven? Just for a beer."

"Well. Sure. You can drop by."

He did and they did and, this time, Michael didn't feel at all bad afterward. He left with Clarence's work number and called him two days later to ask if he could drop by around eleven that night. He brought *The Joy of Gay Sex* with him, having gone ahead and purchased the book that evening. If he was going to do this, he wanted to do it right. Michael couldn't have a book like that in his dorm room, so he left it at Clarence's.

("He's turned into a regular little night visitor," Clarence reported to Ben. "Well, I can't say I mind. I'm too busy doing pre-production on *A&P* to go out looking for sex these days. It just feels weird having a nineteen-year-old using you as a sexual convenience.")

The routine became so regular it seemed to go on for months. Nights when he was going to see Clarence, Michael studied for several hours after dinner, able to concentrate better than before because he knew he'd be taking a break before eleven. His two or three hours with Clarence two or three times a week were a sweet, separate compartment in his life, a hidden compartment that had nothing to do with school or family or reality. The secret made him feel oddly happy about the rest of his life. He started running again—he had run cross-country in high school—going around and around on the indoor track at the gym, tuning up his body now that he had a new use for it. Michael walked around campus that month with a serene look on his face, like the dreamy look of a graceful dancer, his own arms and legs swinging clumsily beneath him.

("No, he's not what I'd call beautiful. He looks like an El Greco with a big head. Of course I'm being safe! You and your— He might be a selfish little pig, but I don't want to chance harming him in any way. I don't.")

They continued like this for three weeks, then Michael went home for Christmas. His family showed him so much love and respect he felt he had betrayed them. He stayed in Phillipsburg two weeks, grew accustomed to feeling guilty, and began to miss Clarence. He missed sex, but he missed Clarence too. Not until he was away from him did Michael realize how much they talked, more than he talked with anyone else in New York. Clarence was a good listener. He was often preoccupied with his own thoughts about the movie he was trying to make, but it was good to have even a half-attentive ear in which Michael could pour his worries about classes and grades and future. Clarence talked about his difficulties too, with his movie and money. He had made other movies, short gay films that he never offered to show to Michael and that Michael was afraid to see. While he was home, Michael wondered what Clarence's movies were like. His new film was to be a parody of something called *Last Year at Marienbad* and was supposed to be harmless enough he could show it to producers and get financing for a feature. Clarence wasn't rich after all. He had inherited a rent-controlled apartment from a roommate, had had a few roommates of his own who moved out when they succeeded. The last one moved out only a month ago and Clarence had been too busy to find a replacment. Michael wondered what it would be like to live with Clarence.

The afternoon he arrived back at school, Michael immediately phoned Clarence at work. He asked if he could come over that night. Clarence said he was busy. What about the next night? Clarence said he was busy all week.

"I could come by even later than eleven," Michael told him. "One o'clock or even two."

"Well, to be honest with you, Michael. I met someone while you were gone. Nothing may come of it, but I want to keep my calendar clear until I know."

"Oh. Okay." Michael thought a moment. "What if I called back in a couple of weeks? Do you think you'd know by then if you were free?"

"Maybe. Yes, call me in a couple of weeks."

Michael hung up and walked toward his dorm. He always telephoned Clarence from outside, not wanting the guys in his hall to overhear his conversations. The day was sunny and frigid. Michael was pleased with himself for hiding his disappointment. But he was more than disappointed. He was hurt, heartbroken, angry with Clarence, angry with whomever it was Clarence had met.

He returned to his room and sat at his desk without taking off his coat. He had a single room, and the painted cinderblock walls and bare mattress disgusted him. He got up, went downstairs and outside to the pay phone, and dialed Clarence's number again.

"Laird, processing."

"I'm sorry to bother you again, but—did you ever think there was a chance I might be in love with you?"

"I considered it. And no, Michael, I don't think you are."

He said it so calmly that Michael was convinced. "Okay. I just wanted to mention that possibility to you. Goodbye."

Michael returned to his room, took off his coat, and began to unpack his suitcase. The presence of his things did not make the room less bare. It was as desolate as the day he first arrived here and Michael remembered the awful months before he met Clarence. He went out and called again, this time from the telephone on his hall.

"What's wrong with me, Clarence? Am I too skinny or stupid or ugly?"

Clarence sighed. "You're fine, Michael. You're too young, that's all."

"I can work on that. Just give me a chance."

"Why?"

"Because I want to see you. Because I might be in love with you."

There was a long, cold pause at the other end. "I'll tell you what, Michael. Come by my apartment at eleven tonight, get rid of this homebound horniness with a nice quick fuck, and then we'll talk about love."

Michael hated hearing that word—the F-word. There had to be nicer ways to describe what he did to Clarence, but all he really heard was Clarence agreeing to see him. "Okay. I'll be there."

He arrived early, had sex with Clarence, and felt no differently afterward, only relieved to see Clarence again. They tried to talk about love, but even Clarence seemed uncomfortable with something so abstract, and talk ran to friendship and consideration instead. Michael was surprised a grown man could be annoyed or hurt by little things he had done, surprised an adult could take him so seriously. He spent the night. He was disturbed to wake up the next morning and find another person invading the privacy of sleep, but the strangeness passed. It was Saturday and Michael didn't return uptown to study but spent the day in the apartment, watching Clarence's movies on his VCR. They were rough and strange and faintly erotic, without being the pornography Michael had imagined when Clarence said they were gay. How could something be gay without being sexually explicit? Clarence seemed pleased when Michael noticed the ways the camera moved in one of them.

They went out and ate dinner in a coffeeshop, then Clarence walked Michael up to Columbia. Michael liked walking familiar grounds with his "lover"—he tried the word to himself. People he barely knew saw them together, but Michael liked that too. He decided not to go back to his dorm after all, and they walked downtown again, buying the Sunday *Times* on the way and reading it in Clarence's bed.

The next day, Clarence said he had work to catch up on and that Michael probably did too, but they would talk that night. Michael was glad to be alone again, yet it was a different kind of alone than before. He tried to identify exactly what made it different from what he and Clarence had before Christmas and all he could come up with was that he knew what he had, which was sex and friendship and—maybe—love. What pleased him most was last night's walk with Clarence, between unconnected parts of the city, and himself, connecting one compartment with another with an ease he had not known was possible.

("I don't know what I'm doing, Ben. I don't feel *romantic* about him. We're so different and he's so young I really feel like I'm using him, not sexually but emotionally. I'm using him for something psychological, like surrogate fatherhood or time-warp narcissism, like I'd *want* to be with myself when I was nineteen, which is an appalling thought. I give it another month, or until someone his own age with the patience of Job puts the moves on him. Well, it's a good distraction until then. But that's why I'm a bit reluctant to bring him to Peter and Livy's Saturday.")

Not until Clarence invited him to a dinner some friends were giving did Michael recognize Clarence's life had other compartments. He was bringing his separate parts together, and Michael accepted the invitation, although he was intimidated by the idea of a roomful of gay adults. He remembered what it was like to stand around, foolish and silent, with the smugly noisy men who were his father's friends. Also, he was not yet over his discomfort about gay people.

A woman, Livy, met them at the door of an expensively bare loft downtown. There were two other women inside, apparently a lesbian couple, but the presence of women of any kind made an occasion more normal. A man with a beard and bags under his eyes looked up in alarmed surprise when Michael entered with Clarence. Another man jumped up from a deck chair, introduced himself as Ben, shook Michael's hand, and grinned like they were old friends. There was a youngish Hispanic man who looked like the Hispanic gunman who'd begun to undress in one of Clarence's films. A Southerner with a red beard handed Michael a glass of white wine.

Almost immediately, they were very friendly and interested, paying complete attention to the answers Michael gave to their questions about life and school. Even Jack, the alarmed one, became gruffly solicitous. When conversation moved on to other subjects, Jack tried to include Michael with muttered asides and quick explanations. Michael was surprised by how comfortable he became. They were adults and he was still young, but he suddenly found adults less inhibiting, perhaps because he was fucking one. But Clarence seemed equal and human here without sex, affectionately teased for faults Michael didn't know he had, or hadn't known were faults.

After two glasses of wine, Michael felt as at home among these people as he did with his own family. More at home, because this family seemed to think it perfectly natural that Michael and Clarence should be lovers.

5

J ACK sat at the typewriter in his kitchen, groping for peeves to turn into metaphors that could be puzzled together into something resembling reason.

He wrote two movie reviews a month for *The Nation*, one book review a month for the *Voice*, then occasional pieces for any magazine that would have him. Now and then, as a political gesture, he wrote under his own name for *Christopher Street*, although he had learned long ago that the so-called mainstream was serenely blind toward gay publications, like an old lady refusing to notice the dogs humping in her roses. Nobody noticed Jack Arcalli was gay except other gay writers, and they didn't care. Gone was Jack's hope of doing his bit for the community by "coming out" in print. Gone were his fantasies of cute young novelists jumping into his bed to get good reviews

—although that would never sway someone as principled as Jack. No, half-visible and unacknowledged, he had to content himself with being just another phantom in the literary unconscious, an anonymous workman on the gothic cathedral of contemporary culture. Always a bridesmaid, never a bride. The remarkable thing was that one could almost make a living from it.

This afternoon was a movie review, the poor, poor movie he had seen yesterday. Books were Jack's real love—they stuffed the shelves and stood stacked like dull rainbows against the walls—but there was more money in movies. And he could slash a bad film to ribbons with less of the guilt that followed even a respectful mixed review of a failed novel: movies were made by banks, but a book was written by someone with a mother. Reviewing books, Jack fretted more over being wrong or sounding vicious. He didn't intend to be vicious; it just came out that way. He cut even when he loved, and was startled by his own goblins of phrase. Who would think such a gentle, bumbling bear of a fellow could have such violence in him? Ashamed of feeling critical of people, Jack unleashed his criticisms on things.

As always when the writing went slowly, Elisabeth Vogler sat on Jack's notes, judging his efforts with her glassy, tinsel-packed eyes. When the electric typewriter hummed to itself for too long, she opened her tiny mouth at Jack in a mute meow. He finally lifted her up, cuddled her soft fur beneath his coarse beard, then poured her to the floor.

"While male adolescents keen for our sympathy like cats in heat," he typed, despite his resolution to ration the cat metaphors, "female adolescents are denied sympathy and reduced to bimbettes or lovely icebergs."

That was for Laurie. Jack tried to let his friends enter his writing, hoping their interests would enlarge his stock of topics and observations. He included feminist remarks for Laurie, political comments for Ben, and technical details for Clarence, still. Jack wanted to stretch his ways of thinking. He often felt trapped by his habits of thought, by the very syntax of his sentences, just as he felt trapped by the neurotic personality that seemed to have hardened around him when his attention was elsewhere. Jack needed to change himself now and then, if only his prose. He liked to believe people could change—he wrote reviews to change their minds—but feared there was no changing anyone, least of all himself.

He stewed over the triteness of his last sentence, longing for an interruption, an interesting phone call, something to distract him. Then the buzzer for the front door blew through the apartment.

"Dammit to hell! Can't people leave me alone!" He eagerly jumped up from the table and pressed the button to talk. "Who is it?"

"Me. Michael."

Jack was stunned. He hadn't expected Michael back so soon, or here. If Michael was here, then Laurie and Carla must have given him their ultimatum. Michael was here to share his mess of emotions. Suddenly, finishing his movie review was what Jack wanted most in the world. But he buzzed Michael in.

The apartment was on the first floor and there was a prompt knock at the door.

"Just a minute!" Jack called out, buttoning his shirt over his hairy belly, sucking the belly in and closing his fly. Working at home, Jack liked to leave the top of his pants undone. Alone and writing, he could forget his homely carcass. He quickly looked around, but there was nothing else to hide. The apartment really was too small for two neurotics and a cat. How could he have been so foolishly guilty as to offer to let Michael live here?

"Michael!" He acted pleasantly surprised as he opened the door. "You're back!"

A boy stood in the hall, looking very mild, blank, and tall. His pale hands were clasped demurely at his waist. His springy hair curled around his ears like hurt feelings. His height seemed oddly touching out there, like the tall, exposed absurdness of a harbor piling when the tide was out.

Jack hadn't seen him all summer and was surprised the boy looked rather appealing. Until Michael spoke.

"You're home, I see. Good. Hello, Jack. Do you still have your tape of *Disco of the Damned?*"

He shook Jack's hand, which was a regression. Michael had become a conscientious hugger during his mourning. But he sounded as arrogant as ever—he spoke as if Jack had come to see *him*—and cryptic, too proud to make sense too quickly, the blunt request for the tape. They were all defense mechanisms, but knowing that didn't make dealing with Michael any easier.

"Come in, Michael. Welcome back. Of course I have the tape. How was Europe?"

"Oh, what I expected." He sighed, solemnly stepping inside and leaving Jack to close the door behind him. "I've had to tell so many people about it, I can't talk about it anymore."

His jadedness was a defense, too. In fact, he seemed more heavily defended today than Jack remembered him being. "Have you talked to Laurie and Carla?"

Michael was judging the apartment, frowning at the number of books. "I spoke to them the day before yesterday, when I got back from Europe. I've been in Connecticut since then, you know. Reading Clarence's letters."

"You haven't talked with them today?"

"I just got back. Nobody was home when I dropped my stuff off."

Jack was relieved. Michael was only being Michael and didn't know yet. Jack was not prepared to deal with that today. Perhaps there was still time for him to get out of his offer to the women.

Michael suddenly looked pained, staring at something: the framed collage of Proust and Charlie Chaplin that perched on the shelf over Jack's kitchen table.

Only Clare, who had never read a word of Proust, could have noticed the resemblance between the author of *A la recherche du temps perdu* and the Little Tramp. The two metaphysical clowns looked like brothers, especially in comparison to the sexy jock in underpants who stood between them. Jack liked to think of the picture as an allegory of their friendship, with Chaplin as Clarence and Proust as Jack, although the picture was probably intended only to represent itself. Jack began to fear Michael wanted the picture, that anything about Clarence belonged to him. Just thinking that made Jack hate him.

Michael blinked his pain away and glanced down. "Oh. I

see you're working," he said. "I don't want to keep you. I just needed to see Clarence's movie today. Will it disturb you if I watch it here? We don't have a VCR anymore, you know."

"Now? Um, sure. Let me set it up for you." It seemed a strange *need*, but Jack was so relieved he didnt' have to deal with his problem yet he could give Michael that much. Living with Michael was going to be impossible, as much because of Jack as because of Michael.

Jack led him into the bedroom. His apartment was an amputated railroad flat, the living room and only windows out front, then the kitchen, then a bedroom in the back, like a dark, oversized closet. The platform bed took up most of the room, the television and VCR at the foot of the bed so Jack could watch movies when he couldn't sleep. The shelves above the bed were piled with videotapes and more books. Jack knelt on the bed and immediately found the tape he had purchased himself. There had been no one to give him a free copy when Clarence's movie came out on video.

"So. How were Ben and Danny?" Jack asked cheerfully as he loaded the cassette. "They behaving themselves in the country?"

Michael winced. "What do you mean?"

"Just knowing them the way I do, I can't imagine them sitting still for too long. I can't guess what they'd do out there except throw dishes at each other. Or drive around propositioning gas station attendants for threeways."

Michael bit his mouth shut and said nothing.

Jack shrugged at his silence. "Okay," he said. "All set. There's no place to sit but the bed, so can you take your shoes off? Would you like some coffee or anything to drink?"

"I don't want to trouble you further, thank you." Michael kicked off his shoes and sat crosslegged on the bed, a lean, sour Buddha lit by the cold light of snow on the television screen. A long toe poked through the hole in one sock.

Jack pressed the button to start the tape. "I'll be in the kitchen if you need me." He stepped into the brighter kitchen as the music for the distributor's logo came on.

His chief thought was to forget Michael and finish his damn movie review. The boy was still Laurie's problem, and Jack should enjoy the respite while it lasted. But when he sat back at the table, he could only stare through the typewriter. Writing, difficult enough when Elisabeth Vogler was present, was impossible with Michael in the next room with Clarence's movie. And Clarence's death.

Et ego in Arcadia sum: I too am in Arcadia. That was Death speaking Latin. Even without the movie, Michael had brought Clarence's death with him, and the review Jack was writing, which had seemed like stupid work to begin with, became worthless and irrelevant. Death threw everything into focus. Jack wondered if closing the door to the bedroom would help, except that the music for the title sequence was playing and he wanted to hear it again.

It was a version of Mozart's overture to *Don Giovanni*, with a disco beat laid in that seemed both sinister and witty. The sequence was one of the best scenes in the movie, the music promising a clever black comedy while the camera glided around couples dancing in a darkness that was like red gold—using the film lab where he worked, Clarence had printed and reprinted it until he had the tones he had imagined. Those tones were lost on Jack's TV, so he didn't get up to look. He only wanted to listen and remember.

Then the Mozart faded out and there was just the disco beat, and the first line of dialogue was read by the would-be actor who should have remained a would-be model: "Has anybody seen my girlfriend? She went to the ladies room an hour ago and I can't find her anywhere!"

Actors were not Clarence's strong suit. Worse, the dialogue by the rich brat who wrote and produced the film was even clunkier than his story. Clarence knew the script stank, but beggars can't be choosers on first features. The brat didn't care what Clarence did to his script, so long as the movie kept its six bloody deaths, frontal nudity (female only), and his screenwriting credit. Clarence cut some deadwood and a homophobic joke, and tried to make the worse howlers seem deliberate, but he couldn't write dialogue either. He had asked Jack to rewrite the dialogue, without credit or payment. Jack had considered doing it, for one minute, then remembered working with Clarence on the script for *Last Night at the A&P*, when he had to fight with Clarence over every line, every word, Clarence unable to say what he wanted, only what he didn't want. Clarence's nonverbal intellect, which some people mistook for gentleness and others for stupidity, came out in all its stubborn glory when he made a movie. Calm, daydreamy Clare turned into an exacting, tongue-tied tyrant. "Our Hitler," Jack called him, sometimes to his face, *usually* with a smile. Jack excused and lied his way out of doing the rewrite on what would always be a sow's ear, believing there would be better, more intelligent projects in the future worth the aggravation of working with his closest friend. Now he regretted not giving himself that month or so of intimate aggravation.

"I don't know what it is, but there's something mighty weird about this club."

That was the hero, played with surprising conviction by an actor named Doug Lipper: he convinced you he was a real actor if not always a real character. Jack had run into Lipper a few months ago at a screening in the Brill Building. Leaving the plush, suede screening room, Jack introduced himself, said he recognized Lipper from *Disco*, and mentioned Clarence. Lipper had already heard. He expressed enormous love and grief for his colleague, as only an actor can, then added, "He wanted me to star in a serious film he was planning. It would've been a great role. This thing has killed yet another remarkably talented man."

An actor's self-serving hyperbole, but Clarence *was* remarkably talented. You could see it in his short films and even in bits of *Disco*, a feeling for image, rhythm, and mood. What he didn't have was a feeling for story, or the ruthlessness that would've enabled him to steal a film from its cocky producer and bully a decent script out of a friend. He might have learned that ruthlessness in time, only then he might not have been someone Jack would want to know. Awful as it sounded, Jack had feared he was losing his best friend to filmmaking long before he lost him to death.

It was a selfish fear. But Jack had been spoiled over the years by his friend's availability and lack of ambition. For the longest time, Clarence ambled through life like a tourist, seeing movies, listening to music, trying out different experiences, getting laid. He might hurt Jack now and then, but he was good, steady company. It was pleasant being around someone who enjoyed life without demanding too much from it. And such passive amiability made Jack feel very serious and successful in comparison. Jack had ambition—being a critic seemed a heroic goal during the struggle to achieve it—and Clarence had life itself; their friendship seemed to make a whole person. The lovers who passed through Clarence's bed were only supporting players to that friendship. They saw each other at least three times a week and talked on the phone every day.

Then Clarence discovered filmmaking. He had always talked about making films, but in the vague, what-if way of anyone who loves movies, too intimidated by the expertise and expense to think it a real possibility. Shortly after he turned thirty, he took a filmmaking class, as just another new experience, and stumbled into the underworld of film gypsies: Super-8 productions, student films, more classes, film cooperatives, film labs—one of which hired Clarence as a timer. He made new friends, ambitious amateurs like himself, most of them straight, and made his own short films. Jack didn't hear from him for weeks at a time. Then he met Michael, who was younger and more dependent than anyone else Clarence had been involved with, but who'd come along at a time when Clarence was too preoccupied to be fickle, or unfaithful. Nevertheless, Clarence suddenly had love *and* work. Jack felt like a failure in comparison, an unlovable grind, an unnecessary acquaintance.

When Jack arrived at the emergency room that night and heard the terrible news, beneath the thunderclap of what it meant, beneath his shock, disbelief, and fear, he had suffered the strangest feeling of satisfaction.

Even now, a year and a half later, he was ashamed and confused over that feeling. As if he preferred to lose his friend to death than lose him to work and success. It was not that Jack envied his friends their success. It was more an insanely possessive love—as if illness and even death might bring Clarence closer to him. Using friendship as a substitute for love produced emotions as grotesque as any that came from unrequited passion.

He looked around for Elisabeth Vogler, wanting to hold and stroke her a moment. The cat was nowhere in sight. A thoughtless, disloyal creature, she was probably curled up on the bed with Michael. Jack stood up, tiptoed to the door, and peeked in. Sure enough, the cat nestled between the boy's legs, holding up her shoulders for the gentle hand that rubbed the scruff of her neck. Michael had stretched out on his back and was watching the movie with his jaw clenched, so intent on the movie he did not look at the cat or glance at the door when Jack's body blocked out the light from the kitchen. Jack wondered what the boy was looking for. Was there really any trace of Clarence in the movie? Already it was lurching into its climax, a long, beautiful sequence filmed at The Saint, where Clarence had once been a regular. Here it was used as a straight dance club in an attempt to recreate the Parisian dance hall scene from *The Conformist*. What failed as imitation became original by default. The camera slithered across the floor, among jerking legs and hopping feet, then craned up until it floated just above the heads of a stormy sea of dancers, lit by strobe as if by lightning. Jack hadn't really wanted Clare to die at the very moment he had begun to use his gifts. The feeling of satisfaction had lasted less than a second. It was only guilt that fixed it in his memory and made it seem important.

A practicing ex-Catholic, Jack was at home in guilt; he was proud of his abilty to live with it. But he knew he should do more than accept guilt, knew he should put it to work, although all he had done so far with it was write a silly little article for *Film Comment.* He stood in the doorway and leaned against the jamb, pretending to watch the end of the movie, stealing glances at Michael.

He shouldn't pretend the boy was still Laurie and Carla's problem. It was time he did something, said something, helped this arrogant boy he disliked so much. He knew he disliked Michael partly because he saw his own egotistical suffering in the boy, untempered by age or self-understanding. Jack understood himself all too well. He owed it to Clarence and the others to come down from his critical height and make some of his self-awareness Michael's self-awareness.

There was a theatrical scream as the sex maniac–killer fell from the catwalk and crashed through the lights. The body hit the dance floor like a side of beef, which was what Clarence had used for the sound effect. Then more dancers arrived, Danny among them in his third role. Not noticing the stunned people staring at the corpse in the flashing, thumping darkness, the newcomers began to dance around the dead psychopath. Fade-out to the closing credits, accompanied by another shrill song from the

East Village band managed by the producer's girlfriend.

Jack stepped into the room and gingerly sat on the edge of the bed. Reverently watching the credits, Michael drew back an inch so they wouldn't touch. Jack knew what he watched for and patiently waited for it before he began the conversation.

There it was: "Special thanks to . . . Jack Arcalli . . . Michael Sousza . . ." Then the disclaimer about the story not representing real people, and the screen went blue and silent.

Jack leaned forward and turned off the set. "And they all lived happily ever after," he joked.

"Get away from me, stupid."

But Michael was only pushing Elisabeth Vogler off him, as if ashamed of showing affection to Jack's cat. He sighed importantly. "I've now seen this sixteen times," he announced.

"Really? I've seen it maybe a dozen," Jack admitted. "It's better in a theater. You know, they're showing it next month at Cinema Village. On a double bill with *Suspiria*." An artsy, incoherent Italian horror film Clarence had hated. Jack attempted a wistful smile. "It's funny. Both of us giving so much time to a bad movie."

Michael looked puzzled. "You think it's a bad movie?"

"It's your basic generic horror film. Except for the dance scenes and some of the camera angles."

"You must not understand it," Michael sniffed.

Jack had intended to use the movie only to talk about what they had in common. He tried to resist the impulse to argue film. "No, it's nicely shot and some scenes without dialogue are striking, only— What do you see in it?"

"It's a disturbing film." Michael addressed the blank screen. "It's full of menace and tension and death. Everybody dies in it. It's like . . . Jacobean tragedy."

Michael knew as much about Jacobean tragedy as Jack's cat did, but Jack did not pursue that. He had been afraid the boy would say the movie was about AIDS. "It's a scare machine, Michael. Like all those movies."

"No, it's only disguised as a horror movie," the boy insisted. "It's more serious than that. I'm surprised at you. That as a friend of Clarence and a film critic you can't see that."

Jack winced. "Well, Clarence said some pretty negative things about it himself."

"Of course. That's his right as an artist. The results never live up to the artist's expectations." Michael sat up on the bed, drawing his knees against his chest and wrapping his arms around them. "All the artist can see is his failure. Clarence worked very hard on that movie. I was with him from start to finish on it. There were nights when he didn't get home until three in the morning, then had to be up again at six. A normal man would've been exhausted, but not Clarence. He was too high on his movie. Because he believed in it."

"He worked very hard on it," Jack agreed. Clarence had claimed he didn't take the project seriously, then threw himself into it completely. Clarence didn't do anything halfway. He exhausted himself on that movie. Which must have weakened his body and triggered the thing that eventually killed him. *That* was what was disturbing about the movie, even tragic: it had killed Clarence. Maybe that was why Michael had to believe it was a good movie: the irony of Clarence dying for schlock was too black for anyone so young.

Jack gently said, "You miss him, don't you?"

"Of course!"

He sounded offended, and Jack was sorry he had brought it up so abruptly. "No, I know you do. I think about Clarence every day," he confessed. "So I can imagine what you must feel."

Michael stared long and hard at Jack. He clutched his folded legs and stroked the long bones. "I wonder if you can," he said. "I wonder if any of you can guess what I'm feeling. You were only his friends. I was his lover."

Jack kept his temper. Michael took what Jack granted him—the possibility Clare's death hurt him more than it hurt Jack—and slapped Jack in the face with it. He could ignore the other bits of arrogance that barbed Michael's conversation, but not that one. And he classed Jack's grief with everyone else's, which stung.

"Maybe. But he was my best friend," Jack said quietly. "We knew each other twenty years, Michael. Friends become more than just friends when you know them that long. They become part of your mind, part of your reality. When they're gone, it's like reality has broken in two."

"That sounds very abstract and neat. What I feel is messy and real."

"What I feel is just as real, Michael." Why did the boy fight him on this? Did he think grief was too valuable to share? A frail emotion that might evaporate if divided among others? "As real and painful as what you're feeling," Jack insisted.

"No. It can't be. Because I *lived* with him. I had sex with him." Michael grew more vehement. "Having sex with someone bonds them to you in a way *you* wouldn't understand. You don't understand his movie and you don't understand love."

You little shit, thought Jack. Don't you know what I've offered to do for you? "I have sexual feelings," he muttered. "I even fall in love. I loved Clarence as a friend. And not that it matters, but I even had sex with him."

Michael glared. "*You?*"

Jack hadn't intended to say that. Repressing other thoughts, he had let that one jump out. Why? "A long time ago, Michael. Fifteen years ago. I don't know why I mentioned it."

Michael narrowed his eyes at Jack, as if trying to picture him with Clarence.

"Only two or three times," Jack apologized. But he had no need to apologize. "It was when Clarence first moved to New York and lived with me for three months. In this apartment, in fact. He'd been to Europe and had lived in D.C. a year. And I was just coming to terms with myself, so he let me experiment with him a few times. We discovered it wasn't what we wanted from each other." Jack remembered the first time most sharply, when he finished too quickly and had to work and work to get Clarence to finish, confused and depressed that the erect cock in his mouth and the naked body squirming in his bed seemed to have nothing to do with the Clarence who was his good friend from college. In sex, too, Clare could be a disingenuous tyrant. That was the first occasion when Jack irritably wondered if Clarence seemed gentle and benevolent only because of his inability to put thoughts into words.

Michael took a deep breath. "I don't care. Clarence slept

with anyone back then. He even slept with Ben."

"And a thousand others," said Jack, getting back at the boy for *anyone*. "Actually, he thought he was in love with Ben, until he realized what he loved was having sex with a guy. Ben was his first." Jack was surprised Michael knew about Ben. He remembered being jealous of Ben that semester, without knowing exactly what was going on between him and Clarence.

"But *you* were never in love with him, were you?" Michael said sharply.

"No," said Jack. "I wasn't." Which was probably true.

"Then it's not the same," Michael concluded. "What you and I are feeling. Because I was in love with Clarence. And he was in love with me. I couldn't care less you fooled around with him. I don't see why you brought it up."

"I brought it up only because—I want you to know he was an important part of my life, too, and I have as much right to grieve as you do. You shouldn't be jealous of us because we knew Clarence before you did."

"I'm not jealous," Michael sniped. "I'm just sick of people telling me what I should feel."

"Nobody's telling you what to feel, Michael." Were they?

The boy gave his head a shake, his curly hair quivering like jelly. "Why can't people let me feel what I feel in peace?"

"We do. We're only offering sympathy."

"I don't want your sympathy."

This time, Jack saw what to do with his exasperation. As gently as possible, he said, "Then maybe it's time you didn't see so much of us."

Michael cocked his head. "What do you mean?"

"If we're such an annoyance to you, Michael, if you think we're always telling you what to feel, then it might be better for you to spend time with other people. People who didn't know Clarence. So you wouldn't feel they were forcing their sympathy on you. You should be meeting other people," Jack said kindly. "People your own age. You're not stuck with just us, you know. We're not your family."

Michael's brown eyes became wide and worried. He lowered the upturned nose that looked faintly piggish when his chin was raised. The arrogant boy turned into a frightened child. "You don't want me around anymore?"

And Jack realized with a start: *We are his family.* Michael had nothing to do with his real family. "No. Not that, Michael. We're your friends. I was just saying we can't be good for you. We're a closed little world and you should get out a bit. Like you did when you went to Europe."

Michael looked nervously around, then looked down and saw his toe sticking out of his sock. He reached down and pulled the hole around so it wouldn't show. He pulled his arrogance back around him. "You think I want a new boyfriend?" he said sarcastically.

"No, I don't," said Jack. "But I do think it's time you started doing things. Maybe some kind of job." He hesitated. "Maybe found your own place to live."

"But I have my own place."

"It's really Laurie and Carla's."

"I don't mind sharing it with them. They give me my privacy."

"Maybe they want a little more privacy?"

"No. We're fine," Michael insisted. "And it's Clarence's apartment. I need to be there."

Jack made a face, wondering how to get around that belief.

"You don't think I really mourn Clarence, do you?"

"What?" Jack couldn't understand where that had come from. "Of course we do. We just feel it's time you went on with other things."

"You think I'm faking it!" Michael said angrily. "You don't think it's real."

"I know it's real. Because I feel something like it. But I go on with my life, Michael. I write my dumb reviews and live my dumb life. You learn to live with it."

"You can," Michael sneered. "But he was the only life I had. You were nothing but his friend. What I feel's got to be ten times worse than anything you're feeling. It's got to be!"

"Then go out and kill yourself if you feel so damn bad!"

Jack could not believe he had said that. Confused by Michael, he had let his guard down and his anger took him by surprise. He should not have said that.

But Michael looked very hard and contemptuous, invulnerable. "What do you know?" he sniffed. "You're nothing but a silly old library queen."

Jack was feeling too guilty to take offense. He accepted the epithet with a shrug. Suddenly, both of them found it very hard to look at the other.

"Speaking of which, I should be getting back to the piece I'm writing."

Michael nodded and scooted to the edge of the bed to put his shoes on. He avoided Jack's eyes, nervously, not contemptuously, as if maybe he were feeling bad for what *he* had said. They had both gone too far. "May I quickly use your bathroom?" Michael asked the floor.

"Certainly. Do you know where the light is?"

Jack was back in the kitchen, standing over his typewriter, when Michael came out. Jack considered apologizing, but an apology might give too much importance to what he had said, which had been a nasty way of hitting someone with the limits of their grief, nothing more. Michael didn't apologize either. They were politely formal with each other.

"Thank you for letting me see the movie."

"Thank you for dropping by," Jack said, opening the door for him. "Give my love to Laurie and Carla."

"See you later," said Michael.

As soon as Jack closed the door, the conversation began to run back and forth in his mind, Jack finding all the places where he had said the wrong thing. He was such a buffoon with people, where you can't do another draft and correct your mistakes. He should have apologized for saying what he said. He should not have said the things suggesting they wanted to drive Michael *completely* out of their lives. He should have given more attention to Michael's sudden fear they thought he was "faking" his grief. Jack admitted the boy's grief must be as real as his own, but exaggerated, or Michael wouldn't be so defensive and insecure about it. The boy strained to love Clarence more in death than he had in sickness. Thinking that, Jack wondered if he too exaggerated his grief. Overdoing an emotion can make it bigger than life, easier to handle, and just a little ludicrous, like the emotions in opera. He wondered if he were exaggerating the importance of his conversation with Michael for the same reason. And yet, he continued to worry the encounter around his head.

He came back to his confession of having had sex with Clarence, and stopped.

It was probably the least of his mistakes, but Jack lingered over it for the sake of the memories underneath. The sex itself was no longer important to Jack. There had been a time a few months after Clarence's death when he tried to use the sex to bring Clarence to life in his imagination, making love to himself with the memory in hopes he could fantasize a sharper picture of Clarence. All that ever gave Jack were his hips and thighs and hairless chest, a face as self-absorbed as when Clarence listened to music. No memory key or madeleine, sex led only into itself. What had been most important about the event, and valuable, were the moments leading up to it.

Jack was the first of his circle to come to New York City, hoping to find an outlet for his love of literature as an editorial assistant at Doubleday. His mother lived only a few hours away in Trenton, but he felt painfully alone his first year in the city. He was overjoyed when Clarence telephoned to say he was moving to New York. Jack promptly told him he could live in his apartment until he found his own place. He had not seen Clare in their year since college, but he had heard the gentle hints from Ben and the rumors from others. He was excited by the prospect of confessing his own sexuality to Clarence.

When they met in Penn Station, Clarence *embraced* Jack. It was 1973 and for two men to embrace in public seemed a bold, beautiful gesture to Jack. They went straight back to Jack's apartment, picking up a six-pack on the way. By the time they finished the beer, they had told each other everything, from the guys they were ashamed of having fallen in love with in college, to their first awkward encounters, to Jack's pathological shyness in bars, which left him horny and full of longing even now when he lived in Greenwich Village.

It was Clarence who suggested they try it with each other.

Jack had considered the possibility only from a distance. But for the long, deep minute while they stood apart beside the bed and undressed, Jack believed this was why he was overjoyed to see Clarence again, that this was what their friendship had been about all along.

But it wasn't. Now, remembering his foolish depression and annoyance while he worked to make Clarence finish, Jack knew for certain he had *not* been in love with Clarence. If he had, he would have enjoyed the work and felt very close to him. Instead, it had felt impersonal and messy.

Afterward, Clarence understood perfectly what Jack was feeling, apologized and offered to sleep on the sofa. The next day they pretended nothing had happened and talked about movies and books, just as they had in Charlottesville. They didn't try it again until a couple of weeks later when Clarence took Jack to the GAA dance at the firehouse—in two weeks Clarence knew more about the gay scene in New York than Jack had learned in a year. They came home drunk and horny, and this time, Jack was the one who proposed it. Clarence tried to make Jack do things Jack wouldn't do; both were very apologetic and embarrassed afterward. Was there a third time? Jack couldn't remember. What he did remember was his relief the nights Clarence went home with somebody and Jack had his apartment and bed all to himself. Nevertheless, when Clarence found his own place and moved out, Jack missed the regular presence of another person in his apartment. It was around then he adopted his first cat, Bathsheba.

Sex and friendship. Jack couldn't decide if the sexual possibility—or obligation—intensified friendships between gay men or simply got in the way. There was no sexual edge in his friendship with Laurie, which might be why they sometimes took each other for granted. And Michael? What kind of sexual memories did he have of Clarence? They had probably had sex so many times the specifics were obliterated, and Michael seemed like one of those people who replace memory with stock phrases and generalizations.

Jack was standing in the door to his bedroom, feeling there was something else he should be remembering now. Then he remembered. He telephoned Laurie.

She wasn't home, so he left the message on her machine: "Jack-o here. Michael came by and I tried to make a start on things, but botched it. No harm done, I think, although I spoiled the cover story about you needing his room. Details at seven. Or whenever you get in. Bye."

Why did they coddle and fret over Michael like this? It was ridiculous. The boy was overly sensitive yet oblivious to the point of invulnerability.

Sitting at the kitchen table, Jack found himself rereading what was in his typewriter. He became interested again, undid the top of his trousers, and retyped the page, working in the sentence, "Requited love can make you stupid." It was too good a line for the movie being reviewed, but he didn't want to lose it.

6

LAURIE played back Jack's message on the answering machine and groaned. She had seen Michael's overnight bag in his room when she came in, and Jack's message was yet another reminder of what they had to do. She wished Jack had succeeded and solved the whole business without them. At least he tried. Hoping Carla would get home before Michael did, Laurie sat at her desk in her alcove and began to sort out the reports and fact sheets from her briefcase before she changed back into her real clothes.

The front door clicked open and shut. There were delicately heavy heel-toe footsteps down the hall, and Laurie's heart sank. The footsteps paused outside their bedroom door, resumed again, and disappeared in the living room carpet. Laurie swung around in her revolving chair to receive him.

"Back so soon from Connecticut?" she said as he came around the corner.

Michael stopped, then took another step forward. He looked as peculiar as ever to Laurie. Boyish and tall, he seemed ashamed of his body and tried to keep his movements very small, almost prissy. He wasn't effeminate, so the effect was just odd, like a basketball player whose body has been possessed by the spirit of somebody's maiden aunt. If Laurie had a body like that, she'd enjoy flinging it around.

He seemed more solemnly serious than he had been two days ago, when he'd been solemnly overjoyed to see Laurie and Carla. But in his hand he held a floppy paper cone full of white flowers. "Here," he said, holding them out to Laurie. "I thought you and Carla might like some carnations."

Laurie took them, suspiciously pulled back the paper, and looked, wondering why. "How thoughtful," she said. Michael was usually so thoughtless, she wondered exactly what Jack had told him. She should have called him as soon as she heard his message. "So? Did you have a nice time with Ben and Danny? Did you get to read your letters?" She found it difficult to think clearly with a clutch of flowers in her hand and looked for a place to put them. The flowers were dripping, and her desk was covered with annual reports. She lobbed the bouquet into a nearby chair.

Michael watched the flowers hit the chair. "The letters were okay. Ben and Danny fought the whole time I was there. I don't understand why Ben stays with Danny."

"Love is strange," Laurie said automatically. In fact, she

thought Danny was the best thing about Ben. That Ben stuck by someone who constantly pricked his pride and pretentions proved he wasn't completely swallowed up in self-importance. Laurie even liked their method of staying together by forever breaking up. It seemed such a dramatic relationship, almost existential.

Michael continued to stand in front of her, apparently waiting for something.

She wanted him to leave so she could call Jack. "When did you get back?"

"Around noon."

"That was a quick visit. What've you been doing since you got back?"

"Walking around. Dropped by Jack's for a bit." He seemed to watch her to see how much she knew.

"Jack have anything to say?" It was like digging a story out of the ten-year-olds Laurie used to teach.

"Nothing much. He was working. I dropped by just to watch Clarence's movie."

"Oh." Laurie hated that movie and thought even Jack took it too seriously. "Well then. I guess that gave you a lot to talk about."

"Nothing interesting." Michael was rocking a foot inside his left shoe, ready to leave but still not taking his eyes off her.

"Good then. Welcome back, Michael. Now if you'll excuse me, I have some paperwork to finish here. You probably still have some unpacking to do." She had to talk to Jack. He could be either devastatingly blunt about things or so subtly tactful not even his best friends understood what he was getting at. Laurie suspected he had been too subtle with Michael, and she needed to find out exactly what he had said.

"Unpack? Yes. If you say so." Michael began to turn around.

The front door opened and closed again. "Pooty! I need you!" Carla sang.

"In here!" Laurie shouted. She smiled at Michael, expecting him to leave, but he only stepped aside and stood there, waiting again now that Carla was home.

The whole apartment rattled as Carla ran jokingly through the living room, hollering "Home!" as she swung around the corner and—stopped dead at the sight of Michael. She straightened up from her pounce position. "Michael," she said crisply. "You're back."

"He brought us flowers," said Laurie, pointing out the bundle on the chair. "What kind did you say they are?"

"Carnations," said Michael.

"Why thank you, Michael. That was very thoughtful." Carla glanced at the flowers, then at Laurie, then Michael. "Oh, but it's good to be home to my haven," she sang as she bent over Laurie and hugged her. "Have you mentioned it yet?" she whispered at Laurie's ear.

"Uh uh." Laurie saw Michael watch their affection with his usual veiled skepticism. She turned away to kiss Carla on the neck. "Jack tried but must not have gotten through," she whispered.

"Ah." Carla stood up very straight, keeping one hand on Laurie's shoulder. "Say,"—she drew a deep breath, ready to get down to work—"would anybody like some tea?

Michael? Come into the kitchen and have some Raspberry Patch tea with us." Carla was determined to get this over with as quickly as possible.

"I have some things I need to take care of first," Laurie said, wanting Carla to wait long enough for her to get Jack's version.

Carla thought she was just procrastinating. "You can do them later. What we need now is some nice Raspberry Patch tea and some serious conversation. All of us."

Michael was blinking at both of them, but he did not look like he suspected anything. His hands hung complacently at his side, and his lips were closed in their natural pout. He took one last glance at his flowers on the chair, lifted his head, and calmly followed Carla toward the kitchen.

Laurie stood up and went too, deciding Carla was right to go ahead with this, no matter what Jack had said. She put the tea kettle on while Carla sat with Michael at the table.

Carla opened her fingers and ran them through her short hair. "Did you have a nice time in Connecticut?" she asked.

"It was all right." Michael sat perfectly still with his hands beneath the table.

"Good." Carla ran her hand through her hair again, then stopped herself by clasping her hands together on top of the table. She was having trouble straddling her natural self and the calm, objective persona she used with patients. "Well. We've been talking about you while you were gone. Laurie and me. And, well, basically . . . we just wanted to know what your plans for the future were, Michael."

"You mean, 'What do I want to be when I grow up?'" he said, almost smiling.

Carla faked a laugh. "Well, there is that. You should be thinking about some kind of job or vocation. But I was thinking more in terms of your living arrangements. How much longer you intended to stay with us."

Michael shifted in his chair but showed no alarm or hurt.

"We wanted to know because we have this friend moving to New York who—"

Laurie cut her off with, "I think we can be honest with Michael." Jack had made it clear they couldn't use their white lie, not even as a way of broaching the subject.

"Ah?" Carla looked across the room at Laurie. "Yes, well, our friend's visit was only the occasion for bringing up something we should have talked about a long time ago, Michael. Before you went to Europe."

"I don't give you enough privacy," Michael said. Or asked, the tone of his voice being so flat it was hard to tell.

Laurie and Carla looked at each other, startled he understood so quickly.

Carla cleared her throat. "Yes and no, Michael. It's a big apartment and all that, and the three of us get along pretty well, I think. Still— We were wondering if you'd given any thought to finding a place of your own."

Michael made no response, showed no response. Thoughts seemed to turn in his head, but they expressed themselves in nothing more than a single blink.

The tea kettle suddenly whistled and Laurie jumped. She recovered, picked up the kettle and poured the hot water into the teapot, pleased to have something to do.

"You mentioned our privacy," said Carla. "There's your

privacy to consider, too. I'm sure there's tons of things you want to do but can't, having two old women constantly underfoot. And it can't be any picnic for you always being 'odd man out,' as it were." She tried another fake laugh.

Laurie was surprised her professional, competent mate handled this as awkwardly as she would have herself. But a good therapist works with questions and the other person's willingness to talk, and Michael seemed complacently unwilling today.

Then he suddenly said, "I understand perfectly."

"You do?" said Carla.

"I've let this go on a whole year. I should have understood sooner." He sounded formal and artificial, but Michael always sounded a little artificial.

"We know you had other things on your mind, Michael, and we respected that," Carla assured him. "We didn't bring it up sooner because we respected what you were going through. And the fact that this was your place before it was ours. Also, it's so little bother having you around, there was no *need* to bring it up. So we just let it go on of its own inertia. Which isn't good, Michael. For any of us. You need your own place. A place where you can be yourself."

Michael looked around at the kitchen cupboards and walls. Sadly? Indifferently? He gave it all a mild frown, then nodded to himself. "When would you like me out of here?"

"Don't say it like that, Michael. It's not like we're throwing you out. No, you should take your time and find a place you feel comfortable with." But that sounded too close to the procrastination and inertia of the past year. "Maybe by the end of October? That's when our friend's coming. If you're not able to move in to your new place by then, Jack said you could live with him for a few weeks, if worse came to worst."

Michael only blinked at that idea. "That won't be necessary."

Carla was visibly uncomfortable with her reversion to "the friend." "And here's our Raspberry Patch tea!" she chirped.

Laurie set teapot and cups on the table and began to pour. "Not to pry, Michael, but what's your money situation like? After your trip?"

"Fine, thank you." Then, thinking it over, he asked, "Would you like me to pay rent for the months I've been living here?"

"Not at all!" Laurie said defensively, although Michael had been perfectly matter-of-fact, not guilty or accusing.

"What Laurie is asking is if you have enough money to get your own apartment. We don't feel you owe us anything, Michael. Not a thing."

"I still have his money. Most of it."

"I imagine you've spent only the interest and haven't touched the principal," said Laurie. "The way you live. The rent and all could run as high as fifteen thousand for the first year. If you decide to stay in New York."

"I'm staying. This is where my friends are," he said calmly.

"Of course," said Laurie. "But you do have enough to cover that and still have money left for personal expenses? Until you start working, that is."

Michael nodded and sat there, contentedly looking at something before him, presumably his future. "No. You're right. I understand perfectly. We've been letting this go on too long. I hadn't stopped to think. I want my own space. It's not like we're family and *have* to live together."

"Families," Carla groaned in agreement. "Most of us came to New York in the first place to get away from family." The majority of Carla's cases were family related and her feelings were less ambiguous than Laurie's.

"But we still expect to see lots of you once you've moved," Laurie told Michael. "We don't want you to think we're rejecting you in any way."

"I couldn't think that," said Michael. "No. No, my only regret is that we didn't talk about this sooner. My living here had gotten to be a bad habit and it's time I broke it. No, this has been a very productive talk." He nodded and smiled at them both, a cordial smile with a bit of pride in it, as though he were pleased with himself for sounding so adult. He picked up his cup of tea and drank half of it. "Was there anything else?"

"No. I think that was it," said Carla.

The three of them sat there and looked at each other, not thinking of anything else to say.

Michael quickly drank the rest of his tea. "Good then. It's settled. I'll try to be out by the end of October." He eased his chair back and stood up. "Thank you both for being so honest with me."

"And thank you for understanding our point of view," said Carla.

"Not at all." He stood there touching the table with the tips of his fingers. "Now, since it's all settled, I think I'll go out for a little walk. Maybe think about what kind of place I want for myself."

"You do that, Michael. Give it some thought. It should be fun to think and scheme over," Laurie lied. "Looking for your own apartment." Some people actually enjoyed apartment hunting in New York, but not Laurie and Carla.

He gave them a slight bow and a smile. "See you in an hour or so," he said as he backed toward the door to the hall, then turned.

A second later, the front door slammed loudly, but they were always forgetting how heavy the door was and letting it slam hard behind them.

Laurie turned back to Carla. "So what do you think?"

"I think it went very well. I think we've underestimated Michael."

"You don't think it went *too* well?"

"I asked myself that," Carla admitted. "I wondered what he might be repressing. But have we ever known Michael to repress anything? He might say it insincerely, but he always said it. Besides, it's not an unreasonable request."

"True. Maybe it's just because I expected him to be all pathetic and theatrical about it that I can't help worrying it's too good to be true." She got up and looked down the hall to assure herself Michael was gone. "He barely mentioned Clarence and never once called this Clarence's apartment. Let me call Jack and find out what *he* told Michael."

Jack answered the phone with the gruff, barely tolerant hello he used when he was writing.

"We did it, Jack. We actually talked to Michael."

He listened to her story, worried at first, then astonished it had gone so well. He sounded as skeptical as Laurie had been, but, arguing with his skepticism, Laurie found herself believing Michael's response had been genuine and sincere. Jack began to give in, expressed admiration for Carla's abilities in such matters, and became sheepish over his failure to do his share of the work. "I was my usual bumbling self with Michael."

"What exactly did you say to him?"

Jack described their conversation, emphasizing Michael's fear they thought he was faking his grief, Jack's brief mention of the apartment and the women's privacy, then how the conversation ended in lost tempers before Jack could pursue anything to its end.

"Hmmm. He never talked about grief with us. What did you say to each other when you blew up?"

"Oh, I told him he exaggerated his grief and he called me a book queen."

That didn't sound so strong, but Laurie suggested Jack may have loosened Michael up, given him something to think about—he had arrived with the flowers—and embarrassed him over his use of mourning. Laurie mentioned all that only so Jack could feel he had played a role in this, but it did seem like a real possibility.

"I guess our next step is to see if Michael actually moves," said Jack.

Laurie admitted it wasn't over yet, but insisted they shouldn't cripple themselves with worry until something went flooey.

"And?" said Carla when Laurie returned to the kitchen.

"He believed it. He sprinkled ashes on his head and said some of his usual your-baby-could-grow-up-to-be-a-heroin-addict things, but he said what he said to Michael and it sounds more plausible than ever." Laurie quickly repeated what Jack had told her of the conversation, identifying things that had reappeared in Michael's encounter with them.

"All right then." Carla clapped her hands together. "Enough about Michael for tonight. Let's go to our Hunan place for dinner. I feel like celebrating and this way we won't have to face Michael over our dinner table. I'm afraid he's going to be all open and intimate after our little talk."

Laurie changed into jeans and a flannel shirt, and they walked over to Broadway and ate in a neat, unpretentious Chinese restaurant that had good broccoli and no yuppies. Laurie liked to avoid yuppies, especially now that she feared she was one herself. She and Carla were co-op poor after buying the apartment, but, doing everyone's taxes, she knew she and Peter Griffith were the only ones among her friends with yuppie incomes. She went out of her way not to say the word aloud. Laurie had noticed you heard the word most often, and said with the sharpest contempt, from hypocrites thoroughly dedicated to the pursuit of yup.

Over dinner, Carla discussed a difficult case involving an elderly lesbian and her "super Catholic" daughter. Laurie discussed her old worries about the impossibility of moral investment: a corporation she had trusted because of their position on South Africa was being accused of anti-union policies. After three days of fretting about Michael, Laurie found it strange to fret about their work again.

Michael wasn't home when they got back from dinner. They assumed he was still out walking, or whatever he did when he disappeared for long stretches of the evening. Not even Michael could stay cooped up in his room twenty-four hours a day. Laurie suspected he might go to bars now and then, not really to meet anyone but just to drink and look and sigh. Jack had told her how easy it was to be perfectly alone for a whole evening in a crowded gay bar. Laurie and Carla curled up on the sofa together and watched their favorite prime-time soap, then Carla read the newspaper and Laurie did some paperwork before they went to bed. Michael still wasn't back.

Laurie had thought she'd want to make love that night, even though they'd made love both of the previous nights—something to do with the tension of having to deal with Michael. But tonight she and Carla simply cuddled a little in their nightshirts and lay very still and close together, Carla's arm across Laurie's breasts, Laurie's nose in Carla's clean hair.

"Maybe he met someone tonight and went home with them," Carla whispered.

"Oh, I'm not worried about Michael. He's out being importantly Michael somewhere. I doubt he's gone home with somebody, though. It would be the first."

"Maybe he did tonight as a way of celebrating the new life ahead of him."

"Maybe." Laurie wondered if the men still did that, had sex with someone the first time they met them. Jack joked that it was now up to lesbians to carry on the tradition of promiscuity. It was a dirty job, but somebody had to do it. "No, I'm sure Michael's fine. But I do admit I'm thinking about him."

"Like what?"

"Not to sound crazy, but I almost regret losing the burden of having him around."

Carla laughed. "You do sound crazy."

"He was my one good deed in the world. Without him I'll be just another greedy corporate woman."

"You're hardly a greedy corporate woman. Besides, you'll still have the burden of me."

Laurie laughed and kissed the top of Carla's head. "You're no burden. But I'm serious about Michael. I know it sounds dumb, but there's all this stuff going on—politically and health-wise and Reagan. And I'm not doing a thing. I just do people's taxes and invest their money. I know he didn't deserve it, but Michael was my 'cause.'"

Carla sighed. "I think you're wrong, you know. I think you do plenty. Why shouldn't good people be able to make money, too? And I know what you mean about Michael. But I've been wondering if maybe we've been making a big mistake treating him as our burden."

"In which way?"

Carla rose up on one elbow so they could see each other's face. "It crossed my mind before, but it really hit home today. When Michael responded so well to our being honest with him. Treating Michael as our burden might be what's made him into such a walking tombstone."

"But we've never come right out and told him he should keep mourning Clarence. We've cold-shouldered his mourning. Even Jack."

"I know. But there's no telling how someone as self-absorbed as Michael will interpret things. If I'd given him the same kind of attention I give to the people who come to me for help I might have picked up on it sooner."

"You have nothing to blame yourself for. Anyway, you were able to fix all that today. I thought you did beautifully."

"You do?" Carla laughed and lay back down beside her. "I felt as bumbling as Jack out there with Michael. It was only because Michael was ready that I stumbled—we stumbled—into what he needed to hear."

Laurie stroked her silky, bumpy head and listened to the silence outside their closed door. "If *you* were to die, I wonder how I'd be."

"Oh Pooty!" Carla tenderly groaned. "Don't be silly."

But she could be silly with Carla, could drop her strength and indulge her fears, real or hypothetical. "I'm sure I'd be fine. That's what worries me. I'd probably go on with my life without any qualms at all," she said guiltily. "Which would mean I loved you for purely selfish reasons."

"You imagining *my* death and not yours proves that's not true. Truly selfish people always picture their own deaths and how people'll respond."

"Maybe I love life more than I love you."

"I should hope so."

"Then you think I don't love you enough?"

"Oh stop splitting hairs," Carla laughed and snuggled into the pit of Laurie's arm. "We love each other really and truly and you know it as well as I do."

Laurie did, but she conscientiously needed to question it every now and then, assuring herself she didn't take it for granted, she wasn't asleep at the wheel.

Carla readjusted her arm across Laurie and prepared to go to sleep. "Anyway, that's not something *we* have to worry about, is it?" she murmured.

Christopher Bram

It wasn't, which was something else to feel strange about—Laurie seemed to want to worry about something tonight, anything—that she and Carla were spared what so many others were experiencing right now. Even Jack, who had not lived the utterly celibate life he suggested with his endless groans about age and fat and solitude, had cause to be fearful. Gay men had become vulnerable and human. Five years ago Laurie found many of them insufferable, repelled by their smug sexuality, second-hand macho, and attitudes toward women, which ranged from benign indifference to a contemptuous air that seemed to say, "Just because I'm queer doesn't mean I'm not a man and superior to any woman." Then she remembered the way Clarence had behaved toward her.

"Relax," Carla sleepily whispered when Laurie's body tensed beside her.

When Laurie met Clarence in college, he was a sweet, innocent goof. Always excited over some painter, composer, or film director he had just discovered, he laughed at his own joy and expected you to laugh with him. His joy in discovering things was infectious, even if it was something you already knew. It was wonderful running into him outside the library or coming up the hill to the dorms, a stack of art books usually under one arm, shuffling along in a sweet, private dream, a newborn aesthete from Danville, Virginia, rawboned and ponytailed—the redneck crewcut had grown out as quickly as his mind, and the big-jawed face was always framed by shaggy sideburns and an unraveling kerchief of tied-back hair. He broke into a grin the instant he saw you, popped out of his dream and shared the dream with you, like a piece of good news: Vermeer, Cocteau, Vivaldi, *Midnight Cowboy*, his first hit

of acid, his first taste of hollandaise. He told Laurie everything, even how as a child he drew plans for elaborate
mansions and palaces and then, because he didn't know
anything else, mentally furnished them from a Sears
catalog. With her other friends so intellectually insecure
and serious those years, it was a relief knowing someone
like "Angel Clare." Laurie had still assumed she was supposed to be attracted to men, but she never mistook her
appreciation of Clarence for anything like attraction. She
was much too serious a person for him.

She saw him only now and then in the years after
college, when she tried political work in Boston and
teaching fifth-graders in Cleveland, and trusted he was
still the same lovable anomaly. Then she moved to New
York with Carla ten years ago, saw more of Clarence, and
realized he had changed. They had all come out to each
other on visits or in letters, and her disappointment that
Clarence's uniqueness might be explained by his repressed sexuality was balanced out by the pleasure of
learning they had something in common. But it felt different in person. Clarence now looked at women, even
Laurie, with polite bewilderment. He smiled down at
Laurie with a blank gaze of "Why're we even talking since
we can't go to bed together?" It was puzzling at first, then
infuriating.

Sometimes Laurie thought she was the one who'd
changed, that knowing Carla had raised her expectations
of what people can be to each other. Sometimes she
thought his friendship in college had been just another
case of "A friend is only someone who got there first," as
Livy liked to say. Whatever the reason, she stopped trying
with Clarence, and he made no effort at all. She saw him

only in the company of the friends they had in common, never alone, never had a long, confessional, one-on-one chat with Clarence like the ones she had with Jack, Livy, and even Danny. She grew accustomed to his benign indifference and forgot their past, expected no more of him than she did of the pesky calico cat Jack fussed over.

Nevertheless, here she was, in Clarence Laird's apartment, lying awake and listening for the return of his widow.

"I wonder how *he* would be now if it'd been Michael?" she asked Carla.

But Carla was sound asleep, her moist breath warming Laurie's side, her arm responding to the sound of words in Laurie's chest with a minuscule shift of elbow.

Laurie shifted down to join her. This was her real life, she reminded herself. All her questions about her past and others were only idle thoughts, luxuries she could speculate on because she knew she had this life and this woman breathing beside her.

They enjoyed waking up early. It was Wednesday, and Laurie worked at home and Carla didn't have to be at the Center until ten. They liked the routine of starting the day together, eating a real breakfast, watching the morning news, exchanging their hopes and dreads for the day ahead. Also, because Michael slept late, mornings were one time when they could be assured of no interruptions.

Not until Carla was ready to leave for work and Laurie walked her to the door did they see that Michael's room was empty. His door was wide open and the bloated leather bag still sat packed on his bed.

"So he did go home with someone!" said Carla.

"I hope nothing's happened to him."

"What could've happened to him? He met another twink and they went off somewhere to *not* exchange bodily fluids." Carla could get rather blunt at times. "He'll come moping in later this morning."

Laurie decided Carla was right and her concern was only guilt left over from last night. She kissed Carla good-bye, closed the door, and went back to her alcove to see what could be done to save a ditsy, neo-punk illustrator from having to sell her mink jackets to pay her back taxes.

It was good, clean, heartless work, going through a Fiorucci bag full of sales receipts, then arranging the figures on a sheet of graph paper. Laurie completely lost herself in it and was almost done when the telephone rang.

"Me again." It was Jack. "I happen to be in your neighborhood and was wondering if you'd like to break for lunch."

"It's too early for lunch."

"It's almost one. Meet me out front and we can go eat lunch and talk about Topic A in peace."

She had forgotten all about Michael. "Yes, well— Could you hold on a sec?" She put down the phone and hurried down the hall. His room was still empty. She would have heard him come in, but she had to be sure. Knowing Jack's love of worry and how it brought out the worst in her, she became concerned again. "Jack? Topic A's still out, so we can talk here. There's stuff for lunch here."

"Where'd he go?"

"Who knows? Well, he went out for a walk last night and never came home."

"*Really?* Hmmm." He said nothing, then very calmly

said, "I'm just around the corner. I'll be right there."

She knew Jack didn't just *happen* to be in the neighborhood; he had come here expressly to talk about Michael. Jack could be oblivious, or he could be overly concerned. If it were the latter today, she would not let herself be panicked into unnecessary worry. Michael was fine.

Laurie opened the door to Jack a minute later. His posture was slumped and casual, but his mournful eyes looked more alert than usual. He bent down and kissed her hello. "Delivered my stupid review this morning. Was going to treat myself to that secondhand bookshop next to where the Thalia used to be." He stepped past her and looked into Michael's room, glancing around with mild curiosity. "He never came back last night?" he said nonchalantly.

"We figure he met someone and went home with him."

"That's probably it." Jack stuck his hands in his pockets and ambled toward the kitchen, doing his baby elephant walk.

Laurie knew both of them were pretending not to be worried, even as they went through the kitchen cupboards together and assembled things for lunch.

"Has he ever gone home with anyone before?" Jack suddenly asked. "Or been out all night?"

"No. Not that I can remember. But there's always a first time. Maybe he fell in love last night."

Still straining to sound nonchalant, Jack said, "How did he look to you when he went out last night?"

"Just fine. He was a little abrupt when he left, but that's Michael's rhythm. He didn't look depressed or suicidal if that's what you're getting at."

Jack looked at her with his mouth open, his tongue

pushing at the back of his lower lip inside his beard.

"What, Jack? You think we should start calling around to the hospitals?" she said with a lightly scornful laugh.

"Nothing. I just—" He pulled a chair out from the table and sat down. "I told Michael yesterday, when I lost my temper with him, that if he really felt as bad as he said he did, then he would kill himself. Or *should* kill himself, I can't remember."

"You really said that?"

"Yes. I hated myself as soon as I said it but, yes, I said it."

Laurie considered it, weighed it in her mind and tried to imagine how it would have sounded to Michael. Jack took words much too seriously—his own especially—and he had a bizarre need to blame himself for things. What annoyed her most, though, was that she found the idea of Michael committing suicide much too plausible. "Has anybody ever done what you told them to do?" she scoffed.

"I know," he admitted. "It's stupid for me to worry about, but I can't help feeling . . ." He stood up slowly. "Where's your telephone book?"

"Why? Who're you calling?" She was getting angry with Jack.

"A few hospitals and the police. Just to put my mind at ease," he grumbled. "What else did Carla say to Michael yesterday?"

"Nothing! What else did *you* say that makes you so damn sure Michael's gone off and blown his brains out!"

"Nothing at all! It's just a feeling I have, dammit!"

They looked sheepishly at each other, bewildered over losing their tempers.

Laurie made sandwiches and tea in the kitchen while Jack used the telephone at the other end of the apartment.

There was nothing like the spectacle of somebody else carrying your own fears to their logical, ludicrous end to make you understand how ludicrous those fears were in the first place. It was ridiculous, she thought. It was comical: poor old Jack fumbling out a description of the pompous little twinkie who had probably gone straight from a one-night stand to his first round of visits to real estate brokers. Jack used the strong, masculine voice he used on the phone with editors and publicists, and Laurie was able to hear him from around the corner.

"White caucasian male, twenty-three, brown eyes, curly brown hair in an expensive haircut, last seen wearing gray slacks and a white dress shirt, white socks, and black tie shoes. That's what he usually wears anyway. And a navy suit jacket. No, no distinguishing marks."

All that was needed to complete the comedy, Laurie told herself, was for Michael to mope into the apartment while Jack was reducing his corpse to a current gay stereotype.

7

MICHAEL had slammed the door hard when he left the apartment, letting slip out the anger he had hidden from the women.

Lying assholes. Greedy bitches. Dykes. The anger filled his head as soon as he was out the door. They thought he was too stupid to see around their clockwork smiles and sagely folded hands. They thought he wouldn't see they only wanted Clarence's place all to themselves. Selfish cunts. *This* was what Jack had been warning him about. Michael knew it the moment the little businesswoman tossed away the flowers he bought her. Why had he bought the pigs flowers?

He was too angry to wait for the elevator, too tempted to rush back inside and tell them what he really thought of their phony concern, like warm spit—he rushed through the door marked Exit. He had carefully hoarded his anger, smiling into their smiles, as cunning as they were, refusing to let them think for a second they could hurt him. They didn't hurt him; they disgusted him. The bleak stairwell banged with his angry hard-soled shoes. If he had shared his anger with them, they would have lied more concern, crawled into his head and tried to argue him out of what he was feeling. They only wanted him out of Clarence's apartment. They only wanted him out of the picture.

It was early evening outside. Above the tattered trees of Riverside Park, the river and sky were still light. Up the hill toward Broadway, streetlamps sputtered on and slowly glowed brighter, washing out the remaining daylight, prematurely turning the evening into night. The air was still mild, but the mixed light suggested winter. Michael stood before the building he had thought was his home and tried to decide which way to go. He walked up the hill into the gloomier light.

Liars, bitches, dykes.

But it was difficult to keep his anger pure. His use of words Clarence had hated no longer stung with the same righteousness. When his anger with the women began to falter, even a little, Michael could sense another emotion beneath it, a feeling or fear he didn't want to feel, something like what he had touched last night in Connecticut.

He had to be angry, he told himself. They wanted to get rid of him; he reminded them of Clarence. They wanted to forget Clarence. Only Michael remembered. And maybe Jack. But he remembered Jack crawling over his feelings that afternoon and how he had thought, "At least the women understand and respect my grief." He had been fooling himself when he thought that. He must have known he was fooling himself, because he realized the women wanted him out even before they started. Jack looked good now only in comparison to the women.

Michael was surprised to hear that Jack had said he could live with him, if necessary. But even that made sense the more Michael thought about it, remembering Jack's claim he missed Clarence as much as Michael did, that he had even gone to bed with Clarence. The fat, horny old critic. He was faking this great grief they had in common as a ploy to get Michael into bed. That was why he sat on the bed and crawled all over Michael's grief. It would be repulsive, like fucking a beached whale. Michael had been too trusting of Jack to even suspect such a thing, until now. He had trusted all of them, thought they were his friends, thought they still loved Clarence. But here they were, the women seizing Clarence's apartment, Jack making a play for Clarence's lover. They were vultures. Michael could be righteously angry and safely above any fears about himself.

With the buildings blocking out the sky and the street lit by shop windows and a river of headlights, Broadway looked sunk into night. Mindless office workers poured out of a subway entrance. Grim mothers rammed strollers full of babies and fancy lettuces through the crowd. Derelicts still stood on the corners and sat on the benches out on the median, annoying Michael with their greasy looks and the idea of their smell and pleas for sympathy. Winter would soon clear them off the streets.

The cool-edged air reminded Michael of school, and he missed the way life had been organized into classes and assignments. The furious neighborhood reminded him of Clarence. Here was the video store where he and Clarence rented movies. Here was the newsstand where they bought their Sunday paper. Here was a young woman walking one of those big baggy dogs Clarence said looked like children dressed up in dog costumes—Akitas. This was *their* neighborhood, Michael's home. How could the women so coldly ask him to move out? Michael's anger with the women changed into sorrow for himself.

He was standing alone at a corner, waiting for the light to change, when the shape of a derelict asked him something, then asked him again and Michael finally looked at the man. It was a blue-faced black in a soiled trenchcoat. He didn't look much older than Michael, until he smiled and showed a mouthful of splayed teeth.

"Sir, sir, 'scuse me, sir?" He spoke very rapidly. "I'm one of the homeless, sir, and I won't lie to you, I do need money, but I don't want you to think I'm asking for a handout or charity, I have too much pride for that."

The media gave these people so much attention they now had an identity and rubbed your face in it. Michael doubted they read the newspapers; seeing the headlines would have been enough.

"I want to give you something of value in exchange for your money, sir, because I have too much pride to panhandle. Now you give me a quarter, fifty cents, a dollar, whatever amount you choose, and in exchange I guess your age and weight."

Michael had never heard this approach. "And if you guess wrong, you'll give me back my money?"

The man smirked as if Michael were crazy. "Of course not."

"Then what's the point?"

"The point is I keep my pride and still get myself some bread."

Michael looked away as he reached into his pocket and found a couple of quarters. He had to get away from the man, and only money would break the creepy bond the man had forced on him. "Here. I don't want to know my age and weight." He dropped the money into the man's hand and stepped off the curb, but not before feeling his fingers brush a cold, rubbery palm.

He reached the other curb, trying to shake the feeling from his hand. He had no business feeling distressed by the encounter. The junkie had suckered a little pity from Michael, that was all. But something lingered in Michael's hand, like a queasiness in the joints. He had to get off Broadway and away from these people.

He crossed Broadway and walked east, down a street that felt treeless and deserted despite a handful of wiry trees and a couple walking their dogs. Accordions of brownstones were squeezed between granite-faced apartment buildings. Here and there in the dead stone peeked windows full of yellow light and comfortable furniture or shifting blue light and television sets: people's homes. They were oblivious of how cruel life could be for those who had no home, like Michael. He paced, listening to the angry click of his shoes. He touched his anger with the women again and drew back from it, as if from a broken tooth. It no longer seemed as solid, no longer promised to protect him.

He saw that he was approaching Columbus and realized where he was headed. He shouldn't want to go there

140

tonight, but he felt too vulnerable to return to the apartment. He did not want to stay alone either, not with the emotions creeping up on him. He stepped into an Asian market on the corner and bought a pack of Winstons. Outside, he adjusted the hair on his forehead and flattened the collar of his jacket in a darkened window full of knives, then went a few doors down and entered the bar.

Immediately there was a numbing roar of conversation and music. A rock video played on the monitor overhead, and people talked loud to make themselves heard. There were oxford cloth shirts, a scatter of important neckties fresh from offices, and several faces still glowing from the swimming pool or gym. It was early yet, and people had stopped here on their way home. The place had the atmosphere of a college reunion for a class that had graduated only a few years ago. Even the men in their thirties radiated college, confidence, health, and promise. Michael saw a pack of narcissistic guppies who didn't know life as deeply as he did.

He set one hand firmly on the bar and ordered a club soda. Even a beer seemed dangerous tonight. He stepped over to the wall roofed with a swatch of chain-link fence and stood between two knots of young men boasting about their jobs, one knot in publicity, the other in fashion retail, and solemnly opened the pack of cigarettes.

A blue-eyed boy in publicity stole a look at Michael, sighed to himself, and looked away.

Michael lit a cigarette, drew a mouthful of smoke—he never inhaled until the fourth or fifth puff—and loftily leaned against the wall to watch a busty woman do aerobics on the video monitor. There was something satisfying about being noticed when you had no interest in meeting anyone, when you were safely above all that. Michael rinsed his mouth with club soda and took another puff.

A clip from a popular situation comedy appeared on the monitor, and everyone stopped talking to look up and watch. Between the deliberate bursts of laughter was a click of billiard balls from the back of the bar. Michael watched but never laughed. The door opened and more people entered, one of them talking very loudly.

"So I told Terry it wasn't love and he was just trying to blowjob his way into *People*—oh!" The talker stopped when he saw the silent crowd facing him; the monitor was just above the door. He quickly recovered with a mocking wave of his right hand. "My fans," he told the two guys with him, coolly readjusted his black-rimmed glasses, then glanced up to see what everyone was watching. "These poor fags," he wearily muttered. "Getting their wit from television." James Teale had been weary and mocking even at Columbia, where he'd been in Michael's class.

Michael stood his ground and waited for James to see him.

"As I was saying," James went on and finished his story out of the side of his mouth while he checked out the room. When he saw Michael he drew his head back in mock surprise and lifted his eyebrows. He smoothly stepped over and stood squarely in front of him, smiling like a cat.

"Mi-chael," he purred, lightly mocking the name by breaking it in two. "Why what brings you here?"

"Oh. Just needed some air." But it was difficult to seem

nonchalant when James's whole manner made even honest expressions seem insincere.

"I haven't seen you here in ages. You been behaving yourself?"

Michael had barely known James at Columbia, but he had run into him here a few times when he started visiting this bar four months ago. Beneath his constantly muted irony, James always seemed to think Michael was overjoyed to see him. "I was in Europe," Michael told him as casually as possible.

"How nice. But how did you manage with the dollar so puny this year? Oh yes, I forgot. You have that boyfriend to take care of you."

Michael had told James back in school he had a lover. Since they started running into each other here, he told him only that his lover had made a feature film, nothing else. He could not share something that important with someone like James. Nevertheless, it was odd finding Clarence still alive in James's thoughts. "I did this on my own," he told James.

"Michael's married," James told his two friends, now standing behind him. "An older man. That *was* your boyfriend I met that night outside the Eighth Street?"

"*When?*"

"Back in the spring. A fat man with a beard."

Michael remembered and shook his head, relieved. "No. That was an acquaintance." James had come up to him when he was in a movie queue with Jack, wearily mocked the movie they were seeing—"I've never heard of it so I'm sure it isn't any good"—mocked the V-neck sweater Michael wore, ignored Jack completely, and sauntered off, fortunately without ever mentioning he knew Michael from this bar. Michael promptly told Jack they knew each other from school. "He's your age and he's like that?" Jack exclaimed. "Is your generation getting into pre-Stonewall retro?" But Jack knew almost nothing about gay men of any generation. James wasn't an old-style queen; he was a minimalist. Even Michael knew that.

"An acquaintance?" purred James, lifting his eyebrows into the pale wing of hair across his forehead. "Hmmm. Michael works so hard to be mysterious," he told his friends. "He has to. He's from New Jersey."

Michael had been worried James might mention Clarence's movie, then remembered that wasn't James's style: it would have made Michael too interesting.

One of James's friends was looking around the room, already bored with Michael. He was a lean, moody runt with a short, casually spiked haircut and sleepy eyes. He wore a brown leather jacket over a tight white T-shirt pooched by a slight tummy. Michael found him attractive, in a blank, annoying way. The other boy had a dark, strong-jawed face and jet-black hair that receded over his temples, although he looked about Michael's age. He stood there with his arms folded, looking at Michael and listening to James, his sealed, lipless smile breaking into a laugh every time James said anything that sounded like a joke. He found the "New Jersey" line especially funny; his laugh caught James's attention.

"I suppose I should introduce everyone," James sighed. "Michael, this is Arnie."

The dark boy reached over James and shook Michael's hand, then frowned as if afraid he'd done the wrong thing. His hand was moist and warm.

"And this is Lloyd. Lloyd, Michael. Michael, Lloyd," went James, making mock of the whole business.

Lloyd nodded his haircut without turning to look at Michael. "What're we doing here?" he grumbled. "I thought we were going to The World."

"We can't go yet," said James. "It doesn't even open until ten."

"The World," Michael said tonelessly, not letting on he didn't know what it was.

"Yeah," James admitted with a pout. "It's Rock and Roll Fag Bar tonight and they have good music. Sometimes."

"I wish they didn't do it on a weeknight. I have to be at work tomorrow," Arnie fretted.

James shared a contemptuous look with Michael, although Michael wasn't sure what they were sharing contempt over.

"What're we gonna do until then?" griped Lloyd.

"We're in a bar," said James. "I suppose we could drink."

"*You* can. I didn't bring enough money to stand around drinking."

James shared a contemptuous look with Arnie.

"I'll buy you a drink," said Michael. He immediately downplayed the offer with a shrug. "I'll buy us all drinks. I just got a big check from home."

The three immediately accepted, careful not to seem too eager.

Michael wanted to buy them drinks, and not just for Lloyd's sake; he didn't find the guy *that* attractive. Michael just wanted some company and buying them drinks should guarantee him their company at least for another half hour. He didn't really enjoy their company, but their impersonality and the challenge of playing their game of cool was the kind of distraction Michael needed right now.

Michael took their requests and made two trips from the bar to bring everyone his drink: scotch on the rocks for Lloyd, sidecars for both James and Arnie—Michael thought they might be putting him on, but the bartender didn't bat an eye—and a gin and tonic for himself. He had no fears about alcohol making him too emotional in this group.

"What do you do, Michael?" Arnie asked, a subtle way of saying thank you.

"Yabba, yabba, yabba," went James. "We're not talking about jobs or rent tonight. We're here to have fun."

So nobody said anything. The four of them stood in a row against the wall and unemotionally drank their drinks.

"Oh! I heard a wonderful piece of dirt today," James announced. With gossip he could allow himself to sound sincere. "You'll never guess who was listed as the co-respondent in the divorce of _____," he said, naming a major movie star above suspicion. After a suitable pause, he named a less major movie star, also male, about whom there were already rumors. "Of course it's being kept very, very secret."

"Wow. Really. Goodness," said Arnie, without irony.

"But how do you know?" Michael could at least assert himself against James with a little skepticism. "People can say that about anyone."

"Believe me. I know. This person I work with has a good friend who's a law clerk and—" James described a complicated procedure involving divorce papers that were sealed in New York but unsealed in Los Angeles and an additional friend, this one the law clerk's, who had a look inside. "They're paying the wife two million dollars so she'll keep her mouth shut."

It didn't sound completely plausible, but it was too good a story for Michael to want to annoy everyone by pointing out the holes.

"Wow. I believe it," said Arnie. "Incredible."

"I'd love to see the look on Reagan's face if he ever heard the star of his favorite movie was a fag," said James. "Even if I did vote for him."

"You voted for Reagan," Michael observed.

"Naturally. He was the best man." James proudly settled his glasses on his nose. "I'm not one of those fags who lets being a fag dominate his whole life, you know."

Lloyd snorted and derisively rattled his ice. "Who gives a shit about politics?" he muttered.

Deciding that was the right attitude, Michael dismissed his surprise that a gay person would vote for Reagan. He had spent too much time among old homosexuals and even James's use of the word "fag" sounded odd to him. He drank his drink and said nothing. The gin and tonic was already giving him a pleasant distance from everything.

James told more stories about "fag" celebrities—the magazine where he worked provided him with a wealth of stories that never saw print. He luxuriated in being on the inside of the real world. Michael pretended to listen, Lloyd pretended not to, but Arnie gave James his complete, rapturous attention. Michael decided Arnie was in love with James, or at least enthralled with him. Nobody fell in love anymore. Arnie was even dressed like James, wearing a robelike cardigan sweater with the sleeves pushed up to show the unbuttoned shirtsleeves underneath. They wore different colors and patterns, however.

Distanced by alcohol and his own silence, Michael found himself peering around the corners of each person's cool, reading their thoughts and looking for a place for himself. Arnie had no room in his thoughts for anyone but James. James was high on holding Arnie in thrall, but he wanted Michael here as a witness to the capture. It was a role Lloyd refused to play. Lloyd's silence and indifference to James endeared him to Michael, created a special bond between them even if it were only the mutual respect of silence. The alcohol was making Michael very quick and perceptive, he thought.

"Want another drink?" he asked Lloyd.

Lloyd shrugged and handed Michael his empty glass. James and Arnie had drunk only half of their sidecars, which were enormous, or Michael would've had to offer to buy them another round. This way he could be impersonally intimate with Lloyd.

He returned from the bar with Lloyd's drink and a new gin and tonic for himself. Lloyd thanked him with a brusque nod. He didn't look at Michael, but made a friendly smile with the corner of his mouth as he took the first sip.

That's all you need, Michael told himself. There was no exchange of intimacy more honest and real than one guy buying another a drink. Everything beyond that was bullshit. People his age understood what was real, were smarter about that than the older generation, who needed to wade around in each other's emotions to feel like they were friends. They only muddied things up with all their talk about feelings and guilt and concern. Michael felt very clear and solid with someone like Lloyd.

"How do you know Teale?" Michael muttered, wanting to build on their shared indifference to James, who now filled Arnie's ear with the rumors of a cat fight between two actresses over the love of a bisexual pop star.

Lloyd rattled his ice again. "Through Arnie. He's Arnie's new boyfriend."

"Ah. And you know Arnie from . . ."

Lloyd twisted his neck as if he had a crick in it. "He's my ex-boyfriend."

Michael glanced over at Arnie, wondering what made him so popular. He glanced back at Lloyd and admired him for being so indifferent. It sounded terribly messy, but people Michael's age, with their gift for keeping emotions simple and real, could handle situations that would reduce older people to nervous wrecks. "It's great you can still be friends," Michael told him.

Lloyd shrugged. "Yeah, well, it's not like I had anything else to do tonight. Hey, Arnie." He leaned around Michael. "We gonna eat or something before we go dancing?"

Arnie was too involved with James to hear.

"You can see her black eye in the photo we used, if you look real hard at the makeup. What?" said James. "I thought you said you didn't need food. That you were broke, remember?"

"Yeah. Just asking," said Lloyd, who shrugged again and settled against the wall.

"I've got money," said Michael. "You want to go eat

somewhere?" The gin and tonics had numbed his stomach, but he remembered he hadn't eaten since morning.

"Nyaah. Just asking to see how long we'd hang out here. Unless *you* wanted to get something to eat," Lloyd added.

"Only if *you* wanted to get something." Michael shrugged.

"Nyaah. That's okay. I only brought enough money to get into The World."

"I said I'd buy." Michael noticed James, then Arnie listening to him. "Hey," he told everyone, "I got a big check from home today. What if I take us all out to dinner?"

Arnie frowned at Lloyd. "You don't have to do that."

"Sssssh," went James. "Mi-chael," he purred. "You serious?"

"Sure. I got money to burn tonight."

"Well then," James told the others. "Wouldn't that be nice? It's not every night one finds a sugar daddy in our midst."

"Yeah," said Michael, liking the idea. "Let me be the sugar daddy."

"You coming with us to The World?" asked Arnie, sounding faintly guilty.

"Of course he's coming. He wouldn't be a sugar daddy unless he had us all night long." James broke into peals of giggles.

It was perfect. He could stay out all night with these guys and never return to the apartment. "I'll be the sugar daddy and the rest of you can be my tricks." He hadn't meant that to sound so nasty, but he was giddy now and could laugh at his accidental nastiness.

James struck a pose and swung the ropy belt of his sweater as if he were a hooker. "That's me, all right. Just a cheap trick. Oh Uncle Mikey. Can't I have just one more drinky?" He really got into the role. "Or I know. Let's go downtown, eat there, maybe drop into Boybar, and then go to The World."

"Sure. Why not?" said Michael. "That sound good to you, Lloyd?"

"I don't care. Whatever you people want to do," he grumbled. "But if we're going, let's quit fagging around and catch a cab or something."

James quickly finished his drink and Arnie did likewise. They all followed Lloyd out the door to the street, where he stood indifferently on the curb and let his friends signal for a cab, Arnie frantically waving one hand in the air like a student afraid the teacher wouldn't call him, James holding his hand aloft with the weariness of a boy who always knew the answer. Their sweaters were lightly blown behind them by the breeze rattling through the trees. The cool air and new sounds around him made Michael more conscious of what was happening. He liked what he was doing; he liked the bit of power he gained in spending money on people he wanted nothing from in return. He tried to remember how much money he had on him. He couldn't pull out his wallet and look, not in front of everyone.

A cab pulled over and the four of them piled into the back. "Make room for Daddy," cried James, pushing his boyfriend against his boyfriend's ex so Michael could sit beside him.

"Let's stop at a Citibank on the way down," said Michael. "So I can stock up and we can do anything we please."

"Anything?" James snapped directions to the driver,

then went into a nasal Long Island accent to tell Michael, "We can do Boy Scouts for you. We can do swim-team-and-the-coach. Priest and choirboys will cost ya extra though." James's voice was nasal to begin with, so he only sounded like himself without the veneer of cool.

The driver didn't even glance at his rearview mirror.

The cab stopped outside a bank on lower Fifth Avenue and Michael went in alone. The room with cash machines was empty and as bright and barren as a public restroom. Michael used his card and five-letter code and pressed buttons until the machine gave him thirty dollars, his usual withdrawal. He realized that wouldn't be enough and started all over again, using the code to enter his savings account, where most of his money was. He seemed to be drunk, because he found himself imagining all the layers of information and memory that must be shifting around beneath the green fluorescent screen while he waited for his money. The machine tsk-tsked for an incredibly long time counting it out behind the shiny cylinder. Then the cylinder began to rotate: Michael saw a stack of bills an inch thick. He grabbed the money and tried counting the tens and twenties, which were so new they seemed coated with clay. He had to read the screen to find out how much he had in his hand: "I have just given you $500.00."

He hadn't intended to take that much. Then he read what was left in his account: "$30,497.02." Laurie was right; he'd been spending the interest and had barely touched the principal of what Clarence left him, even though it was just normal bank interest. Michael had deposited the check into his bank account and left it there, not wanting Laurie to invest it for him, not wanting to think about the money, never giving it much thought except when he withdrew the fat amount for his trip. Only when he was staring at the impossible figure on the screen and remembering where the money originated did he remember what his five-letter code meant: C-L-A-R-E. He had used the code so many times his fingers knew it as a sequence of positions on a keyboard, nothing more. How could he have forgotten?

He frightened himself. He had forgotten Clarence. He didn't deserve to stay in Clarence's apartment, and the women were right to throw him out. He looked at the thick stack of bills in his hand and wanted to feed it back into the machine. It was too late for that, so he hid it in his wallet for now, only the wallet wouldn't close. It was like a steel spring with so much money in it.

He was startled by a furious drumming out front. He turned and saw James outside, pressing his body into the window and making faces like a polyp against the glass. Arnie stood beside him, doing anything James did. Lloyd sat in the cab, still idling at the curb.

Michael smiled and wagged his stiff wallet at them, then slipped the wallet upright into the inside front pocket of his jacket. He walked out the door. "Daddy's loaded," he announced.

"All for us?" James laughed and patted the thickness over Michael's heart. "Oh Uncle Mike. Not *another* evening of champagne cocktails and caviar."

"If you love Daddy you'll drink every last bit," said Michael in a low, worldly voice. What movie was that from? James's silliness allowed Michael to be silly and he suddenly felt wonderful.

Lloyd watched coolly as they crowded back into the

cab, but showed something like a smile for Michael.

James ordered the driver to take them toward Broadway and Houston. "We'll know where we're going when we get there."

"Odeon?" Lloyd said listlessly.

"Don't be jejeune. They wouldn't let us in with you dressed like that."

"How about that Thai place?" Arnie suggested.

"You're really in a rut. Uncle Mike's giving us a chance to try something extraordinary tonight. Aren't you, Uncle Mike?"

"We've got money to burn," Michael assured them. He remembered something about the money bothering him at the bank, but it seemed to have floated off. He really was drunk. Money to burn, he thought with satisfaction. What did he need it for anyway? What would happen if he spent it all? Not only what was on him but what was in the bank, interest, principal, everything. Well, for one thing, the women couldn't so blithely expect him to find his own place. He wondered how one went about spending so much money at once. Maybe spending this five hundred dollars would show him if it were a real possibility or not. A large sum of money with no future and no past was intoxicating.

They arrived laughing and stifling laughs at a downtown building with two limos parked out front. Michael felt even Lloyd was laughing now, although whenever he remembered to look at Lloyd he found the guy as cool and solid as ever. A twenty from Michael got them into a series of rooms like the brothels Michael had seen in paintings in Paris, but maybe he thought that only because there was a table full of people speaking French. Everyone here kept glancing up and looking disappointed, as if they'd just missed seeing someone famous. They all seemed to have come here for a fabulous party, only nobody knew if they were too early, too late, or even at the right address.

Michael didn't care. he had another gin and tonic in front of him, then a plate of roast beef and parsley, but those weren't important to him either. His euphoria was much grander than the sum of its parts. He could walk through walls, he was so drunkenly happy. James nodded at a woman across the room and said, "Actress-slash-model," which Michael found hysterical although he had no idea who the woman was. Arnie laughed, too, but laughed even harder when Michael got his attention with a stern look, then let out a loud belch. Lloyd, looking utterly at home here despite his white T-shirt, methodically ate a lobster.

The fashionably dressed woman who waited on them brought the bill and Michael paid it: just a little over two hundred dollars even with the tip. James was impressed, Arnie was embarrassed, and Lloyd didn't look.

Out on the street, a man in a green plaid sports coat stood beside one of the limousines and read the *New York Post*. Michael walked right up to him, shouted, "Taxi!" and burst out laughing.

The man looked up. He had a youngish face and a little middle-age mustache. "You boys going somewhere? I got an hour to kill. Arriving in this vehicle will get you into any club you can name. You interested?"

"How much?" asked Michael, still laughing. When the man said forty, Michael pulled out his money and paid him. "Hey fellas! Look what I got!"

The man checked his watch and opened the door for them. Lloyd promptly climbed in, but James had to hustle Arnie through the door, holding him under one arm and laughing something at his ear.

"Hey." The man wagged a finger at them. "I'm cool. But no monkey-business, hear?" He gently closed the door after Michael.

They sat sealed in a silent bubble of tinted glass and leather upholstery. All sank back and sighed, even Lloyd. The ticking of the dashboard clock made James and Arnie giggle. The man climbed into the front seat and asked where they were going.

"Boybar," said Lloyd and told him where it was. "Wait until they see me pull up in this."

They rolled through the street, everything altered by the tinted glass and smoothness of movement, as if they were floating through a dreamed city. All too soon, they dollied down a familiar street with sidewalks full of people, only it looked like an aquarium through the limo windows. People glanced and looked away, pretending not to notice the limousine.

"Can you pull up another foot?" said Lloyd. "So they can see me through the door when we get out."

The man looked at the anonymous entrance to the bar and parked just so. He got out and professionally opened the door on Lloyd's side. "Have fun, boys."

Without the tinted glass, St. Mark's Place looked shabby and grim, like a room lit by a naked light bulb. If the three bouncers inside the glass door to the Boybar were impressed or surprised by the limo out front, they didn't show it. There was a five-dollar cover charge and Michael paid it for all of them. They went down the hall and stood in a bare space with a long crowded bar at one end.

"This place sucks scissors," said James. "All that East Village attitude. We should've gotten that guy to take us straight to The World. But nooooo. Mr. Lower East Side had to play showdog for all his little Boybar buddies."

Lloyd finished looking around for faces he knew. "You wanna go to The World, we'll go to The World. I don't care."

Michael grinned and sang, "I don't wanna set The World on fire—"

Something was wrong; nobody laughed.

Michael tried a little attitude. "I don't know about you guys, but I'm going to The World." He turned around and walked toward the door, immediately followed by the others. "Too Bridge-and-Tunnel," he told the sullen bouncers as he strutted past.

The limousine was gone, of course. They had to walk over to Second Avenue to catch a cab, through street vendors, future and former junkies, and a pocket of heavy metal music. Arnie flagged down a cab, and this time Lloyd sat up front with the driver. Michael resumed humming his song, waiting for somebody to get it.

Another fare, another bill from his wallet, only the wallet remained as stiff and bulky as ever, even when Michael paid more money to a doorman or bouncer in the dark, rundown lobby of what once had been a theater. And he kept finding the smaller bills he received as change wadded up in his other pockets. His clothes seemed infested with money tonight.

Lloyd went off to check his leather jacket while Michael followed James and Arnie up a big staircase that looked like it had been left out in the rain. The red wall beside it was badly water-stained and a few scabs of gold gilt remained on the bannister. There was music upstairs, pounding like a heart, a raw kind of disco except nobody called it disco anymore. Climbing stairs toward music immediately reminded Michael of the dances at Earl Hall, where he had finally entered and climbed a long bannistered stairway toward a ballroom, and The Saint, where he climbed industrial stairs into a flashing, futuristic dome full of—

There was no dance at the top of these stairs. The enormous dance floor beneath the lofty ceiling was deserted. Music pounded from two speakers the size of refrigerators on the empty stage at the far end of the floor, but the twenty or so people here only stood around on the balcony overhead or at the bar in the back. The high ceiling looked badly scuffed, as if people had once danced up there.

"Oh damn. We're too early," James whined.

"Well, some of us have to work tomorrow," said Arnie.

"I don't have to be anywhere," Michael said with a grin.

He was bouncing on the balls of his feet to the music. The beat of the music, the sight of so much open, empty space in front of him: he couldn't stop himself. He stepped out on the floor, almost skipping to the music, and began to dance, lifting his knees and flailing his arms. People told him he danced like a spastic chicken, but he didn't care, not tonight, not even when he glanced up at the balcony and saw a few people coldly looking down, watching a skinny kid in a dark suit, white shirt and no tie dancing alone on this great pale floor. It felt good to let go with his body, just as he'd been letting go with his money. He looked back at James and Arnie, wanting them to join him out here, dancing toward them and back out again, trying to draw them out on the floor.

They stayed where they were, barely glancing at Michael, pretending not to know him. It seemed money bought you the right to only so much silliness.

Michael promptly stopped dancing and casually walked back to them. "You guys need another drink," he told them. "We all need drinks. Where's Lloyd?"

Nobody knew and nobody cared. They went to the bar, where Michael was tempted to let the two twits buy their own drinks. They had grown too accustomed to Michael's money and were not showing the proper appreciation for his company. Then he remembered that spending this money was supposed to accomplish something that had nothing to do with James and Arnie, although he couldn't remember exactly what. James and Arnie ordered beers and Michael stuck to his gin and tonic. "Never mix, never worry," he said, then winced when he recognized the phrase was his father's.

More people arrived but nobody was dancing yet. Michael stood with James and Arnie against yet another wall and watched people. A pack of boys, three or four years younger than they were, stood in the opposite corner in jeans and jerseys. They had a tough, loud quality that made them look like gaybashers. Only the self-consciousness of their haircuts was gay.

"Hmmm," went James. "The younger generation. Killer twinkies."

"Isn't that Lucian Whatzits over there?" said Arnie.

"Lucian Brock?" said James. "It can't be. I heard he's real sick."

"I know. But I'm sure that's him. Over there in the Armani jacket and gray sweatshirt."

Michael looked with them and saw a lean man wearing an elegant jacket over a sweatshirt and jeans, a haircut like peachfuzz and hollow cheeks. He knew the name only as that of someone in the art scene, a painter or dealer or something.

"Why does he have to be here?" said James. "I mean, shouldn't he be at home in bed?"

"Maybe he's in, what's it called when you feel better for a while?" asked Arnie.

"Remission," Michael said. He closed his eyes and turned away. "What's upstairs?" he asked, pointing at the balcony.

"Another bar. More people standing around looking cool," said James.

"Let's go up there. I want to check it out." Michael wanted to get away from the man they said was sick. He wasn't afraid of the man; he just didn't want to look at him. He stole another look at the man as he led James and Arnie toward the stairs.

The balcony was narrow and the rose-colored light made the people who stood up there look like waxworks. Around the corner was a large dark room with another bar and a woman bartender, the woman's face and glassy bottles behind her all lit from below against blackness. Michael finished his drink so he could order another.

"And two Heinekens for my boys here," he told the woman.

James set his half-full bottle down so he could take a new beer, but Arnie held up the bottle already in his hand and said, "None for me. I'm fine."

"*Two*," Michael repeated and paid for the beers and his gin and tonic with a twenty. "Keep the change."

"Go ahead and take it," James whispered to Arnie.

But the new bottle sat on the bar, Arnie pretending not to see it, yet ashamed to know it was there. Trying to hide his shame, he swept his hand over his receding hairline and blandly smiled toward the music outside.

"What's wrong?" said Michael. "You all of a sudden don't *like* my money?"

"What?" went Arnie. "Oh no, I'm fine, Michael." He showed the half-finished beer in his hand again. "I just—You don't need to spend any more money on me."

Michael suddenly hated him. He wanted to obliterate him and James with money, buy them a thousand drinks and see them passed out in their own puke. "You and your fag sweaters," he sneered. "You been sucking off my money all night. Two little whores."

Arnie gazed dumbly at him, then looked at James, needing James to let him know what to say or feel.

"Uh oh, Uncle Mike's on the rag," teased James, shifting his eyes uncertainly inside his glasses.

"You fags make me sick," Michael spat. "I've been wasting my money on two silly fags." He turned and sailed out of the room.

He felt wonderful for telling them off, as if he'd been wanting to tell them off all night. Tricks, he thought contemptuously. Hiding their nothingness in attitude.

He stood on the balcony and waited for them to trail after him, the way they had trailed after him and his money before. When they didn't, when he found himself alone on the balcony with his back to the barroom, his wonderful feeling began to fall. He lifted the full glass in his hand and swallowed, gripping the low balcony parapet with his free hand while he gulped a coldness that tasted like pine, something that should lift him above his emotions and turn feelings into mere thoughts. When ice began to knock his teeth and burn his upper lip, he lowered the glass and looked down and saw a few people below, dancing.

A dozen guys danced down there, almost in pairs, with enormous spaces around each person. Most of them were the "killer twinkies" James had pointed out, but there was one boy dressed almost like Michael: the white shirt buttoned at the collar, the lightweight jacket from a dark suit, and then, a sweetly young touch, a pair of baggy gray shorts that hung over his knees, like knickers. Michael was so eager to join the dancing he wanted to vault over the parapet to get down there. He knew it was further down than it felt, knew he was as drunk as a ghost. He balanced his empty glass on the lip of the balcony and hurried downstairs to find someone to dance with.

Down below, it felt less simple and more intimidating than it had appeared from above. Michael scuttled around the edges of the dance floor, looking for someone who stood alone and moved slightly to the music, as desperate to dance as Michael was. He saw Lloyd again, a white T-shirt slumped against a shadowy wall, a lazy look of boredom on his face that seemed intended as a challenge, or invitation. Michael was through with those jerks for tonight, Lloyd too, and he walked by that white shadow without even looking at him. Instead, Michael found himself looking at Lucian Block or Brock, whatever his name was, the man they said was sick.

He stood on the risers in front of the downstairs bar, talking to another man as Michael approached him. He seemed more gaunt than ill, but the idea of his illness made him more real than anyone else here, unnervingly real. The other man was thin and balding, with an anemic mustache that also suggested illness. Once the idea of illness appeared, everyone seemed suspect, the way seeing an amputee on the street can make you feel for the next few minutes that any arm or hand that isn't in plain sight might not be there. Everyone *was* suspect, but being told this man actually had it concentrated the reality on him. As Michael walked past, he heard Lucian say, "... a little ice chest for my medication."

He had intended to get as far from them as possible, but he suddenly stopped, just twelve feet beyond them. He remembered he had cigarettes and decided he had stopped here to smoke one. Lighting a cigarette, he could watch the two men, Lucian in particular, who was turned toward him.

He did not know what he was watching for. He did not know why he was afraid of the man. He was not afraid of the disease, not really, not after what he'd been through. Not anymore. But he was afraid of the man and fascinated by his fear, which seemed to be why he stood here and looked. Despite the last drink, his thoughts had turned back into emotions, but he was too drunk to find or invent plausible causes for what he was feeling.

A cheer ran through the entire room. The lights had

dimmed, except over the stage at the other end where two smooth young men in white underpants now stood and danced. Michael noticed them, then returned his full attention to Lucian.

The guy with the anemic mustache laughed and leered over the boys on stage. Lucian remained calm and perfect. He had a genuine cool, nothing like that of James or the others when their masks were in place, but a genuine cold wisdom that put him beyond pleasure. Michael felt it must be the death sitting just beneath the man's skin that made him so silent, handsome, and terrifying.

Lucian nodded at his friend and walked away. He walked by Michael—so close Michael could've touched him if he'd been ready—and went to the bar.

Michael followed. He stood just behind him, studying his long thin neck and the freckled scalp visible through his short downy hair. The wrist that stretched from the sleeve of the elegant jacket when he paid for his club soda was like a bundle of wires sheathed in skin. He turned around, settled his back against the bar, and calmly sipped, without seeing Michael.

Michael stepped up to the bar and stood beside him. Not looking at the man, he felt his presence more strongly than ever, like a center of gravity. He turned around, too, glimpsing an enormous speckled ear, settled his own back against the bar, and faced the dance floor, which was so crowded now you couldn't tell who danced with whom. Because he was drunk, everyone here seemed drunk tonight, drunk and weightless, everyone but the man beside him.

Bodies jostled on Michael's right as somebody forced

his way up to the bar. Michael was pushed against Lucian. He was knocked against the man and imagined he felt bones covered with clothes and virus. He knew that wasn't so, knew touch was only touch and his terror groundless, but the terror excited him and left him as breathless as the first time he deliberately touched another guy, when he was too frightened to feel anything sexual.

"S-s-s-sorry," Michael stammered and pushed against the body on the other side of him to give the man room.

"No problem," said Lucian, his voice deep and whispery, without looking at Michael.

But he had spoken to him and Michael wanted to keep him speaking, so he said the only thought he found in his head, "Would you like to dance?"

Lucian turned a calm smile on Michael. "Thanks. But I'm not much of a dancer these days."

"Then will you fuck me?"

Calm and smile broke. "What?"

"Fuck me. I want you to fuck me," Michael pleaded.

Lucian shot frightened looks around the bar. "You know who I am? You mocking me, asshole?"

Breathless and grinning, Michael leaned in closer. "I want you to fuck me, Lucian. I want you to shoot inside me with everything you've got!"

"You little psycho!" He pushed Michael away with both hands. "Get away from me you drunk little creep!"

"But I want you to fuck me! Please fuck me!"

"Who put you up to this? Whose sick joke is this?"

And Michael finally realized what he'd been saying. He was horrified. Then he burst out laughing, letting himself know it was only a joke, a disgusting failed joke that now had him laughing hysterically as he backed away from the man. There were people dancing around him, and Michael began to lift his elbows and stamp his feet even as he continued laughing.

The man glared at him, appalled and confused, and turned to the bar, folding his arms across his chest. The man with the anemic mustache hurried over to see what was wrong with his friend.

Michael stopped laughing and slipped between dancers. He moved deeper into the crowd, wanting to lose himself in them, needing to hide from the man he had insulted for being sick. It had been a vile, heartless joke. He couldn't understand why he had said such a thing, except he was drunk.

There was a small clearing in the dancing crowd. Michael began to dance, hoping to lose himself in that. He felt foolish dancing alone, so he tried to dance with some of the bodies sawing and swaying around him. Nobody looked at Michael. He tried to dance with the two boys in jockey shorts swaying on the bright stage. Their eyes were wide open but they kept their gazes locked above the crowd, like they were dancing alone in their own private rooms without even a mirror for company. Michael closed his eyes and danced in the dark room of his own head. He wanted it to be like running cross-country in high school, when he could disappear inside himself for miles on end, without thought or feeling, just a soothing dreamless sleep carried along by the beat of his track shoes.

He was rocking his hips, moving them in a way he

never moved them except when he was dancing or fucking.

"Oh, but I love being fucked by you," Clarence said again and again.

"You shouldn't have anything to worry about," he said later. "I only did it to you once or twice and never without a rubber, right?"

And later still: "I'm not asking you to have sex or even kiss me. Won't you just let me *hold* you for a few minutes?"

Michael opened his eyes, but nothing outside seemed as real to him as what he was thinking.

Won't you just let me hold you?

It felt dreamed or imagined, only it came to him with live emotions attached, not just remembered but reborn emotions, feelings that seemed to have been perfectly preserved while frozen in forgetting. Just outside his remembering seemed to stand a mass of forgotten incidents and moments, but all Michael experienced now were the emotions: fear and guilt and more fear. Of Clarence.

He had been too frightened to share his bed, too terrified to touch him. He had hated being in the same room with the illness.

Michael was barely dancing now, just shifting his knees and absently flipping his hands to the music. He did not want to remember this yet. He would remember it later, when there would be a sober calm where he could look at it straight and defend himself against what he'd felt and how he'd behaved. He danced harder, trying to shake away the memory his dancing had shaken loose.

"Watch it, prick!"

167

He had lost the beat of the music. He moved more wildly, trying to catch up with it again. He spun around and his flying hand hit something.

"You dumb shit!"

Hands pushed him away. An elbow hit his jaw. The crowd suddenly capsized and Michael was on the floor.

He deserved to be on the floor. He wanted to be stepped on and kicked. He had not loved Clarence sick. He had been too selfish and afraid to love a dying man. He looked around and saw a forest of writhing legs. It was like he was inside Clarence's movie. He had remembered the movie without remembering his fear of the man who made it. It was like he'd been drunk his entire life, to have behaved the way he had and then forgotten it.

He threw himself flat on his back and waited to be trampled into the floor. When nothing happened, when the bodies towering overhead stepped around him, Michael began to bang his head against the floor, wanting to knock himself out.

"Kid? Get up from there, kid."

A bald head with a handlebar mustache plunged toward him, and Michael felt his shoulders being lifted. He was rising up like Clarence's camera and he expected flashes of lightning up there, where he would float like a spirit over the bobbing crowd. But he didn't float and there was no lightning, only a handlebar mustache, a bald head as smoothly angular as an apple, and a set of darkly kind eyes.

"You okay, kid? Helluva place to take a nap."

"I'm fine. No nap. Fine."

"Let me walk you out of this stampede."

The man's concern was such a surprise Michael almost hugged him. But he remembered he had no right to hug or touch anyone. He pulled his arm out of the man's gentle grasp. "Don't touch me. I'm scum. I'm shit."

"You're shitfaced, you mean. Somebody's had tee many toonies. Here, let me get you over to some friends."

Again Michael jerked his arm from the man. "I don't have any friends. I don't deserve any. Go on with your dancing. I'm fine. Just fine."

The man looked back at another man with a similar mustache who had continued dancing while he watched them. "Okay," said the bald man. "If you say so." He patted Michael's shoulder and set him walking toward the nearest wall.

Michael stepped stiffly through the crowd, straining not to touch anyone. The man's kindness pained him. The man hadn't understood. If he understood he would have let Michael lay there and kicked him. Michael looked for Lucian, wanting Lucian to kick him, hurt him, do something to him to punish Michael for what he had done to Lucian and Clarence and everyone else. All he saw in the enormous room were dancing men, an army of friends who would never turn away from each other in sickness or fear. He did not deserve to be among them.

He hurried along the wall and past the bar, then down the stairs and through the lobby. He stepped out of The World into a silence so sudden and deep it was like stepping out of time. But then there was cool air, stark buildings, and the huge strange thoughts again, and Michael ached to step out of the world and time for real.

8

MEMORY is imperfect knowledge. People often remember only what is safe to remember or, when they need
to punish themselves, what hurts them most.

It began as a cough Clarence developed sometime
between shooting his movie and editing it. A dry, insistent cough, he blamed it on the shouting he had done
during the shoot—Clarence was unaccustomed to shouting. Michael blamed it on too many cigarettes and tried to
scold Clarence into cutting back on his smoking—his
scolding was more a rite of intimacy than an expression of
real worry. Clarence was too immersed in the movie to
pay much attention to either Michael or the cough.

He edited for fourteen and sixteen hours at a stretch,
coming home every night from the cramped, windowless
editing room near Times Square goofy with fatigue. He

obsessed over specifics, how shots didn't cut together, how certain scenes dragged, how his only hope was cutting more rapidly and cheating with the soundtrack. Despite his griping and the way he ground his teeth in his sleep, he clearly loved the work and enjoyed his suffering. He was both intoxicated and hung over with the movie. Michael grew tired of hearing about it, and a little jealous, as if Clarence were going on and on about an impossible infatuation with another guy. He tried to ignore Clarence's movie to devote himself to his last semester at school.

When Clarence finished, he screened the final cut for the boy-producer, the producer's post-punk girlfriend, and Jack and Michael. The event he had worked toward for the past six months took place in a grim screening room with folding chairs, a linoleum floor with missing tiles, and film canisters stacked in the corners. Afterward, the producer was quite proud of *his* movie and strutted around the room like a bantam rooster while he talked about his vision, his talent, his future as a filmmaker. He thanked Clarence for helping to bring his vision to the screen before he and his girlfriend hurried off to get to a party at Nell's. Clarence only exchanged weary, knowing smiles with Louise, the assistant editor. She alone understood what they had been through, but they said goodbye to each other as casually as two construction workers after a bad day.

Clarence remained distant even when he was alone with those closest to him. Jack complimented him on technical details and didn't have a single word of criticism for the film, a sure sign he hadn't liked it. Michael had been disappointed it looked like any other horror film and that none of his suggestions for the script had been used, but all he said was, "It's a real movie," an assessment promptly seconded by Jack. Yet Clarence didn't seem to care what either of them thought. He was numb to the movie now that it was done, relieved the work was over, and stoically amused by all the fuss that had preceded this confusingly empty moment. He insisted he wasn't depressed, only exhausted, and said he wanted to go to sleep for the next two months.

Only when he had time for it did Clarence get sick. The cough became a cold or some kind of flu; Clarence joked that it was his body's way of insisting he take a vacation. He spent most of the day in bed or on the sofa, taking long naps and listening to classical music. Michael enjoyed the domestic routine of babying the invalid a little, bringing him glasses of orange juice and cups of soup, picking up flowers and treats for Clarence on his way back from classes. Final exams were coming up and Michael did most of his studying at home. It was wonderful having Clarence around the apartment again after he'd been gone for so long.

After two weeks of this, Michael was awakened one night by Clarence talking in his sleep. It was not the usual nonsense questions that, once answered, would be followed by a reassured mumble and sound sleep, but a furious, absurd monologue about lost footage in Danville and a shot he had forgotten to include so that everything was out of sync. The bed around him was soaking wet and his body was like an oven. Michael tried waking him, but couldn't. He telephoned Jack, who sleepily told him it must be the fever breaking and he should let Clarence sleep. When Michael got back to bed, Clarence was still talking, his words now hammered apart by a chattering of teeth. The telephone rang. It was Ben. Jack had called him after thinking about what Michael said; Ben was better informed about the dangers here than Jack. Ben calmly asked Michael questions about Clarence's condition, then told Michael not to worry but they should get Clarence to a hospital tonight. He was to dress Clarence in warm clothes and have him ready when Ben came over in a cab. They could get him to a hospital sooner than an ambulance would.

There was no room for self-consciousness or thought that night. The crisis made thought impossible. Ben was at his best in a crisis, giving orders to the cab driver, demanding assistance at the hospital. Michael did everything Ben told him to do. They spent that night and most of the morning in the waiting room at St. Luke's Hospital. Jack arrived and he and Ben told Michael to go home and get some sleep, but Michael wouldn't leave. He feared a doctor would appear any moment to tell them Clarence was dead. Death was easy to imagine in the abstract space and bright white light of the hospital—he remembered Clarence hating the ugliness of fluorescent light. Jack brought the morning newspaper with him, shared it with Ben, and asked Michael if he wanted the crossword puzzle. Michael shook his head, confused they could think about anything else, surprised they could read the news and even comment on things to each other. Danny arrived, clean and shaved and looking like daylight. He sat with Michael while Ben and Jack went out to get some breakfast, held Michael's hand, told him not to worry, then left for a cattle call downtown when Ben and Jack returned.

When a doctor did appear, a woman with an Indian accent, she took them into a tiny office and told them it was pneumocystic carinii pneumonia. Which meant AIDS, which was what Ben and Jack had been fearing. It had only been a vague possibility to Michael, another name for Clarence's possible death. AIDS had been a regular presence the past four years, a condition considered and talked about as constantly as politics, almost as abstract as politics. But when Michael heard the word attached to Clarence, when it sank in, it seemed less frightening than death, more specific and concrete. It made Clarence's condition more public, tragic, and important for Michael, and somehow easier to bear. Ben and Jack took their own turbulent feelings of shock and helplessness and focused them on Michael, treating him with tender respect as someone tragic and important.

There was nothing they could do once they had the terrible news. Clarence was in intensive care and they weren't allowed to see him. They would be notified of his progress, the doctor informed them. Michael went home with Ben, where Ben tried to distract them by playing Danny's records of Broadway musicals. The silliest, sappiest songs would start Ben crying. The sight of Ben's tears helped Michael to find his own.

Michael spent two nights at Ben and Danny's, then stayed with Peter and Livy, who had more room. He didn't want to be alone and the others respected that. While time stood still, he was unable to do anything except watch television and look through magazines, forgetting then remembering the cause for his sadness. All of them ran out of ways to talk about Clarence, but nobody could talk about other things for longer than ten or fifteen minutes before thoughts of Clarence crowded back in, ending conversation. Finally, they could at least visit Clarence.

He was barely there during the first visits, a pair of glassy eyes looking up from a large livid face on a stone-white pillow, a dry flaking mouth that sometimes worked itself into a polite smile. After a few days he gained a little personality, made jokes about the "food"—an IV bottle suspended over the bed—and said the last week had been the worst acid trip he had ever experienced. "Who gave me that bad acid?" he joked, several times each visit, forgetting he had already said it. Then, quite suddenly, his alertness and good humor would vanish, as quickly as the skin of steam on a cup of tea, and he lay there looking confused and miserable.

In the second week he became Clarence again, or a reasonable facsimile, reporting his goofiest dreams or longings for fantastic meals while he grinned at his own foolishness, describing the dress and quirks of the patients and nurses who populated his world with a kindly appreciation of such human cartoons. Now and then, a new crankiness would break out, a resentful remark or bitter sneer, but it quickly passed and he went back to being himself, or rather the self his friends were accustomed to. Danny brought him a coloring book and crayons, just as a joke, but they were the gifts Clarence seemed to enjoy most. He never read the novels Jack brought him or looked at Ben's skin magazines. Michael felt the situation was too important for gifts or words. He sat beside the bed each visit, held Clarence's hand, and let the others do the talking.

Compared to what Michael experienced later, this was a pure and simple time, fear and the anticipation of grief housed by a hospital, made real by it yet contained by the daily visits.

He was ecstatic when Clarence was allowed to come home; he looked forward to taking care of him. It was the end of May and school was over—he had missed final exams, but that became trivial in the face of this—and Michael could devote himself completely to Clarence. Talking with Ben and reading everything he could find about AIDS, Michael had decided Clarence would be one of those cases whose remission lasted for years. He might die, of course, one day. Michael knew that, but in the way most people know they too will die, eventually. He fed Clarence, monitored his medication, and indulged him, doing everything he could that first month to get Clarence over this last hill into good health. Clarence remained in a quiet limbo of naps, fatigue, and restlessness. He seemed removed from Michael's efforts, amused and touched by them. The one time he tried to talk about death, Michael wouldn't hear of it. He scolded Clarence for thinking about it. He wouldn't even let Clarence talk about his past life, talk that suggested his life was almost over. Michael told him to concentrate instead on his next movie, the strange project Jack encouraged him to make called *Murder in the Faubourg Saint-Germain*. Marcel Proust investigated the murder of a duchess, doing most of the work in the confines of his cork-lined room and coming up with nothing more conclusive than that Time did it. Jack even wrote a few pages of script to give Clarence something to storyboard. The point of the story was beyond Michael, but he was pleased it made Clarence think in the future tense.

They tried to have sex, just hands and kissing, but Clarence's body couldn't respond and Michael felt bad, as if he were taking advantage of an invalid. Clarence tossed and turned in his bed at night, and they agreed it would be better if Michael slept in the bed in the spare room.

It was around this time that Michael came out to his family. It was the wrong time and Michael hadn't intended to tell them, but he lost his temper one night during a telephone conversation with his father. Mr. Sousza couldn't understand why his son had missed his exams, why he made no effort to make them up, what it was about "this hippie bum" from whom Michael had rented a room for three years that made Michael put aside his life to look after this guy while he was sick. Michael was feeling very righteous and noble. "This guy *is* my life," he told his father. "He's my lover and I'm gay. I'm gay, Papa. I'm gay and you're stupid, or you would've understood that years ago."

He didn't tell him what Clarence had. He hoarded that fact as something too important to share with any of them. If Mr. Sousza had been less emotional and more aware, he might have figured it out without being told, but he blocked out that idea just as he had blocked out his old suspicion his son might be gay. He felt insulted by Michael's confession and too angry to continue. All later conversations were with Michael's mother or his older brother, who called him a degenerate and an ingrate, accusing him of taking the family's money under false pretenses to come to New York to become a faggot. His mother called him only during the day, when the men were at work. She too was angry and upset with Michael, but spoke as if all this would pass, her husband's anger if not her son's homosexuality. She timidly asked about the state of Michael's "friend," although she never pressed for details and didn't mention AIDS, as if afraid to know. Everything happened over the telephone. Michael could not go home to Phillipsburg, and nobody came to see him. Mrs. Sousza told Michael to give his father and brother a little more time, but he thought her patience was misplaced. Besides, he was relieved to have his connections to his family severed. His life was now centered on something more dramatic than the small-minded people who had raised him.

But very slowly, without Michael noticing when it happened, his life with Clarence ceased to be dramatic. It became daily life: normal, troublesome, and a little boring. Michael wasn't the only one to feel this. Clarence's friends from *Disco of the Damned*—Louise, the assistant editor, George, the cinematographer, a couple of actors, although not the leads or the boy-producer—visited Clarence his first weeks home, then stopped coming, accustomed to his condition and able to forget it while they went on with other projects and ambitions. His friends from life continued to come, but even that became routine. Ben bought groceries twice a week, Laurie came over to work out Clarence's health insurance with him, and Jack dropped by simply to talk, yet all were slightly impatient with being there, treating Clarence as another duty in daily rounds already full of duties. And Clarence himself became accustomed to his condition, and bored with it.

He slept late, then diligently shaved and dressed for the day ahead, although most of his day was spent on the sofa in the living room. When the weather turned warm he found he was more comfortable in his underwear and bathrobe; he no longer bothered to get dressed except when there was company. He spent his time sleeping, eating, and listening to music, methodically working his way through his record collection. He lost interest in the storyboards he'd been sketching. Michael rented movies for them to watch on the VCR, but all Clarence could see in other people's films was the immense work that had gone into them for such paltry results; he couldn't watch more than an hour of a film without becoming so exhausted he had to go to bed. He left the apartment only when Michael took him to the doctor or clinic. There was no other reason for him to go outside that hot, miserable summer. They waited for something like health, but Clarence remained the same, getting neither better nor worse, his T-cell count fluctuating slightly with no visible effect.

Alone with an invalid all summer, Michael found his own rhythms slowing down until he became more and more like Clarence. Danny took him out dancing twice, but Michael felt guilty and lonely in a happy crowd without his lover; he came home early both times. Through an AIDS volunteer support group, Ben arranged for a "buddy" to come by the apartment once a week, just so Michael could get out. Michael spent his first free night idly walking around the city, noticing the sunny faces and worked-out bodies of guys his age, the baggy jams like long boxer shorts that were the fashion that summer, feeling as lonely and foreign as he had felt those first months before he met Clarence. He came home to find Clarence happily chatting with the volunteer, a pudgy serious guy in his late twenties, asking the guy about himself in a way he no longer asked Michael—Clarence already knew all there was to know about Michael. Michael was hurt to see him so talkative and friendly again. It was the fake friendliness Clarence showed with strangers, nothing more, but Michael was jealous. Whenever the volunteer came by after that, Michael only withdrew to the guest room, where he worked on poems about his father. He had discovered emotions that lent themselves to the broken phrasing he mistook for poetry, and enjoyed unleashing all his resentment toward his father. He attempted to make friends with the "buddy," but the guy was officious and condescending with Michael, as if he thought he had replaced him in a job Michael neglected.

Clarence continued to thank Michael for every little thing, which felt strange. Now and then he spoke in the short-tempered voice of his filmmaking self, demanding Michael find a misplaced record jacket or answer the door or reheat food that had grown cold while Clarence talked on the telephone. He always apologized afterward. Most of the time he was the gentle, undemanding fellow he had been before his movie, although Michael began to feel he was only impersonating that fellow. His real self seemed elsewhere; perhaps his real self had always been elsewhere: Michael began to doubt he had ever really known Clarence. It was as though illness had loosened Clarence's personality just enough to suggest it was nothing but a mask, that he had never been as gentle, undemanding, accepting, and innocent as he appeared. Instead of feeling closer to his lover as they spent more time alone together, Michael found an unreal space growing around Clarence, a deep strangeness where everything seemed questionable or imaginary. He took Clarence only on trust.

Only then, when reality became as elastic as thought, did Michael experience what most people go through when they first encounter just the idea of AIDS: he feared for himself.

The fear was more common than the disease. Here was this disease people read about in newspapers or heard about on television, a disease so new and vague it registered first as a fear, a dread which easily worked its way into the imagination because it was so vague and general. People inured to old-fashioned worries about cancer or heart disease fell prey to this new fear. Anyone whose mind was already ajar with personal unhappiness or a neurotic disposition suffered it even more, experiencing a furious paranoia, a psychotic hypochondria intensified by the fact that one had good cause to be fearful, particularly if one was gay. There were hours of anxiety and many sleepless nights before one grew inured to the fear, just as one grew accustomed to the fear of nuclear war. People then went on with their lives, sometimes thoughtful, sometimes thoughtless, the thoughtful ones keeping the fear in perspective, worried but no longer debilitated by panic. The more passionately thoughtful turned their fear into anger.

Michael had not yet experienced the fear; he had skipped that phase of knowledge. Before he knew he was gay, he thought only gays and addicts caught AIDS. When he discovered he was gay, he was too relieved to find love and sex in his life to be afraid—and Clarence was unobtrusively careful for both of them. When Clarence was diagnosed, Michael was too overwhelmed by the fact it was Clarence to think about his own vulnerability. Only when the situation lost its urgency and Clarence was no longer quite Clarence did Michael become afraid for himself.

He developed a sore throat. He thought little of it the first few days, except to note which cups and glasses Clarence used so he wouldn't use them too; he couldn't give his cold to his defenseless lover. One night Michael lay on his bed in the guest room with the sheets kicked back. He had to do it quietly. They left their doors open in case Clarence needed something in the night; Michael felt funny about doing this alone again, his partner at the other end of a silent, open apartment full of corners, shadows, and the soft glow of the night light in the hall. He hurried himself along by remembering sex with Clarence, the first times, then the routine times past counting, then the hidden, half-forgotten times—nights they began making love in their sleep, teasing each other the next morning with accounts of similar dirty dreams. Michael used his memories of that to finish now, then found himself alone and pointlessly naked in the empty bed. Listening for the familiar sandpapery breathing in the distance, he began touching the glands beneath his jaw. Had they always been safe during their half-awake dreams of sex? Michael repeatedly swallowed, exploring the soreness in his throat, then fingered the nodes beneath his arms. Hours passed while he worried the possibility around in his head, and it became a fear.

In the days that followed, Michael forgot his fear while he waited on Clarence or spent any time with him. But when Clarence was asleep and Michael was alone, the fear returned: he had it too. He thought he had understood perfectly what Clarence was experiencing, but Michael had accepted much of it on trust, the way one accepts another person's statement they have a headache or other private pain. Now he imagined suffering what Clarence must suffer, and he was terrified. He wasn't afraid of death; he couldn't imagine death. What he feared was sickness, the condition he had lived with for three months without ever feeling it himself. His fear was like a terrible sympathy with Clarence.

Michael told himself he was crazy to believe he had AIDS—his glands weren't swollen and his sore throat was nothing—but he could not reason himself out of his fear. All he had read about the disease, all the unanswered questions, only made his anxiety worse. He couldn't share these worries with Clarence, but he was too ashamed to talk about them with Ben or Jack, either. It was too selfish and self-important a fear to share with anyone. Early on, Jack had mentioned the possibility of Michael getting himself tested. Ben argued against it, citing political reasons as well as the fact that, at the time, there was nothing they could do if you tested positive. Worry was only turned into a feeling of doom, and false-positives were so common as to make the whole procedure psychologically dangerous. But Michael was already crazy with worry. Without telling anyone, he went to a clinic one evening while the volunteer was with Clarence and had himself tested. On the appointed day, he telephoned the clinic while Clarence took a nap, gave his code number, and was given the results: negative.

He was relieved at first, then guilty over his relief, then began to feel he had somehow betrayed Clarence by being tested. It might have been worth the guilt if the fear had been completely dispelled, but fear only moved into a deeper, more irrational place. The disease was all Clarence's now. Michael's fear became a fear of Clarence.

He began to pay more attention to not drinking from a glass Clarence had used than he did to not letting Clarence use one of his glasses. When Clarence kissed him good night on the lips, Michael had to fight the urge to turn away so Clarence only kissed his cheek. He knew he could not catch the disease from saliva or touch, but the new fear was more impervious to reason than the first, even though it was more specific: an actual phobia for the body in his care. The harder Michael fought what he felt, the stronger the feelings became. Much of the time he could hide his feelings in a brusque, businesslike manner while he fixed the meals or cleaned the apartment—he became obsessed with keeping inanimate things clean and neatly ordered—but he betrayed himself when he was unoccupied and alone with Clarence. He found it difficult to speak to him except when he was telling Clarence to take his medicine or finish his food. He couldn't sit on the sofa with Clarence's head in his lap anymore, then he could not sit on the sofa at all. And he turned his head to the side when Clarence kissed him good night. Soon he was finding things to do in other rooms when it was time for Clarence to go to bed, then things that took him out of Clarence's reach whenever it looked like he might touch Michael.

He was ashamed of what he felt and how he gave in to it, but shame only fed the phobia. He made a point of not being in the same room with Clarence when Ben or Jack or anyone else came by, for fear they would see what he felt and know him to be selfish, perverse, and inhuman. He succeeded so well in hiding his emotions that Jack thought him young and oblivious while Ben thought he was being strong.

Clarence noticed the change, of course, but he watched it guiltily, as though it were something he had done wrong. He never mentioned it to the others and seemed to gently accept it, then placidly ignore it, like a good Southerner not wanting to offend his host. He became more polite and undemanding than ever with Michael, looking out at him from his bubble of illness with a mild smile that suggested both understanding and indifference.

One night he sat on his bed, bony and grandfatherly in the striped pajamas Laurie had bought him, and watched Michael snatch up the pieces of dirty clothes scattered around the room. He had ignored Michael's command to lie down and get under the covers.

"It's funny," he said. "I miss cigarettes more than I miss sex. But almost as much as cigs, I miss hugging and kissing. You must miss it, too."

Michael held the handful of empty clothes away from his body and moved toward the door. "No need to get mushy. There'll be time for hugging and kissing when you're feeling better." He heard the coldness in his voice and looked back at Clarence, intending to hide the coldness with some kind of smile.

"I'm not asking you to have sex or even kiss me, Michael. Can't you just let me hold you? For a few minutes?"

Michael was startled to be caught in his fear, stung and ashamed. It was as though he had believed the man was too sick to notice or care. But this was Clarence: of course he would notice. He found Clarence calmly watching him, without anger or resentment, not even sitting up straight to make the accusation.

"Don't be silly," Michael told him. "Of course you can hold me." He looked around the room, as if his only concern was to find a place to put the clothes he held in his hand. He carefully set the clothes on a chair and approached.

He drew a deep breath, bent down, and laid his hands on Clarence's back. He sensed the bony back through the pajama top, cool and moist like cheese, and his ear brushed hair and another ear he knew were powdered with dead skin. He felt himself freeze inside, sick with fear. When he thought enough time had passed to prove his love, he removed his hands and pulled back.

But Clarence had his arms around Michael's neck, and he held Michael there, kept Michael's face close to his and whispered, "Poor Michael. You're in over your head on this. You deserve ease and happiness at your age, don't you?"

He seemed to mean it kindly, but Michael detected bitterness and sarcasm behind the words, as if the words were thoughts Clarence attributed to Michael. He leaned into Clarence's mouth and kissed him, angrily, getting his tongue into the mouth and licking at the roof.

Clarence received the kiss from far away. He ran his hands over Michael's clothes without passion, only curiosity. He gently pulled Michael back and shook his head. "I'm sorry. Hugging is all I'm good for anymore. It must feel peculiar to you. Like that old joke about kissing your aunt and having her slip you some tongue?"

Michael slowly straightened up. He did not know what he had hoped to prove with the kiss. It had been sexless and angry and he didn't know who the anger was for. He could not imagine how he had once kissed and touched Clarence with nothing in mind but the pleasure of kissing and touching. "You just need to get well," he told him. "You don't have to worry about me."

"You don't hate me for being like this?" Clarence could say even that with matter-of-fact calm.

"No. Of course not. You don't hate somebody just because he's sick. Here." He pulled back the covers. "Lie down and get some sleep."

Clarence obeyed him, scooted up the bed and climbed beneath the clean sheets. He lay there like a child while Michael tucked him in. "But it gets boring, doesn't it? You must be bored out of your skull. I know I am."

"Don't talk nonsense. Get some sleep. You'll feel better in the morning." Michael bent down and kissed him on the lips, lightly. He gathered the dirty clothes from the chair and held them against his chest while he reached for the light switch. "Sweet dreams," he called out, looking at Clarence looking at him as he pulled the switch. The room went black and Clarence disappeared.

Michael was relieved he was gone, but he stood in the door until his eyes adjusted to the darkness and he could see Clarence again.

Michael's fear of Clarence subsided a little after that, although the handful of words and even the kiss felt so inconclusive they were easily forgotten. The fear itself and all memory of it were completely forgotten in what followed a month later. The weather changed and there was another attack of pneumonia; Clarence was rushed back to the hospital. It seemed almost routine now, and nobody spent the night in the hospital waiting room. Michael was expecting Jack the next morning so they could visit the hospital together, when the telephone rang. The news came in a commonplace telephone call.

The shock of death temporarily obliterated all that preceded it. When memory returned, Michael's past was rearranged around his grief: memory short-circuited around his time of fear and guilt. As more time passed, Michael sensed he had forgotten something, but assumed what he missed was Clarence. He returned from Europe afraid he was forgetting Clarence, and he read the letters, saw their friends, watched the movie one more time, hoping to find something to fix Clarence in his thoughts all over again. But what he missed, and what he found, was the memory of himself. When his forgotten piece crowded into him on the dance floor at The World, it seemed more terrible and unforgivable than it had been when Clarence was alive. It came back to him isolated and magnified by the year of forgetting.

Out on the street after fleeing the dance, Michael walked quickly with no sense of where he was going, wanting only to outwalk memory. Lifeless buildings like cold blocks of mud squatted in rows along a wide, deserted street. The endlessly overlapping streetlights illuminated a long waste of bone-gray pavement, fences blowing with newspapers, and glinting spirals of razor wire. He was still drunk, but so accustomed to being drunk he felt only the self-hatred binding his neck and blocking his thoughts. He remembered his fear, but little of what had preceded or accompanied it. He could not remember hugging Clarence the night Clarence asked to be hugged. As if in revenge for being forgotten, the memory came back to him with the final piece missing. He wanted to believe he had done what Clarence asked, but that seemed like only another lie now that Michael knew how selfish and cowardly he had been, a lie even if he had hugged Clarence.

He tried telling himself he hadn't understood. He hadn't really known Clarence would die. If he had known—but it was too late now to do anything with his knowledge.

Three men like clothes tied into knots stood in a broken doorway, eyes like broken glass hidden in the shadows of their hard swollen faces. Michael noticed them watching as he walked by. He hoped they would follow him, pull out knives, and demand his money; he could resist and be stabbed. They would cut out of him everything he was feeling. But Michael heard no footsteps or breathing at his back, nothing to take him out of himself for good.

He hated himself for forgetting how hateful he had been. How could he have forgotten that? His forgetting seemed as criminal as what he had forgotten. No wonder the others treated him as a phony who was only faking grief. His grief seemed just a lie now, an exaggerated monument used to cover his selfishness and cowardice. Love should be selfless and heroic. Michael had seized Clarence's illness as his chance to be heroic, noble, and good. But he had failed Clarence; he had failed love.

Michael suddenly grabbed at the idea he hadn't loved Clarence. Not really. It had only been sex and gratitude for sex and the absence of hassles that Michael had mistaken for love. He wanted desperately to use that idea to excuse himself for behaving the way he had. But thinking that thought pained Michael more than the memory did. If that too were a lie, then Michael was nobody, nothing. No, he could not let go of his belief he had loved Clarence, not even to save himself.

He heard the steady rumble and sigh of a highway up ahead and sensed water somewhere beyond it. He walked toward the water without thinking what he would do there, and found himself crossing on a fenced-in overpass, cars and trucks bowling through a concrete canyon as bright as daylight under his feet. He stopped and looked down, just as he had looked down from the balcony at the dance, and imagined himself falling. He gripped the diamonds of the chain-link fence and looked up to see how far he would have to climb. The wind was blowing hard. His jacket was flying out and dancing behind him like a tangled flag, and the air whistled and rattled in the hair around his ears; it was easy to imagine dropping from the sky like a dead spirit.

Teeth and jaw would break apart when they hit. He liked that, but the thought sobered him enough to think about the future as well as the past. Nobody would know why he did it. He wanted them to know. He felt his pockets for a pencil or pen. He found only money.

And he remembered the others: he was not alone. He could not throw himself from his life as if he were the only soul on earth. He had to do this, but he suddenly wanted to do it in a way that would prove to the others he loved Clarence, even as he proved it once and for all to himself.

9

A LOPSIDED wing of afternoon sunlight lay folded in the corner of the alcove. Jack gently placed the telephone receiver into its cradle one last time and stood up. He returned to the kitchen, where Laurie sat at the table with two neatly cut sandwiches on a pair of unmatched plates. Her arms were folded and her elbows on the table. "No," he told her. "No emergency cases or bodies matching Michael's description."

Laurie unfolded her arms. "There. What did I tell you? Michael's fine. He'll come waltzing in just when we don't want to see him. As usual."

Jack nodded and sat down to his sandwich. "The police said I might check Central Booking downtown. I'd have to go there in person to get anything. But that's only if Michael's been arrested for something."

"If Michael got arrested, we would've heard from him by now."

Laurie was being sane and objective, which was exactly what Jack wanted from her. With her flannel shirtsleeves rolled loosely above her elbows and her pale eyes glancing up at him through her pale eyebrows, she looked competent and cool yet concerned. But she must have worried some, because she hadn't touched her sandwich while Jack was on the phone. She ate now, but very slowly. Laurie was usually a slow eater because she was busy talking, but she was being quiet.

Although Jack thought he wasn't hungry, his sandwich was gone almost as soon as he sat down. "Do you think I'm silly to be worried? You're worried, too, aren't you? A little?"

"Mostly because you've got me worried," she said. "But okay. Yes. I was a little worried before you showed up. It's probably just guilt over asking Michael to move. Just like your worry is probably guilt over losing your temper with him."

"Maybe. Guilt *is* our element," Jack admitted. Intelligently rational adults, they were fairly adept at explaining their worst thoughts to themselves and keeping them at bay. Jack's anxiety had subsided while he heard himself sounding like an idiot on the telephone; it began to return to him now that he wasn't doing anything with it. "I just wish the idea of Michael killing himself wasn't so damn appealing. No, not appealing but— You know what I mean." Jack realized he did find the idea *appealing*, as if some part of him actually wanted Michael to kill himself.

"Plausible," Laurie said, the right word and proof she had

seriously considered it too. "I wonder why? It's not like Michael's been giving us signals or acting more depressed than usual. He's been strange since he got back, but more stuffy than unhappy."

Jack *couldn't* want Michael to commit suicide. "The thing is," he said, 'I don't really believe in Michael's unhappiness. Which I know is wrong of me. And his possessiveness about Clare annoys me, which is wrong too. So I've reacted against my doubt and annoyance by overcompensating and believing Michael to be so unhappy he really could kill himself. Yes?" he asked Laurie. "Does that make sense? Is that all my worry is?"

"But Michael has good reason to be unhappy," Laurie insisted. "After what he's been through. But being unhappy isn't synonymous with feeling suicidal. And experiencing death firsthand like that should cure anyone of wanting death for themselves. Shouldn't it?"

"I remember what I was like at his age." Jack looked at his fingers and wrists on the table. "You're not used to being utterly miserable, and death seems like such an appealing, easy way out. When you're older, you realize every mood passes, even the bad ones. But I remember a couple of times when *I* came very close—" He was talking about himself at the wrong time and backed off with a nervous laugh. "If I'd been raised Protestant instead of Catholic, I might not be here today."

Actually, he still thought about suicide now and then, whenever his attacks of loneliness became too much for him to bear. But it had become a kind of therapy for him, an alternative that put his despondency into perspective and made it tolerable again. Laurie accused him of enjoying his loneliness, but Jack felt this was a part of his life she couldn't understand: she had a lover and he didn't. Nevertheless, Jack realized he hadn't once considered suicide since Clarence's death, and had suffered none of his old attacks of bottomless melancholy over the past year. Then why did he imagine—or intuit—it for Michael?

Laurie looked very deep and thoughtful opposite him, following her own thoughts in silence. She suddenly shook her head and groaned. "I don't know, Jack. Michael stayed out all night. Big deal. With anybody else it wouldn't mean a damn thing. But he's not in a morgue. There's nothing for us to really do except be patient and wait for the inconsiderate dope to show up."

"You're right. I know you're right," Jack told her.

"You want another sandwich?"

"No thanks. Uh, you going to finish the rest of yours?" Half of her sandwich sat untouched on her plate.

"No. You go ahead." She pushed the plate over to him.

"I hope I haven't alarmed you," he said while he ate. "I should be letting you get back to your capitalist duties." He pictured himself leaving and going home and not giving Michael another thought for the rest of the day. And he realized he couldn't do that. His anxiety for Michael, temporarily stilled while he chattered rationalizations, grew stronger than ever. He could not do nothing. "You wouldn't happen to have any pictures or photographs of Michael around, would you?"

Laurie looked blank, then made a face. "Why? You want to put Michael's face on a milk carton?"

"Yes, I know it's stupid. But I'd rather be stupid than

spend the rest of the day sitting on my hands. I thought maybe I'd drop by a couple of bars on the way home and ask if anybody's seen him."

"Oh Jack." She gave him a pitying, condescending look, shook her head again, and stood up. "*We* sure the hell don't keep any pictures of Michael. Let's see if there're any in his room."

He followed her down the hall to Michael's room, surprised she was doing this. Laurie promptly began to pull open drawers in the dresser. Jack watched over her shoulder a moment—it was all socks and underwear—then went over to the windowsill, which was used as a bookshelf, and looked through the row of textbooks and notebooks. There was no photo album, and nothing that could be read for pleasure; Michael was as illiterate as Clarence had been. The narrow room was starkly utilitarian, with no pictures or posters on the walls, nothing but a yellowed medication chart still taped to the closet door. Jack turned to the packed overnight bag left on the bed. Unzipping it seemed a weirdly intimate, almost sexual act, especially after Jack pulled out a boyishly small pair of white jockey shorts.

"*Now's* when Michael will probably walk in through the door," muttered Laurie, going through the bottom drawers.

Jack was feeling something similar. He did not so much believe in the efficacy of action as hold certain superstitions about it: whatever you want will come about at the worst possible moment. The phone call you've desperately waited for all day will come only when you're on the toilet. The guy you've sighed over for months will show interest in you only when you've fallen in love with someone else. But Michael did not choose this moment to return.

"What's this?" said Laurie. "Ugh. They look like poems." She handed Jack a sheaf of looseleaf notebook paper.

"Oh yeah. Michael's my-father-didn't-love-me poems," said Jack, looking through them and catching a line here and there.

"What if we called them? Maybe he's gone out to see them or they know where he might be."

"No. They don't have anything to do with him and vice versa. And no wonder. 'You toad of the church, you hypocrite,'" Jack read aloud. "'I came and went from you like a fly on shit.'"

"I didn't know Michael was another ex-Catholic."

"Apparently." Jack read more closely, looking for something that sounded suicidal, but all he found were strained rhymes and a few more scatological epithets. The poems might be insane or they might be just bad writing. He passed them back to Laurie, and she returned them to the drawer where she had found them.

"Well, no photographs at all," she said. "Not even a picture of Clarence. Which is strange when you consider how fixated he is on him."

"It is, isn't it?" But Jack himself had kept no photographs of Clarence, quite deliberately. He believed photographs get in the way of how you remember something or somebody; after a time all you can remember is the photograph. He was amazed to think Michael might feel the same way.

"That solves that," said Laurie. "It's just as well. There's no way you would've been able to find him, Jack. Really."

"Did he ever mention going to a particular bar?"

"He never mentioned going to bars, period. Let's just forget it. If he doesn't show up tonight, then maybe we can—" She shrugged, not knowing what they could do.

Wherever Michael was, Jack imagined the words "Then go out and kill yourself if you feel so bad" burned into his thoughts.

"No. I can't do nothing," he said. "I'm going to check out the bars on Columbus, then swing by Uncle Charlie's when I get downtown. I just might run into somebody who knows him or remembers someone like him acting funny."

Laurie rolled her eyes and bobbed her head about in acceptance of Jack's foolishness. But she was gritting her teeth. "Dammit, Jack!"

"I'll leave you alone and you can get back to your work. This is just something I have to do for my own peace of mind."

"You get me all worked up over Michael and expect me to go back to my arithmetic? Thanks but no thanks. Let me get my shoes."

"I don't expect you to go with me," Jack called apologetically after her. "Maybe you should stay here in case Michael comes back."

"It'll serve us right if he comes back while we're out looking for him!" she shouted from the other end of the apartment. She loudly returned wearing work boots. "I think we're just jacking-off, *Jack*. But anything's better than sitting around here fretting over that stupid twerp. Don't look at me like that. Let's just go."

He felt bad about dragging Laurie into this but was glad

to have her with him. She made him feel less crazy. Now that he was doing this he felt like a fool again, but he preferred being a fool to being indifferent.

"Anyway," said Laurie when they were out on the street, "it's a lovely day for a wild twinkie chase."

Which it was, the air warm in the sun but cool in the shadows, the September light as clear and restful as water in a glass. Outdoors and moving, Jack could stop worrying so much about Michael. He was startled by the presence of another world in the streets, something he forgot when he'd been writing or thinking for too long, and he was stunned by the sheer number of people, most of whom must have inner lives almost as complicated as his own. He and Laurie passed through the scattered afternoon crowds along Broadway, then walked east, Jack lugging along, Laurie bobbing beside him. He imagined they looked like Mutt and Jeff in public. When they talked, they didn't talk about Michael but about an airhead illustrator whose taxes Laurie was doing.

The green trees in the park behind the Natural History Museum were speckled with yellow leaves, like eyes. Jack led Laurie to where he thought Cahoots would be, but the neon sign in the window said The Works, a bar Jack remembered being in a different block. He wasn't sure if it was his memory or the city that played tricks on him. Jack hated bars and never went to them alone; it had been years since he visited the bars on Columbus with Clare, before Clarence met Michael in fact.

They went inside and the young bartender and two solitary drinkers at the bar turned and stared. Jack thought they must look like a straight couple, despite Laurie's shirt and hair, which she'd pushed to one side in its boyish mode. Jack didn't think he looked gay, which was sometimes cause for relief but more often an annoyance—you had to be svelte and young to be gay. Jack was calm enough over Michael to feel self-conscious again.

"Looking for someone?" the bartender asked without being prompted. He was svelte and young, with cheeks like a chipmunk.

With Laurie standing back and looking around the bar, Jack stepped forward, explained they were hunting for a friend, and tried to describe Michael.

"Sorry, sir." His respect made Jack feel old. "I wasn't on last night and know only a couple of regulars by name. And this Michael person sounds like half of the boys who come in here."

"No, I understand that," said Jack. "But there's no harm in trying, is there?" He wrote out Michael's name and his own telephone number on a notepad the bartender handed him, although he suspected the piece of paper would be peeled off and dropped into a wastebasket as soon as he left. He asked about other bars on the street and was told Cahoots and The Wildwood no longer existed, but he might try an adult bookstore with a French name the bartender said he couldn't pronounce.

"Oh, you mean Les Hommes." It was one place in the neighborhood Jack did know. "Yes, that's a good idea. Thanks again for your time. Goodbye." He nodded to Laurie and they went back out to the street.

"I thought gay bars were more butch than that," she told him. "It was almost elegant in there, despite the hurricane fence in the ceiling. Where to now?"

"I don't know. This really is rather pointless, isn't it?"

"We knew that when we started, Jack. I've decided to treat this as my little tour of how the other half lives."

Her blitheness annoyed him, and there was her old condescension toward gay male sexuality and its rituals. Jack could be pretty catty about it himself, but it was different coming from an outsider, even someone as close to him as Laurie.

Les Hommes was on a cross street several blocks down. It looked both seedy and silly in the light of day, just a door with a sign in a blank wall. Jack was embarrassed to stand outside it with Laurie.

"Maybe you should call the apartment while I go in here," he told her. "See if Michael's come back."

"Michael wouldn't answer the phone if he were back. He never does. What's the matter, Jack-o?" she said teasingly. "You don't want to be seen in here with me?"

"No, I—you won't be comfortable in here, Laurie."

"Aw, Jack. Come on. You got me curious. I'm a big girl. I know all about gay men and their dumb little sex fetishes."

Jack snapped. "This is serious, Laurie! I'm worried about Michael and you treat this like it's all a joke!"

Laurie looked startled, as if she'd been slapped. She grimaced, kept her temper, and said stiffly, "We're doing this to keep our nerves intact. Remember? I'm worried. *You* got me worried. But I'm not going to get pious and frantic while we go through the motions of hunting for the little jerk." She drew a deep breath. "If you need to enter this holy inner sanctum without me, go ahead. I'll wait here."

Jack lowered his head—she understood him before he understood himself. "It's just that I feel odd having you in there," he admitted. "I used to come here. Now and then. That's why I lost my temper. I apologize."

"I figured as much." She sounded more tolerant than forgiving. "No, go on in. I'll wait out here. Or no, I'll wait over there at the corner, where I won't look so inappropriate."

He thanked her, apologized again, and told her he'd be right out. He waited until her back was turned before he opened the door and went inside.

There were no windows in the front room, the store portion of the place, and the fluorescent lights buzzing overhead turned the afternoon into two o'clock in the morning. The right half of the room was sealed off behind a scratched and smudged wall of plexiglass, like a derelict bank, a man at the window beside the turnstile reading *Soldier of Fortune* magazine. There was nobody else in the room. On the wall opposite the plexiglass stood a display case full of apparatus, the most prominent being a row of dildos arranged by size from the vaguely human to what looked like a stuffed moray eel. All attempts at verisimilitude—flesh-colored rubber, wet glaze, and swollen veins—only made them look more grotesque, so the handcuffs, leather masks, and cockrings seemed homey in comparison. Jack had wanted to cite the dildos as an example of the limitations of realism in fiction or film, but no review had come up where dildos would have been suitable.

He went up to the window. "Excuse me. I'm looking

for—" He gave his description of Michael and asked if the man had seen anyone like that last night or today. "It's important. He's a friend of a friend and he's disappeared."

The man looked up from his magazine with a weary smirk.

"It's a family emergency. Really." Without Laurie beside him, he must look and sound like a lovelorn chicken-hawk chasing down a recent trick. It was a repellent thought.

"Young preppy type?" said the man. "Sure. I think we got one of those today." He nodded at the curtained door on the other side of the turnstile. "Five dollars."

"You don't understand. I'm not looking for a *type*. This guy has curly hair and is very long and skinny."

"That might be the one. Maybe."

Jack knew the man was hustling him, but there was a chance Michael might be back there; he wanted to see to make sure. "Can you let me run in, have a quick look around, and come right out again?"

"Sure, pal. Five dollars."

It was the answer Jack expected and he knew it was pointless to argue. He paid the five dollars just so he could get this over with, and the bastard let him through.

Jack read the new sign posted by the curtain—it forbid sex *between* persons on the premises—and pushed through the curtain toward the sounds of moaning and heavy breathing. The sounds were the porn movie playing in the video room, a dark room with a dozen theater seats facing a video projector and screen where the granulated image of genitals squished and heaved. Jack hated the close-ups anyway, but he found the image sexless and absurd because he was here for something else. The video was the ultimate today in impersonal sex: it played to an empty room.

Beyond the little theater was the real space, a large room full of curtained booths and false walls arranged to form a little maze. It seemed like the sexual labyrinth of your own head when your mood was right and the maze was full of men. This afternoon there was nobody in the first leg of booths. The light was all red, which had caused him to quip, "People developing photos here?" the first time he visited with Clarence. Clare had laughed, drawing indignant stares all around. The men who came here were piously humorless, as if lust were so frail it could be shattered by a giggle.

Slowly, carefully, Jack stepped along the row of empty booths, afraid of making a sound while he wondered if he were the only person back here. The place was as hauntingly silent as it was when full of men looking through each other.

There had been a clump of men groping each other in the dark corner beyond the booths when Jack came here with Clarence. Clare laughed at Jack's joke, then, without any apparent shift of thought, eased himself into the grope, closing his eyes and smacking his lips when the dozen hands and half-dozen mouths gradually turned to him. They focused on Clarence not because he was attractive but because he was so appreciative. He was the only person Jack ever met who actually smacked his lips—over food or art or sex—with utter conviction. He was *almost* attractive, which made him look available in the eyes of men who'd be intimidated by anyone beautiful.

203

That, anyway, was Jack's theory about Clarence's sexual success.

Jack had hung back with the handful of others who coldly watched the little orgy. Clare's closed eyes and grin weaved in and out of the light, the rest of him a long red shadow between the shirt bunched under his arms and the jeans binding his ankles. Jack considered stepping in to ask Clare if he wanted him to hold his wallet, but resisted the urge and went back out to the little theater— it was movies instead of video then—and waited for Clarence, feeling very unattractive, stupid, and moral. He was twenty-six and righteously clung to his belief sex should be connected with love, or the chance of love. When Clarence came out, his hair was tangled and his face red with whisker burns, but he acted as though he'd done nothing more than had a nice relaxing swim. His capacity for pleasure endowed him with something like a self-healing innocence; Jack couldn't condemn him. Clare was genuinely sorry to hear Jack hadn't enjoyed himself and tried to make up for it by talking about books with Jack over cheeseburgers in an all-night diner.

Had they ever talked about anything besides books and movies? Jack suddenly wondered if Clarence had only been humoring him all those years.

No. Jack couldn't think that. From college days on, Clarence loved to hear Jack describe the novels he couldn't read himself, either because he was dyslexic or simply lazy—dyslexia was a concept Jack couldn't understand. Clarence didn't fully understand the nickname Jack gave him in Charlottesville until years later when Roman Polanski made *Tess*. "Angel Clare is a terrible person," he indignantly announced after they saw the movie. "Is that how people see me?"

"It was just a bit of sophomore cleverness," Jack assured him.

Clarence wasn't stupid. He always asked good questions and had interesting comments about the novels Jack described to him. The night after they went to Les Hommes, Jack talked in great detail about Flaubert's *Salammbo*, and Clarence said, "Sounds like a Maria Montez movie directed by Stanley Kubrick." Which was perfect.

That might have been the same night they argued about the phrase "guilty pleasure," an idea whose point Clarence refused to see. "Maybe it's just me, but I've always found that phrase a total contradiction." He laughed and added, "I'll bet you think it's a—what's the word? Redundancy."

Jack had smiled and nodded at that. He didn't go back to Les Hommes until a month later, without Clarence.

Jack turned the corner and started down the next leg of the maze. He had not anticipated finding the past here. When his thoughts swung back into the present, he was confused enough to imagine Michael was actually here. He stepped more quickly down the back aisle, hoping to catch Michael off guard even as he convinced himself he was alone in this place. Then he found the boy in a booth.

A hightop sneaker stuck out from under a curtain, pressing and twisting against the floor. Jack grabbed the curtain and yanked it open. A boy sat inside, a boy with bad skin and long hair lit by the video flickering on the little monitor. He bared his teeth and glared at Jack, looking like the kind of boy who'd throw empty beer bottles at you from a car with Jersey license plates. But the fly of his torn jeans was open and he was working an erection in his fist.

"Pardon," said Jack and he jerked the curtain shut.

Jack hurried to the end of the aisle, becoming more flustered. Seeing what he'd seen blew away what little reality the place had, although what had he expected to see at Les Hommes? It was finding nobody here but a street tough—maybe nobody else went to backrooms anymore—that made the sight so shattering. He remembered Laurie outside, and that grounded him back in reality. He gave his head an agitated shake, and left.

The fluorescent light of the front room was a sickly blue-gray after the red light inside—Jack didn't even look at the man in the window. The daylight outside was blinding, and Jack stood there blinking until he saw Laurie down at the corner. She leaned against a telephone booth with her arms folded, looking thoughtful and human. He walked toward her, shaking his head and holding out empty hands.

"No, huh?" she said, without surprise.

He expected her to make a crack about what took him so long, but she wouldn't, of course, not after what they'd said to each other earlier.

"You okay, Jack? You look a little funny."

"No, I'm fine. It's a strange place back there, that's all." Actually, he found Laurie strange after what he'd seen inside. Her boyish hair was confusingly sexual. If he didn't know her so well, he might even find her body sexual. Sex and Laurie were two halves of his life that had nothing to do with each other, happily.

"I made a couple of calls while I was waiting," she said

unimportantly. "Livy, who said she hasn't seen Michael since they ran into him in Paris. I didn't say anything to get her worried. And I called Ben and Danny."

"They're not back from Connecticut, are they?"

"I guess not. But I left a message on their machine. So. Where to next?"

Jack shrugged. "No place, really. Maybe we should go back to your place, see if Michael's returned, then I'll just go home. I might go by Uncle Charlie's when I get down there."

"Let's go downtown now. I'll go with you. We can swing by the Center and talk to Carla about this."

"Oh?" Jack liked and respected Carla, but was intimidated by her rocklike sanity. He suspected she thought he was a fool, or worse, without any of the self-recognition and sympathy that enabled Laurie to find him occasionally foolish yet still worthy.

"I've been thinking while you were in there, Jack. We're making each other positively nutty over Michael. We should hear what Carla makes of all this. She *is* more experienced with potential suicides than we are."

"Maybe." Jack was still anxious about Michael, but eating away at his belief was his ability to feel so many other things at the same time. Yes, Carla might be the person to shame him out of his worry. "All right. Sure. Let's go talk to Carla."

They walked west toward the 72nd Street subway station, Jack reviewing his thoughts to himself while Laurie remained oddly silent. She retained the air of seriousness that had come over her while Jack was in the bookstore, as if she had been thinking about something else besides talking to Carla. Laurie's silence was so rare it was suspenseful. Not until they were beneath the street and standing on the long, narrow subway platform did she share what was on her mind.

"Jack? Being brutally honest about this—" She sounded gentle and tentative. "If you were Michael, would your life be so empty without Clarence that you'd seriously consider ending your life?"

He bent his eyes at her, wondering what she meant.

"I just can't imagine him being such great company when he was alive," she explained. "Maybe I'm wrong, but I always assumed it was nothing but sex between them. I mean, what did they have to say to each other?" She hesitated. "You don't have to look at me like that. I bring this up as just another argument for why we shouldn't be worried about Michael."

Jack limited his anger to an exasperated sigh. "Just because a couple aren't like you and Carla doesn't mean they're not a real couple."

"It's *not* because they're not like us." She folded her arms and settled her back against the girder beside them. "You knew Clarence better than anyone else, Jack. Right? You know what I'm saying. Do you feel your life is over because he isn't around anymore?"

"An important part of it is, yes." He said it firmly, proudly.

Laurie pinched her mouth at him. "Jeez, Jack. I feel I've spent half of my life hearing you complain about Clarence. How self-absorbed and irresponsible and forgetful of his friends he was. You're as bad as Michael playing the widow. You are."

"Laurie, he was my best friend. You wouldn't understand. I don't have a Carla in my life. I miss him. I even miss complaining about him."

She was silent again, and he wondered if it was because he called Clarence his best friend instead of her. But then she said, "I think you love him more now that he's dead than you ever did when he was alive. It's easier now."

That stung and infuriated him. He kept control and firmly said, "No. It's clearer now, that's all."

"And it's why you're jealous of Michael's grief."

"I'm not jealous of Michael!" He was taken by surprise and his anger jumped out. "You don't feel jealous of grief!"

"Jack! You don't see that? You're jealous of Michael. Why else would you hate someone so much who isn't worth hating?"

"I don't hate Michael! Would I be running all over the city after the little asshole if I hated him?" He looked around and saw the other people on the platform glancing toward him and Laurie. He lowered his voice and said, "Michael's just a nuisance to me. But I know something of what he's feeling and I'm worried for him."

Laurie lowered her voice, too. "Maybe. Although I've been wondering if you're all upset and anxious about him today just to prove to yourself you don't hate him."

Jack bit the corner of his mouth and chewed his mustache. It was the kind of psychoanalytic nonsense he had expected from Carla, although Carla was too professional to say it outright. "Everything doesn't *have to be* a symptom of something else, you know."

"I know," Laurie admitted timidly. "It was just a suggestion. Just a possibility. And it made more sense than you being paranoid for Michael out of guilt over losing your temper with him yesterday."

"Maybe it's not just paranoia," he claimed. Their train was grinding, then roaring into the station, and he did not have time to toss off any valid reasons for his worry. "Maybe I have ESP!" he said sarcastically, raising his voice. "Maybe it's my woman's intuition!"

Laurie smiled, as if his joke were a return to the old Jack, and they stepped into the crowded subway car.

But Jack found he was still angry with her on the ride downtown. The train was too loud for them to talk without shouting, and Jack was afraid shouting would put him in closer touch with his anger. What gave her the right to say he loved Clare better dead than he had loved him alive? He stood shoved against her among the slack bodies coming home from work, able to see her only as a reflection in the darkened window. Jack never knew what to do with his anger. It debilitated him, left him feeling empty, helpless, and stupid. He was far more comfortable with guilt.

The Lesbian and Gay Community Services Center stood on West 13th Street, an enormous abandoned school the city sold to the jumble of gay and lesbian organizations that had sprung up like a bureaucratic boomtown over the past ten years. The building's tall brick front looked as plain and quaint as an old warehouse on the street of brownstones, and the inside still looked like an abandoned school. Beneath the intimidatingly high ceilings— the school had been built in an age when there was the desire and money to awe occupants with the power of an institution—everything looked secondhand and temporary. The maintenance fees alone were exorbitant, and there was never enough money left over to make the place more than habitable. The public spaces were bare of anything new except the crowded bulletin boards and numerous posters and the occasional coat of fresh paint. It was Danny's contention the Center had been carefully redecorated in High Lesbian.

Jack remembered the joke without smiling as he followed Laurie through the reception area, where a bearded volunteer with an ear punched full of studs and doodads sat at a chipped wooden desk and answered the telephone. Jack came here only when he was meeting Ben and Danny or Laurie and Carla for dinner, although he lived just a few blocks downtown from the Center. The social activities never appealed to him, and they attracted a class of gay men that made Jack uncomfortable. All manner of women came here, but Jack thought the men were almost always the ones you never saw in bars—the shy or middle-aged or homely or fat, all of which Jack knew himself to be, but he didn't like having his nose rubbed in it.

He followed Laurie up the long stairs in the cavernous stairwell, telling himself he had nothing to fear from Carla, that there was nothing she could say worse than what Laurie had told him. He remained angry with Laurie, but it was a quiet, tolerant anger. He knew he was worried for Michael in spite of his dislike for the boy, not because of it, and that he had loved Clarence alive; he had.

The offices for LGMH were on the second floor and looked more permanent than the space downstairs. The four desks in the main room matched at least, and the walls were a single shade of pale lavender. A potted plant slouched in the corner.

"Hi. Is Carla Peterson free at the moment?" Laurie asked an elderly gentleman in a necktie and cardigan sweater who sat at the first desk.

"Carla? Oh, Carla. The woman." The first desk was often occupied by volunteers who weren't familiar with the rest of the staff. "I don't rightly know, my dear."

"Laurie. Hey." A handsome black woman looked up from her desk in the corner. "Carla's still out. Some kind of meeting with a shrink down at Bellevue. She should've been back half an hour ago. You want to wait for her, her office is empty."

"Thanks, Jocasta. Hmmm. What do you think, Jack? Do we wait?"

Jack looked around the room and shrugged. He was ready to forget the whole business and simply go home.

Just then, the door behind Jocasta opened and out stepped Ben Slover. "Jo! You got a pen? There's no pen or pencils on my desk! Who's been snitching my pens while I was gone?" he said in a rush, then saw his friends across the room. "Jack! Laurie! Can't talk now. Important phone call. Thanks," he told Jocasta when she wearily thrust a fistful of pens at him. "Come on back. I'll be finished in a sec," he called out, and disappeared back through the door.

Jack and Laurie glanced at each other, then went back to Ben's office. It was a windowless cubbyhole with doors at each end, perhaps a cloakroom when the building was a school. Ben sat wound up at his desk, the telephone receiver pinched between his shoulder and head while he used both hands to pull things out and write things down.

On his desk was a photograph of him and Danny in coats and ties, chatting with Ed Koch.

"Uh huh. Uh huh. That's all perfectly well, Councilman, but there's going to be five hundred people demonstrating outside Gracie Mansion tonight whether the police approve it or not. Be easier for the cops if they were there just to stand by than it will be if they have to haul five hundred people off to jail. It's in everyone's best interest if we get the permit."

Ben was still dressed for the country, sweatshirt and jeans, but he looked utterly at home on the telephone. His voice turned conciliatory, indignant, or mournful from one moment to the next, but a corner of his mouth remained curled in delight over the game he played. Jack had watched this before and decided it was the political equivalent of phone sex.

"Okay, Jim. You do that. Yes, I'll be here. Call me back as soon as you finish with him." Ben hung up, took a deep ecstatic breath and solemnly faced Jack and Laurie. "Another crisis," he groaned. "What brings you guys down here?"

"We came to see Carla," said Jack.

"What's up?" asked Laurie, nodding at the phone. "You and Danny weren't supposed to be back until Friday."

"Haven't you heard? Don't you people listen to the radio or read the papers? The stupid sonovabitch really stuck his foot in it this time." And Ben indignantly reported a statement by Mayor Koch about "AIDS chiselers," people Koch claimed pretended to have the disease in order to take advantage of the city's resources for people with AIDS.

Jack recognized it as the kind of careless, insensitive

remark frequently tossed off by the mayor. After he was criticized for a day or so in newspapers whose animosity toward Koch was stronger than their indifference toward gays, Koch would call a news conference, claim he had been misquoted, and say more carefully what he had really meant. Jack didn't believe it was a real crisis, at least nothing like the personal crisis he was involved with today. Politics seemed so distant and illusory anyway, Jack often dismissed the whole business as an enormous fiction.

"So I hurried back first thing this morning—Danny's still in Connecticut—got the phone tree in action, the word out, and we're going to raise a stink outside Gracie Mansion tonight. Get a little media attention for how *little* the city does for PWAs." He eyed the telephone, expecting it to ring. "What about you guys? Have a nice September?"

"Fine," said Laurie. "We better be going. You've got your hands full and we only dropped by to see Carla."

"Oh, no. Please stay," said Ben. "I can't do a thing until this person calls me back. And it's good to see you both. It is." He reached out and carefully touched Laurie's hand, then Jack's arm. "So everything's fine? Connecticut was nice. A bit boring but restful."

"Actually," said Jack. "Everything's not fine. Michael's disappeared." He had intended not to mention it, but Ben's good spirits and air of self-importance brought it out of Jack.

Laurie frowned at him and told Ben, "Well, not disappeared exactly. But he hasn't come home since last night."

"When Laurie and Carla told him it was time he found his own place," Jack said pointedly.

"After Jack told him he should kill himself if he felt as bad as he said he did," Laurie added.

Statement by statement, the subtle accusations of each other giving way to a flat description of their doubts and fears, they filled Ben in on what had happened in the past twenty-four hours. Laid out for the benefit of a third person, their worry sounded even more unjustified than when they had tried arguing themselves out of it. Ben listened, mechanically lifting and lowering his eyebrows at each of them, continuing to steal glances at the silent telephone. But then he began to rub a finger over his upper lip, as if missing the mustache he once wore.

"I wonder if Michael's still upset by—?" Ben shook his head at himself. "No. He's fine. The boy's probably just been out tomcatting around."

"What?" Jack jumped at Ben's bit of guilty wondering. "Something happened when he was with you and Danny? Something he said or how he behaved?"

"He seemed okay when he was with us. He even seemed to be getting over Clarence. Read some of his letters, but he seemed bored by them. Didn't even want to talk about them or hear about Clare in college."

"But something upset him," said Jack.

"Well, yeah. We should've known better. But"— Ben rolled his eyes—"We tried a threeway with him one night and it didn't work out." He suddenly looked at Laurie, uncomfortable to have her hear about this. "Which sometimes happens when the involved parties aren't all in the right mood," he insisted. "I realize this might sound somewhat sordid to a woman, but it can be perfectly natural and friendly given the right circumstances."

Laurie glanced worriedly at Jack.

He had told her all about Ben and Danny's hobby, repeated stories with amusement, disapproval, or envy, depending on his mood. But what he felt today was righteous anger. "Damn, Ben! You and Danny pounced and Michael freaked?"

"No. That's not what happened," Ben said defensively. Seeing the door to the main room was half open, he stood up and closed it. He leaned his back against the door. "Michael got into bed with us one night. He said he didn't want to sleep alone. One thing led to another, and *Danny* was the one who freaked. He didn't freak, exactly, but he couldn't go on and he went down to the kitchen. I didn't want to go on without him, and Michael went back to his own bed. The end."

"So what does something like that mean emotionally?" Laurie asked both of them.

"Yes," said Jack. "How was Michael after you got him worked up, then kicked him out of bed? If it was me, I'd have felt like shit."

"It wasn't you, Jack. It was Michael. And he seemed fine. He was disappointed and I was apologetic. I think Danny and I felt shittier about it than he did. We hugged him goodbye at the train station the next day and everything was fine."

"I'll bet," said Jack. "We know how attuned you are to people's feelings."

Ben looked hard at Jack, then glanced down at the telephone. "I haven't got time for this. I'm in the middle of something much more important than your fine-tooth combing of moral nits. Danny and I were in the wrong, all right? But Michael's stronger than you give him credit for.

He hasn't thrown himself under a train somewhere, and he certainly didn't do it because we kicked him out of bed."

Laurie groaned. "Jack's *not* saying it's your fault. We don't even know if anything's happened for *anybody* to be at fault. We want to know Michael's state of mind, that's all."

But Jack could not help feeling it was Ben and Danny's fault. To be kissed and touched by someone you knew, then pushed away—it would be devastating, leaving you vulnerable to any accusation or rejection that followed. There must have been some hidden signal in the boy's eyes or vibration in his voice yesterday that alerted Jack to his condition, unconsciously, without Jack recognizing how he knew what he knew.

"And I'm telling you his state of mind was fine," Ben claimed. "Christ almighty. You people. You in particular, Jack. Here we are in the middle of a war"—he gestured at the telephone—"and all you can do is fret like a mother hen over a boy who's fine. Who's too oblivious to be anything but fine. You've gone on and on yourself about how oblivious Michael is."

"Maybe I was wrong," said Jack. "Maybe it's all been an act."

Ben shook his head. "You take Michael much too seriously. The way you've babied him? He's just a kid who got in over his head on something, but it's over now and he did fine. He was perfectly cool, competent, and mature the six months he had Clarence on his hands. I admire Michael for that. The only thing off about Michael is that he's got no gay identity."

"Unlike those who have nothing *but* their gay identity," Jack told him. It was part of a longstanding debate between them, but Jack used it now in anger.

Ben frowned. "Jack, I wonder how much you're really worried about Michael. The more you go on about him, the more I think he's just your newest way of grieving for Clarence."

"No, you wouldn't understand my grief, would you?" sneered Jack. "Some of us remember our friends. And not just when it serves our political purposes the way it did in your so-called obituary."

"Guys!" cried Laurie. "This has nothing to do with—"

"Yes!" Ben barked at Jack. "There was more politics than Clarence in that obituary. So what? We're not talking about somebody who died in a car wreck, dammit! This wasn't a private death that's over and now there's nothing to do but grieve! It's time you got over your idiotic notion Clarence's death was strictly personal, involving just him and you—and Michael. We're talking about something that's still going on, that can kill Danny, me, even you, Jack."

Jack stood up straight and said, "He was my best friend. He deserves to have one person who remembers who he was now that he's dead. Personally. For his own sake. And not just as a statistic or pawn in some political career."

"My career, as you call it—" But Ben was too furious to finish that. "You would've done better by Clare if you'd done more while he was sick."

"What're you saying? I did things."

"Yeah, you dropped by now and then. You were around. But you weren't involved the way I was, Jack. Or the way Michael was. You visited now and then. Big deal."

Jack was stopped; his mind went blank.

"Ben, don't," said Laurie.

But Ben was into his next thought. "Which must be why you're such a fervent mourner, Jack. You use this fancy personal grief to compensate for all you didn't do while he was alive. But I was there, Jack. I was involved from start to finish. Hospital and groceries and medications and all the arrangements. I was able to work off my obligation to *my* best friend. I can go on and work for the living because, unlike you, Jack, I know I did all I could for the dead."

"Ben!" Laurie cried. "Shut up! Will you shut the fuck up!"

Ben went silent, and looked amazed.

"Both of you," Laurie snarled. "You're being real assholes about this. What does any of this crap have to do with Michael?"

Ben seemed amazed by all he'd said, and ashamed. He suddenly couldn't look at either Jack or Laurie. He stepped to his desk, pulled out the swivel chair, and sat down. "All I was saying—" He shook his head at himself. "That was stupid. All I really meant to say was I'm sure Michael's fine. After all he went through with Clarence, and handled very well, he's not going to flip out over the little things we've done."

Jack lowered his head and said nothing. He was still engaged in the argument in his head, searching for things he had done for Clarence. There were the visits, the few hours spent at the hospital, the article in *Film Comment*, and not much else. Ben was right. Ben had done far more, with the thoughtless busyness with which he threw himself into any activity, yet he had been in the middle of it while Jack drifted in and out, "visiting," watching Clare's dying from a distance. Suddenly, Jack's grief felt thin and dishonest, and his concern for Michael completely misplaced.

"I had no business saying all that," Ben apologized. "I don't really believe any of what I said. I said it only to protect myself against things you said, Jack. It was a painful experience for everyone. It's idiotic for us to argue over who did how much."

Jack nodded. "I shouldn't have said what I said, either. I apologize." But the apology did not make him feel less miserable or stupid the way apologies usually did after he lost his temper.

Laurie tried to smooth things by mocking both of them. "Really. You sounded like two Vietnam vets bickering over who had the worse tour of duty." It was a favorite analogy of hers, and Jack noticed she left out her line about both vets spending their tours as typists at headquarters.

"I was overreacting," said Ben. "Real silly. And my mind's on other things right now."

But nobody knew what to say next. Both Jack and Ben knew not to believe each other's denials of what they'd said. Jack had suspected all along that Ben thought his grief was a foolish luxury, but beliefs and differences that could be ignored when held in private seemed impassable now that they'd been said aloud. And Jack feared Ben was right: his grief was only the unfinished business of failing to do more while Clarence was alive.

The telephone began beeping. Ben looked but didn't reach for it. He guiltily glanced up at Jack. "I really should take care of this," he said. "But we'll talk later. When we can laugh over how that goofy kid made us all a little nutty today." The telephone beeped again. "Laurie, I'll bet you go home and find Michael grumping in your living room, as usual." Not until they both nodded at him in agreement did Ben answer the phone. "Slover. Hey, Jim. So what's the word? They want it rough or do they want it easy?" He winked and waved at them as they went out the door.

Jocasta was gone from her desk, apparently finished for the day, and the volunteer at the first desk said no woman had come in since they arrived. Laurie wondered aloud if Carla had gone straight home after her meeting. She didn't mention the exchange with Ben until they were going down the stairs.

"Oh Jack-o. You poor guy. First you get it from me and then you get it from Ben. This isn't your day, is it?"

Jack shrugged, wanting to show he thought he deserved it. He could not protect himself against Ben's accusations the way he had against Laurie's. The rebuke hurt too much for him to talk about it yet. "He's right about Michael though. After all the boy's been through, it's crazy of me to think anything we've done could push him over the edge. Especially a few words from somebody like me."

Laurie frowned, but said nothing until they were outside on the sidewalk. "Still want to swing by Uncle Charlie's?" she asked, doubtfully.

Jack shook his head. "No. I don't need to play that game anymore."

"Then would you like to get a cup of coffee somewhere?"

"Thank you, no. I think I've stirred up enough bad

feeling in myself and my friends for one day. If you don't mind, I think I'll just go home."

Laurie looked up at his face and studied it sadly. "Okay," she said. She put a hand on his shoulder and held it a moment. "You did what you could, Jack. Ben was familiar with the brass tacks about the thing. And Michael was his lover. There's nothing more you could've done without pushing Michael out of the way."

"I guess." But acknowledging Ben knew things Jack didn't only made Jack aware of his uselessness. Maybe he wasn't good for anything except grieving and fretting and criticizing. "Well, thanks," he said and bent down to kiss the top of Laurie's head, his beard snagging strands of her hair. "I'll give you a call in a half hour or so. So you can tell me if Michael's back or not. Let him know how thoughtless he was for not telling us where he was, but don't let on that some of us got a bit hysterical."

"I won't," Laurie said. They walked to the corner together, touched and patted each other goodbye, faked sardonic smiles over the whole affair, and Laurie headed uptown toward the subway station.

The sun was setting and the shadows of buildings were pressed like paper cutouts against the glowing orange brick of St. Vincent's Hospital on the other side of Seventh Avenue—the neighborhood was dominated by the hospital the way medieval cities were dominated by their cathedrals. Jack was painfully conscious of the hospital as he walked past, although this one had nothing to do with Clarence.

He was such a buffoon, he told himself, a foolish, self-important buffoon. He often found refuge in that description—you cannot be blamed for your failings when you are by nature just a buffoon—but the tag gave him no relief today. He had thought he was being so selfless and wonderful, panicking over a boy who meant nothing to him. But it had only been an elaborate self-deception, a bit of buried guilt disguised as love, the excess emotion of a spectator at a movie. He felt so worthless and bleak as he walked home, he slapped himself with the thought that it would've been better if he had died instead of Clarence. He knew it was a silly piece of romantic masochism and didn't take it seriously, just as Laurie had known not to take his despondency too seriously. Like so much else in Jack's life, it too would pass.

This side of the street was in gloomy blue shadow, and Japanese tourists were already snapping each other's pictures under the awning of the Village Vanguard, the strobes of their cameras flashing like heat lightning. Jack walked one more block to Charles Street and turned west toward his apartment, an oyster returning to his shell. At the far end of his street, pinched between the rows of brownstones and the shaggy roof of trees, the peephole of the river glowed like a fireball, the sun setting today in that impossibly precise spot. A stick figure crossed in the distance and threw a quick shadow up the entire length of the street.

Jack noticed somebody sitting on the front stoop of his building in the next block. After spending the afternoon looking for Michael, he immediately thought it was Michael. He sneered at himself for being able to think that still, and ignored the person until he reached the foot of the steps, and saw it *was* Michael.

The boy was asleep, leaning against the sun-gilded balustrade, his hands clutched between his legs, his upper lip
and chin speckled with beard, like black pepper. There
was a jagged tear in the black leather of one shoe and a
chalky mark on the shoulder of his navy coat. He had a
brown paper bag at his feet and looked like a young
derelict. Jack stood on the sidewalk and gazed, still not
believing it was Michael.

Then the boy stirred, cracked open an eye, and bolted
awake, as if frightened by a terrible dream. He stared at
Jack as if Jack were that dream.

10

THE DAY had begun with a glimpse of what he thought was the morning star.

Still standing on the overpass but away from the edge, Michael had looked around to see where he was. In the pale sky above the black East River, above four smoke-stacks like the fingers of a buried hand, there was a bright pinhole of light, brighter than any star he had ever seen. He rarely noticed stars in the city.

This star seemed to float, almost drift in the sky. Michael saw another star, and still another, both fainter than the first, stars that did not hold perfectly still in relation to each other, but seemed to slip—a constellation slowly collapsing together, like the end of the world.

Then the morning star abruptly changed direction and sailed across the sky. They were planes, not stars. The air above Queens was swimming with them, white landing lights hovering and darting. Michael was disappointed.

He turned his back on the sky and walked west, toward buildings and streetlights. He knew what he had to do. The heaviness inside him drew him inward, deeper and deeper, as if he were collapsing into himself. But not here. Not yet. He needed pen and paper first.

He walked quickly. He was afraid he might procrastinate to the point of doing nothing at all, but the decision remained with him. He tried to decide how. The image that came to him was of mind and life blowing out of his skull like a final sneeze. He poked a finger into his temple and repeatedly snapped his thumb as he walked. But Michael didn't know where he could get a gun. Other methods repelled him. To jump and fall was too much how he had lived his life. An overdose of something meant he'd sleep through his own death. Hanging seemed more a torture than a death; his head already ached and the idea of blood trapped and pounding in his head sickened him. He wanted to lose his blood, get it out of his body and throw it in the faces of those who didn't believe in him.

The street was drained of color; it looked like a bad print of a silent movie, gray and unearthly. Only when Michael glanced back and saw the paling sky behind him could he believe the light was natural. A taxicab rattled out of nowhere, banged around a corner and was gone, leaving a deeper silence behind. Michael never came to The World. Either he was on the wrong street or it had vanished while he was gone. He came to a broad avenue that seemed eerily deserted compared to the traffic and crowds he knew. A few trucks rolled past and two or three people were visible up and down the long sidewalk, but people disappeared in such enormous space. Trees stood on the median like motionless billows of smoke. In the darkness inside a gated window stood the white shadows of wedding dresses.

It was another city, another country. The only times Michael had been out at this hour were when he'd been dancing with Clarence, when Clarence had shown him the life he led before he gave himself to Michael and film. They stumbled out of The Saint, exhausted and satisfied, and Michael was always amazed to find it light outside. Once, watching for a cab, they drifted along the curb in a daze and a car with its radio blaring stopped at a traffic light. Forgetting where he was, Clarence automatically began to dance again. The car pulled away; Clarence realized what had happened and burst out laughing. And he resumed dancing, without music. And Michael danced with him, guessing at the beat from the way Clarence moved, neither of them making a sound to cue the other. They danced in silence on a street corner beneath a hundred darkened windows, in the middle of a city still asleep on a Sunday morning. Michael had been beautifully happy. He was ashamed of himself now for having been so happy.

He thought this colorless light was all there was, until he saw a fan of yellow light stretched over the sidewalk up ahead. It was as if he had forgotten color. The yellow light came from a little all-night market, the kind run by

Koreans. They would have what he needed. He stepped under the awning and stopped.

Beneath the awning, bins of yellows, reds, and greens glowed like a box of paints. The colors were so intense they hurt. There was something frightening yet beautiful about so much color, something crazy. Michael had to pick up an apple to assure himself it was only fruit. He gently set it down again and gave it a pet. Buckets of flowers crowded beside the door and Michael bent down to sniff them, never sure which had a scent and which didn't. He liked the idea of flowers and enjoyed giving them, but he never understood what other people saw in flowers, not even now. Already his deep feeling over the color of things was subsiding. He drew a deep breath and went inside.

A stout Korean woman stood at the counter doing some kind of paperwork. She might be the last person he ever spoke to. There was gray in her neatly tied black hair; she wore a quilted jacket over a man's flannel shirt. Her fingers were stubby and her round face was abstractly cheerful, like a smiley face. A tape player on the shelf sing-sang something Asian—Clarence had claimed that if cats were musical they would sing songs like this one.

The woman finally looked up from her work. "Yes?" she said, with an abstractly cheerful smile.

"Yes. Do you sell ink pens?" He was startled by how young and loud he sounded; it was as though he hadn't spoken in days.

The woman proudly gestured at a cup full of pens beside the cash register.

Michael hesitated, unable to choose, then realized how

insane it was to care what color ink he used. He plucked out a red pen. "And paper?"

She took down a box of envelopes, then a handful of little spiral notepads, and shrugged to show this was all they had.

Michael pointed at a spiral notepad. "And razor blades."

She looked straight at him and, for a second, Michael thought she knew.

"For a safety razor. To shave," he explained and mimed shaving, finding a light stubble on his chin.

"Oh shaver! Yes." The woman slapped her cheek and bashfully laughed. She reached toward a cardboard display of disposable razors.

"No, no. Just blades," said Michael. He almost mimed doing something to his wrists.

"Yes?" She held out a tiny carton of ejector blades.

Michael had been picturing the old-fashioned razor blades he remembered his father using, double-edged, paper-thin, the dangerously flimsy blades Michael had handled very carefully as a boy to trim the plastic and decals of model cars and helicopter gunships. He hadn't imagined anything as familiar as the ejector blades he now used himself. Of course they would do.

He watched the woman add everything together on the register. He pulled crumpled bills from one pocket, carefully smoothed them out, and paid her. When she gave him his change and passed him the bag, he said, "Thank you. Thank you ever so much," and suddenly thrust his hand at her.

She smiled, gladly took his hand, and gave it a firm shake, as if it were perfectly normal for a customer to want to shake hands. Her palm and fingers were warm and smoothly leathery.

Outside the bright store, the street had acquired a little color. The trees on the median had gone from gray to gray-green; the sky was lighter and there was a dusty pink glow along the edge of a cloud overhead. Michael felt different now that he carried a bag with everything he needed. The pressure to do what he was doing no longer had the same desperate urgency. There was no longer the horrible emotional weight behind it; Michael felt no emotion at all. He even thought he didn't *have* to do this, for a second. Then he rebelled against the thought. He would stick to his decision. If his emotions were no longer involved in it, it would enable him to be more rational, clear, and patient than he had been before.

He sat on a long concrete step in front of a closed, caged shop to write his note. The step was perforated with tiny windows of thick glass, disks like eyeglass lenses, which glowed from the light in the basement below. It was like sitting on eyes. While he composed his thoughts, Michael began to go through his pockets, pulling out money, smoothing out bills and stacking them together, then adding them to the money still in his wallet. He found he had over fifty dollars left. It was strange to have so much money and be sitting here on the street like a common derelict. A suicide note should be composed in peace, even in comfort. Michael realized he was hungry. He should eat and write his note in a suitable place, a special place. This was the most important thing he had ever done, and he did not need to rush into it. He stood up and resumed walking, wondering where he should have his last meal.

More traffic, people, and light stole into the city as he made his way uptown. This was the last time he would ever see New York, and he thought things should be as furiously present as the fruit outside the Korean market. Instead, the city seemed to dissolve in the bright sunlight that kindled the tops of buildings and slowly made its way down toward the street. All colors became thin and transparent, like the burned-out colors of an overexposed photograph. Even time seemed to thin itself out, so that Michael had no sense of how long it took before he stood outside the Algonquin Hotel, half-reflection and half-shadow on a plate glass window, smoothing his hair with both hands.

In his four years in New York he had never been to the Algonquin, but he knew where it was, knew what it stood for. Ben used to tease Jack for treating their circle as "a homo Algonquin Club." By coming here for his last meal, Michael felt he was proving something, striking at something, although he was uncertain what. The other fancy places he knew had no meaning for him at all.

The lobby was comfortably dark and rich, all oak paneling and pools of dim light. A few well-dressed men sat reading newspapers and drinking coffee among chin-high partitions of wood and etched milk glass. With his paper bag folded neatly under his arm, Michael walked up to the front desk and curtly told the clerk, "I'm meeting a relative and I'm early. Is your dining room open?"

"Yes, sir. Straight ahead, sir."

Michael gave the man a cold nod and strode back to the restaurant. He requested a table for two, adding that "an uncle" would be joining him later but that he would be eating alone. He was seated at a table around the corner with his back to a rose-colored wall. A fatherly waiter took his order. The table setting opposite him was left in place, silverware on the starched white tablecloth outlining the presence of someone who wasn't there.

Sitting very still, Michael slowly looked up. The few diners scattered around the room chewed and swallowed in silence. It was so quiet Michael imagined he heard a click of teeth and squish of tongues. Waiters in black moved about on soundless feet, the only clear sound in the room the muffled tinkling of porcelain. Coffee in a bone-white cup and saucer appeared on the table. Michael lifted the cup, sipped, and carefully reseated the thing in the indentation in the saucer. The coffee tasted like school and the morning after an all-nighter before an exam. He took the notepad and pen from the bag and set them on the table. Beneath the table, he took out the little packet of blades and turned it around in his fingers, looking for directions printed on the box. He returned the packet to its bag and eased the bag into his coat pocket. He opened the notepad and tested the pen on the first sheet of paper, writing, "Goodbye cruel world."

He read it and almost burst out laughing. He was amazed by his wit. Because it seemed genuinely witty to him, a brilliant, cynical joke. To kill yourself and leave nothing behind but a cliché?

But people would misunderstand. They would think it was only smartass, think even his death was smartass. It defeated the whole purpose, didn't it? Michael turned the page, took another mouthful of coffee, and tried to muster his reasons. The pen hovered over the blank page for a long time, then he gave up wanting to put it all in words. He wrote simply, "I cannot live without Clarence Laird. I want you to understand. You never understood before."

He sat back and read that. It seemed a poor, bare thing. He imagined Jack scoffing at it, sneering at it for its artlessness the way he had sneered at Michael's poetry. That fat library queen, that critic. Michael decided to leave his note bare and flat, just to show he didn't care what Jack thought. The opinion of that nonentity should mean nothing to him.

He leaned down again and wrote, "All money left in my bank account is to go to my father to pay him back for everything." Would the bastard get the anger in that phrase? Michael added, "Let him know whose money it was and how it came to be mine." That felt perfect, like he was paying his father with Clarence's blood.

"Sir?"

He clamped his hands over the notepad.

The fatherly, long-faced waiter stood over him with a plate of bacon and eggs.

Michael snapped the notepad shut and held it in his lap while the waiter slid the plate in front of him. He sat with his head lowered until the waiter was gone. He set the notepad and pen to the right of the plate, picked up the fork, and slowly remembered how to use it. The eggs were porcelain white and lightly puddled with butter. When he applied the fork to one, the yolk burst and the plate was flooded with yellow.

Eating distracted him. He found a nicely physical hollowness in his stomach, and the food was soothingly real, full of tastes and different textures that came apart in his mouth. He loaded the sticks of toast with strawberry jam, needing the sweetness. He kept adding salt to things, wanting to increase the salty wetness flowing in his mouth. Looking around the room, he was pleased to be eating here after what seemed a lifetime of eating in the kitchen in Phillipsburg. He opened the notepad again and read and reread his words while he ate. He hadn't noticed when he was writing that the ink was red; the note seemed written in blood. He reread it until the words became opaque and beautiful, like poetry. He didn't bother to cover it when the waiter came by to refill his coffee cup. He wished he could read it aloud to the man.

When there was nothing left to eat, he methodically wiped off his fingers with the napkin, then picked up the pen and signed the note. He added their last address and gently tore the sheet of paper from the wire spirals. He began to pluck the paper crumbs from the ragged edge, but decided he liked the effect and its suggestion of something severed. He folded the paper in half, then in quarters, and slipped it into his shirt pocket, where the police would find it when they found his body.

Where would they find his body? Writing the note made him feel the deed was already done, but he still had to decide where. He thought about doing it here. Not in the restaurant but in a hotel room. He could rent a room and do it here, and people would know he had come to the Algonquin before he died. They would realize he had done this not in a desperate fit of insanity, but reasonably, even civilly, with a nice breakfast before he went.

He pictured his body being found on a wide, blood-soaked bed—or maybe in a bathtub. Only here it would be strangers who found him. The others wouldn't see him until they came down to the police station or morgue, if then. That made it too easy for them, too neat. He didn't want to set his death outside their lives, just as Clarence's death had been safely outside, in a hospital. To bring it all home to them, he should do it in one of their homes. Ben and Danny. Laurie and Carla. Jack. Even Peter and Livy. His bitterness toward them was so strong he regretted not being able to kill himself four times, a death in each apartment.

He signaled the waiter for the bill. "I've changed my mind," he told the man. "I won't be waiting for my uncle after all." He needed to get out of the hotel before he changed his mind again and did it here. This was the wrong place. His act would be wasted here. He pocketed the notepad and pen, left twenty dollars on the little tray, and left.

Stepping out into a shock of bright sunlight, he squinted around at the street and started walking quickly. It was as though he were fleeing from the hotel. He wondered if his decision not to do it there had been his subtle way of deciding not to do it at all. Each step he took toward the act made the act feel less necessary. Would he go on with his life by procrastinating his death? But as soon as he imagined that, as soon as he conjured up a tomorrow, a next week, a next month, all his pain and self-hatred came back to him, a nausea in his bones and skull as if his own body were sickened by the person it housed. Michael couldn't live with such loathing. It was only the thought he soon wouldn't live at all that made this minute and the next minute bearable. No, he knew what had to be done and couldn't live with himself if he didn't do it.

Standing on the corner of a broad avenue, he kept turning around and feeling the outsides of his pockets while he tried to decide which way to go. Enormous faceless buildings towered overhead, grooved like machinery. All around him streamed men and women on their way to work or already out on coffee breaks— Michael had no sense of what time it was. When a pack of people behind him stepped off the curb and into the street, Michael stepped with them. He continued in that direction and realized he was walking downtown.

Jack lived downtown.

Jack worked at home. Yes, he would go to Jack. He wanted to prove himself to everyone, but he suddenly understood he wanted to prove himself to Jack most of all. His thoughts kept coming back to Jack. Who was alone, like Michael now. Who had been closer to Clarence than the others. Who would be the chief executor of Clarence's memory when Michael was gone.

That last thought distressed Michael. In Jack's mind, he'd be remembered as only a minor episode in Jack's long, dreary friendship with Clarence, nothing more. The past would close over Michael as if he had never lived. He considered going on with his life simply to spite Jack. The only other alternative was to make Jack part of his death, blocking out Jack's memories of Clarence with something more memorable and awful. He wanted to take all memory of Clarence with him.

The light was so harsh and Michael's eyes so tired all he could see clearly on his walk downtown were individual shadows isolated in the brightness.

The angle of light looked like noon when Michael climbed the front steps of a rust-colored sandstone building on Charles Street and pressed the button labeled "Arcalli." He could hear the buzzer blare inside the building, but there was no answer. He pressed again, then stepped outside to lean over the balustrade and see what he could see through Jack's window. The apartment was on the first floor and the front windows a few feet to the left of the stoop. The windows behind bars were opened a few inches, and a radio softly played in the darkness inside. Michael knew Jack turned his radio on only when he was out, to discourage burglars.

Something suddenly hit the window from inside, rattling the blinds.

It was Elisabeth Vogler, bounding up to the windowsill to see who was there. She gazed wide-eyed at Michael through the hazy screen and opened her mouth at him without a meow coming out.

"Hello, cat. Happy to see me?" Michael said sweetly. He wanted to hold her, run his fingers through her fur, even bury his face in her warm silkiness. He leaned out and lightly scratched at the screen with an outstretched hand. "*You* love me."

She lifted her nose to the hand, glanced sadly at Michael, then folded her forelegs beneath her chest and settled on them, pretending Michael wasn't there.

He sighed and drew back. He stepped down and sat on

the stoop. Jack had probably gone out for food or to Xerox something. Michael could wait for him.

When he leaned against a vase-shaped pillar that was part of the balustrade, things in his coat pocket pinched his side. He reached into the pocket and brought out the notepad, pen, and bag with the packet inside. Could he do it? Would he? He seemed to have made and remade his mind a dozen times, and it angered him to find he still had room for doubt. He was angry with Jack for not being home and forcing him to prolong this anxious doubting.

He put the pad and pen in the bag with the packet and left the bag at his feet. Settling back with the pillar between his shoulder blades, he discovered he was exhausted. He had never gone to sleep last night, had he? He wondered how much that fact had to do with how he felt, yet the burning in his eyes and stretched state of his nerves—like violin strings tuned so tight their pitch was too high for human hearing—felt nothing like sleepiness.

This street seemed sleepy, however. It was so quiet the rustle of air when an occasional car drove past was indistinguishable from the steady breathing of the trees full of leaves like big paper stars. The tree trunks lining the curb looked badly scarred, sycamore trees with patches of gray and yellow bark. The long building across the street looked scarred too, patched red stucco full of cracks and seams, a wall like a mass of sunburned faces.

If he slept, would he wake up without his pain and self-hatred? He imagined sleeping, then awaking to find everything fine again, his craziness gone, his real self lovable and loved again, his memories only a bad dream. Perhaps Clarence would even be alive when he woke up.

Knowing Clarence was dead instantly killed the fantasy about sleep. He could not undo that fact. He turned to a new fantasy, wanting to hold himself to his decision: he imagined meeting up again with Clarence in death. It was a sweet, beautiful fib, perfect for funerals and widowed grandmothers, and Michael could not believe it for a second. He did not believe in life after death, not for himself, not even for Clarence. Which was what made death so attractive, as appealing as the idea of sleep was to him right now. He felt he was already dead. This blind groping inside his head was the initial stage of death, the front stoop, the foyer, the front door. It was a minor annoyance to know a physical act was still necessary to make this state of mind final.

The front door squeaked open. Michael turned and saw Jack Arcalli standing in the foyer, looking down at Michael and gesturing for him to come in.

Confused, Michael stood up. Jack had been home all along. Or no, Michael had fallen asleep and Jack had returned, walking right past Michael and not seeing him because Michael was sound asleep, or not recognizing him because he had never seen Michael sleeping.

"I looked out the window and thought it was you," said Jack, leading Michael down the hall and into his apartment. He seemed genuinely glad to see Michael.

With all the lights on, the apartment looked bigger than usual. Jack had bought the Sousza's kitchen and brought it here from Phillipsburg. It was late and Michael was wearing pajamas, the buttons on the fly disappearing and reappearing each time Michael checked them. He

stood by the peninsular counter while Jack fixed a sandwich, carefully arranged it on a plate, and left it on the
kitchen table with an opened can of beer. Noticing
Michael's baffled look, Jack said, "He still comes by late at
night. I like to leave a little snack for him."

Michael wanted to hide in the cupboard under the sink
and wait for Clarence, just to catch a peek of him and see
how he was. But before he could explain what he needed,
Jack took him by the hand and led him to the bedroom.

They became naked when they embraced and kissed on
the bed. Michael felt funny doing this with Jack, but his
body enjoyed it so much he couldn't stop. Jack's beard was
as soft and chewy as cat's fur, and his skin felt like warm
sunlight. People walked past on their way to the bathroom, Ben and Laurie among them, politely averting their
eyes. Michael's only real worry was that by doing this he
might miss Clarence.

Then the warmth left their bodies, like the sun slipping
behind a cloud, and Michael found an extra arm, an extra
shoulder, and a familiarly knuckled hand here with him
and Jack. Clarence was somewhere in the bed! Michael
kissed and held Jack harder, wanting to conjure up more
of Clarence, enough so he could see and talk to him, and
apologize for still being alive.

Clarence's hand gripped Michael's. Overjoyed, Michael
opened his eyes to see Clarence.

And he saw Jack standing in front of him.

Everything was framed in bleared reddish gold light—
sun shining through the balustrade on Michael's eye-
lashes. The tilted shadows of trees were stretched like a
net across the building behind Jack Arcalli. Jack stood on

the sidewalk, staring in astonishment at Michael. As if he had watched every minute of Michael's dream.

Michael was stung awake, hurt it was only a dream: the forgiveness and the sex and the affection for Jack. Here was the real Jack, stolid and baggy, his shoulders and the circles under his eyes heavy with judgment. Jack's stare seemed sharp and indignant, as if he couldn't believe Michael had the gall to be here.

There was no possibility of sympathy, no chance of understanding. There was no way to get through to him except to do what Michael had intended all along.

11

"MICHAEL?" said Jack. He was thrown by the way the boy looked at him, eyes wide and mouth open for air, like a frightened child, a heartbreakingly ugly look that turned him into an entirely different person.

Then he pulled his hands from the space between his legs and rubbed his face, as if he'd had his real face balled up in his hands and was putting it back on. "Dozed off," he muttered behind his hands. "Bad dream." He lowered his hands and looked like himself again, aloof and self-important despite his bloodshot eyes. "Where have you been?" he said sharply.

"Just out," Jack said guardedly. Michael's insolent tone made him feel like a fool for fretting all afternoon. He already felt like a fool after Ben's accusations and was sure he looked like a perfect fool to Michael, standing here and gawking the way he did. He refused to confess his foolishness to the boy. "One might ask the same of you. Laurie and Carla were wondering where you disappeared to last night."

"Out," said Michael. "Dancing and stuff."

"Dancing?" What an idiot he'd been to imagine this arrogant twit was capable of dangerous emotions. "You could've at least given them a call and told them where you were."

Michael responded with a bored sigh and stared past Jack.

Jack wanted to slap him. He propped his hitting hand against the front post of the stone railing and stood there, making a special point of not inviting Michael inside. "So what brings you to this neighborhood?"

Michael continued to look past him. "I wanted"—he cleared his throat—"to take a bath."

Jack snorted and smirked. "You've got a perfectly respectable bathtub at home, Michael. Why're you really here?" As soon as he asked, Jack realized he didn't want to know, but a bath was too absurd a request to be a disguise for something else.

"Didn't they tell you?" Michael said contemptuously. "I don't have a home. They threw me out."

"They didn't throw you out." Was that why he was here, to ask for sympathy? "I've talked to them. They asked you to start looking for your own place. That's all. You shouldn't be so melodramatic about it."

Michael glared at him. "I'm not being melodramatic. I'm angry at them and I'm not going back there. Not tonight anyway. I came here to bathe and shave, and then I'm going out dancing again. I'm not going back to those . . . women until I'm good and ready."

There was so much false drama to wade through with Michael. He may have stayed out last night to get back at Laurie and Carla, or maybe he simply never thought to call them. Jack suddenly wondered if "dancing and stuff" included spending the night with someone. It must, if Michael intended to do it again, although he didn't look like he'd had much sleep the night before. The idea of Michael going to bed with another man infuriated Jack. Because of the worry he had wasted on the little shit, he told himself.

"Well?" said Michael. "Can I use your bathtub or are you rejecting me too?"

Jack's anger had reached the point where his automatic reaction was to go against it, bury it and be polite. "Don't be silly, Michael. Come on in," he said wearily. "Scrub-a-dub-dub."

Michael slowly gathered his limbs together and stood up as Jack climbed the steps past him. Michael continued to stand on the steps and look out at the street when Jack opened the front door and waited for him.

The sun had dropped below the horizon while they talked. The gold light and shadows were gone, and the buildings seemed to crowd closer together. The electric light in the foyer and hall was brighter than the street. Michael stood with his back to Jack, then finally bent down to pick up the paper bag at his feet and came up the steps to the door.

"Been shopping?" Jack asked, trying to be civil.

"Toiletries," said Michael.

When Jack opened the door to his apartment and turned on the kitchen light, Elisabeth Vogler thumped to the floor in another room and promptly slithered around Jack's ankles.

"Cat!" cried Michael and he bent down and scooped her up in his arms, leaving his bag on the floor. "Fat cat. Pretty kitty. Hello there," he baby-talked, brushing his cheeks against her whiskers. He closed his eyes and smiled. His change was so abrupt it seemed schizophrenic, the way people often change around animals. Then, just as abruptly, he looked up and demanded, "What's that?"

Jack glanced around, until he realized Michael meant the radio, which was left on and tuned to a classical station. A plaintive, familiar melody for flute was playing. "Oh, uh. Cocteau used it. Eighteenth century. Seminal opera." Jack had to recite facts to himself before he could remember the name. "*Orpheus and Eurydice.*"

"Yes," Michael said solemnly. "Clarence liked it."

"Clarence liked almost everything." Jack hadn't meant to sound sarcastic. He usually turned the radio off the minute he came home, but he left it on for Michael while he took off his jacket and hung it on the coatrack. "Let me use the toilet quickly and the bathroom'll be all yours."

He hurried back to the bathroom, wanting to get this peculiar visit over with as quickly as possible. Standing over the toilet, he glanced around to see if he'd left out anything that was too revealing about himself. There was something disturbingly intimate about a visitor using your bathtub.

When he finished and opened the bathroom door, he saw Michael still standing in the middle of the kitchen,

Jack's cat still bonelessly draped in the crook of his arm, his fingers lightly stroking her fur. He had the trancelike look of somebody listening to music, only the music was over and a sophisticatedly emotionless announcer was now talking.

What a ham, thought Jack, but he had to say, "Michael? Are you okay?"

Michael didn't respond, but Elisabeth Vogler did, suddenly squirming around and jumping out of Michael's arms. Michael rubbed his arms and said, "I'm just tired and dirty. I need a bath."

"Well, all yours." Jack gestured toward the bathroom, where he'd left the light on. "The shower works fine if you'd rather take a shower. A shower's quicker."

"No. A bath," Michael muttered, but he stood where he was, gazing through the dark bedroom at the white rectangle of light as if it were a mile away. "When Clarence was sick—," he began, and stopped.

Had the music set Michael off on Clarence again? If they were going to have another argument about who felt what, Jack was prepared to keep his temper. "Yes?"

"When Clarence was sick, did he resent anyone for how they behaved? Hate or blame or resent anyone for how they acted?"

The little bastard, thought Jack. He spoke stiffly, impersonally. He hadn't said "you," but it was clear he meant Jack, hitting him where he was most vulnerable now. "He never said anything. Not to me anyway. I hope not. But I don't really know." Jack realized he didn't want to know. This was worse than what Ben had said to him. To be judged by someone who had died was worse than being judged by the living; there was no way of knowing what the dead really thought of you, no way of arguing with them or yourself. Had Clarence felt Jack avoided or neglected him? "Did he ever say anything to you?"

Michael narrowed his eyes at Jack, a critical, skeptical look. "No," he said.

"We did what we could," Jack insisted. "All of us. Although I know some of us could've done more."

Michael winced and turned away, as if he were ashamed of what he'd used against Jack. "I'll try not to make a mess," he said and headed toward the bathroom, taking his bag with him. When he closed the bathroom door, he had to close it again and again, until the bolt finally clicked.

The noisy closing of the door hurt Jack: it sounded like an accusation he was someone who might steal a peek at a boy taking a bath. Jack turned off the radio and sat down at the kitchen table. There was a rumble of water filling a bathtub. No, he hadn't done all he could when Clarence was ill. But does anyone truly believe they did all they could for someone who was dead? Even Michael, beneath his self-important grief and overwrought drama, probably felt he hadn't done enough. Ben was right; Michael had done plenty. Who was Jack to feel critical of the boy for behaving the way he had during Clare's illness when Jack had done so little? But even Michael must feel he hadn't done enough.

With a closed door between them, Jack worried about Michael again. It was neurotic. Irritated beyond words by Michael in the flesh, he again felt sympathy and even fear for him in the abstract. Something bothered Michael today, maybe just guilt for having gone out and had a good time last night. Jack wanted to talk to him, patiently, firmly. But he recognized the violence in his desire to get through to the boy; cracking open the false drama to get at any real drama inside was analogous to cracking open Michael's skull. Were his good intentions genuinely good? Jack feared he could be moral only when he was alone.

It was the saddest hour of the day, still light outside the living room windows but dark in the living room, pitch-dark in the bedroom, the electric light of the kitchen feeble and lonesome. This was the hour when Jack felt most melancholy and immobile. He sat in his chair and sighed. Leaning forward, he could see the thin crack of light along the bottom of the bathroom door. He wanted to say something friendly to Michael, but he didn't know what. He hoped to rise out of his stupor and find a kind word by the time Michael finished his bath.

After he got the door to shut, Michael turned the little paint-caked knob that locked it. He turned around and saw himself in the mirror above the sink, a gray pinched face in a bright room of white tile. The ceramic fixtures were black. The toilet seat was black. There was a pattern of black little squares in the ceramic tiles on the floor. Everything else was white, but a white that looked less clean the longer Michael looked at it. A gray film of dirt coated each horizontal surface: Jack was a pig. Michael felt dirty. There was a black rubber stopper for the tub. Michael plugged it in and turned the hot water on.

The bathtub was low and modern, an elongated round-ness inside a rectangle. Michael had imagined a bigger tub, a deep boat with clawed feet. This would do, he insisted, and hung his coat on a hook on the door. He watched himself in the mirror while he unbuttoned his shirt, his blank face blurring into a mask as the glass fogged over, his wild hair hovering like smoke. With his shirt still on, he turned and stood over the toilet. He always needed to pee before he saw a movie, took a test, or had sex, anything that excited him. Water drilled water for a long time, the bubbles multiplying and crowding out. He remembered standing on his father's shoes so he could get high enough to pee into the bowl, his father holding him by the shoulders so he wouldn't fall in. He had been three years old.

A louder drilling of water thundered behind him. Would this be like drowning? Would his whole life flash in front of him?

Without flushing, he lowered the lid and sat down to untie his shoes. There was a gouge across the top of one shoe. When did that happen? His fingers felt too big for the knots and he finally pried the shoes off and tossed them in the corner. There was a magazine rack between the corner and the toilet, a wooden box stuffed with *The Nation*, *New York Review of Books*, and *Stallion*. Jack, he remembered. Jack the jerk. Jack the judge. "Some of us could've done more," he had said. He judged Michael as someone so worthless he couldn't even say "you" when he accused him. Jack was outside the door, already worming in a book or feeding his face straight from the refrigerator, already forgetting Michael was here, never imagining what Michael was about to do to him. Michael would show him. Michael would show all of them. He remembered to pull the note from his shirt pocket before he tossed the shirt into the corner.

He tossed all his clothes onto the floor in the corner, proving to himself he knew it didn't matter now if they got wet. He hesitated before he pulled down his underpants, as if this were sex where complete nakedness was the point of no return. Then he pulled them off and felt nothing different, not even naked, only long and bony. His body looked sickly, a hollow chest, a pale stomach that bellied out from his skinniness, a penis like a vulnerable pipe of skin. He touched his testicles and ran his fingers through the coarse kink and curl of hair, wanting to remember how much his body had meant to him once, but everything was numb or ticklish.

He was ready, but the water was still too shallow. He turned on the cold water with the hot, sat on the edge of the tub, and waited. There was no window and the little room was steamy and warm, yet Michael felt cold, his skin tightening around him. He picked up the note he had left on the corner of the sink, opened it, and read it, sitting with his arms and legs bunched together. The note made no sense, as if somebody else had written it, then made perfect sense. "I cannot live . . . You never understood before." It was like a note to himself, a reminder. He had to do this. He set the note on the lid of the toilet, flattening it out with both hands. He took up the paper bag and took out the little box. He broke open the box—it was like peeling back the shell of a shrimp. He set the plastic and metal dispenser on the edge of the tub—it looked delicate there, almost electronic.

He reached over and turned off both faucets at once.

The silence was sudden and perfect. Yet he was still conscious in this small white room, still alive. He lifted one foot over the bathtub wall. The water burned. He brought his other foot in. The water lightly lapped against the tub. He slowly lowered himself, his body freezing, his teeth chattering until he sat on heat, then in heat, then sank until warm water rose up to his neck and he was warm all over. Heat flowed into every fold and corner. It was like the sex in his dream, sex without any genitals involved. Maybe his dream hadn't been about sex at all but about this. The clear water gently swung back and forth, his body dissolving in warmth. It would be beautiful, like a slow drowning in self.

Michael sat up and took the dispenser from the edge of the tub. He drew back the tiny shuttle and pushed it forward to squeeze out a blade. The first blade popped out, flew from the tub, and landed on the ceramic tiles with a surprisingly loud ping.

The deep pounding of water suddenly stopped, getting Jack's attention. He listened to the silence and thought about baths. He often took a bath himself when he was depressed or wanted a long, deliberate wank—usually one and the same thing. He heard the slosh of water as Michael stepped in and a subtle change of pitch as the water rose. Then there was calm, perfect silence, so quiet one could hear a pin drop. Yes, a bath did make you feel—

Jack *heard* a pin drop.

He actually heard something small and metal click on the tiles.

Like a razor blade?

As soon as Jack thought it, he wondered why he thought it. "If you feel so bad you should..." His imagination had been crying wolf all day, but the idea jumped back into his head, stronger and clearer than ever. He leaned forward on his chair and listened closely, as if one could actually hear a soft whisper of skin being cut with a razor.

What if it were a razor blade? Michael had said he needed to shave. The toiletries in his bag: he had dropped a new blade on the floor. And why suicide? Why did that idea keep coming back to Jack? It was almost as if he *wanted* Michael to kill himself.

He tried out that possibility, imagining he knew for certain Michael was in there slashing his wrists and Jack would sit out here and let him do it. It was like a ghost story you invent to scare yourself, Jack trying to frighten himself out of his neurotic worry with the sickest scenario he could imagine. "I must be insane," he thought, sitting back and settling into himself again.

Michael reached out to pick the blade off the floor. He used his fingernail to lift the metal sliver up enough to get a finger beneath it. It was such a tiny thing. He held it tight between his thumb and index finger, an inch and a half of sharp edge. He knew a common mistake was to cut across, when the correct way was to cut across and down, in a J. How did he know that? He wondered who had told him.

Blue lines were buried beneath the pale white skin of his left wrist. The tendons went flat when he bent his hand back. His hand looked new and unfamiliar, purplish lines in the joints of his fingers, the tips covered with fingerprints like the lines for mountains and ridges on a topographical map.

He was frustrated he was still seeing and thinking. He had to stop thinking. He steadied his arms by pressing his elbows against his sides. The razor blade touched his wrist, then broke contact, without cutting. The razor blade wavered, like a pen hesitating over a signature. Where was his blinding pain and self-loathing when he needed them? Michael closed his eyes. Now. Or now. Or maybe now—

"Jack will be fine." The crowded subway car trembled and swayed, Laurie swaying with the bodies pressed around her. "I should have said more but Jack can cope. Hope Carla's home. Unload some of this crazy, jerky day on Carla." She assumed Michael would be home too, his presence a nuisance that forced them to speak in whispers.

Carla sat in the gathering dark of the living room, enjoying the peace and quiet she had come home to. She briefly wondered again where everyone was, but it felt so nice to sit and think nothing after going against the bureaucratic mind at Bellevue all afternoon.

"We do not grieve for the living." Or, "We do not grieve for the sick?" thought Ben, buttoning up the white shirt he had borrowed from the elderly volunteer—it would not do to speak at a rally in a sweatshirt. No, "We do not grieve for the living," then words about grief being premature and the sick needing anger and care, and then his introduction of the speaker from Bailey House.

"My life is harder than yours," Danny told the blue-eyed, angel-haired dog in Connecticut. "I get only twenty-three roubles a month, less what they take out for my pension, but I don't wear mourning." He was using his solitude to rehearse lines, but his heart wasn't in it. An open-mouthed dog made a poor audience, and Danny was still miffed over Ben's flight into town. He wondered if Ben's political rah-rah was only an excuse for getting even with Danny for screwing up their threeway. He began again. "Why do you always wear black?" Chekhov could be so Hispanic.

"I wonder how they're doing?" said Peter, watching the nightly news. "We should have everyone over for dinner soon, now that we're all back." Washing lettuce in the kitchen, Livy muttered, "I guess. Although we can't have them without having Michael." "Michael's all right," Peter claimed, then groaned and added, "Poor Michael."

And Jack, sitting at his kitchen table, thought, "Arcalli, you're nuts," wondering how he had gone directly from fear for Michael to annoyance with him, without even a moment of relief when he found the boy alive and sitting on his front stoop. He suddenly remembered the look Michael gave him out there when Michael snapped out of his dream. A look with none of the arrogance Michael usually hid behind. The look of a frightened child. What kind of pain and confusion did Michael mask with his arrogance?

Jack listened carefully, and heard no slosh or dribbling of water. You're a buffoon, he told himself. A dotty, stupid buffoon. But he stood up and walked across the kitchen. He stood in the doorway and listened more carefully. He felt ridiculous, like a father worried that his son was playing with himself. But he drew a breath to call in to Michael.

Michael heard someone coming to stop him. He pressed his wrist against the blade and pulled.

He felt nothing, then a mild sting across his wrist. Watching a dark red globule appear at the center of the cut, he became frightened, excited. The globule broke. A drop rolled off and fell into the water, where it slowly opened like a rose.

"Michael?"

Jack was outside. He had to finish this or he would look like a fool to Jack, a coward, a wimp. He cut lengthwise and more blood welled up. It was hypnotically beautiful, his own blood dark on his arm, bright red in the water. The stinging through his arm was clean and satisfying.

"Michael!"

"What!"

There was a pause, then a sheepish, "How much longer will you be?"

"I'll finish when I finish," Michael called out.

Strings and skeins of red floated beneath his arm, unwinding through the water like smoke. He was sorry he would never see the look on Jack's face when Jack found him here. He remembered the note. Had he said enough? It was too late to rewrite the note. And the fingers of his left hand were getting numb. He should do his other wrist while the fingers could still hold a blade. Very carefully, he passed the metal sliver from the fingers of his right hand to the fingers of his left. He cut across again. The thin red line looked like a little mouth before the incision filled with blood. The note was unnecessary. He was giving himself extra mouths to say what he needed to say.

He finished his right wrist and laid the blade on the edge of the tub. He sat back and sank down, wanting to taste every second of his going. His arms lay in the water, a warm constant stinging, a comforting release of pain, as if his whole body were weeping through his arms. The water turned pink, then red. Time passed quickly even as it seemed to stand still, the way time passes when you watch the second hand sweep around the face of a clock. He was frightened he might change his mind before he was finished.

A book thumped shut.

Jack was still out there. Michael was annoyed he had to think about Jack. There was something else he should be thinking about now. But he had to keep Jack away. He had to assure Jack everything was fine until he was finished here. To assure Jack things were fine, Michael began to sing:

Row, row, row your boat, gently down the stream.
Merrily, merrily, merrily, merrily—

Jack remained in the doorway, chastened by Michael's "I'll finish when I finish," but unwilling to go back to the kitchen. He automatically pulled a book from the stuffed bookcase there, just as he often pulled a book on his way to the toilet. He opened it and actually read a page before he realized what he was reading—Gore Vidal—then read another page to stop himself from thinking. Feeling distracted and calmer, he snapped the book shut and wedged it back on the shelf. He was returning to the kitchen when he heard Michael singing.

A child's song. Sung cheerfully? Mockingly? Its tone was so different from everything else about Michael tonight, the song sounded bitterly sarcastic, then deranged. Michael sang it over and over, the song running down like a motor, then speeding up again. He sang like someone having a nervous breakdown.

Michael kept singing, not knowing how to stop once he started. He was getting lightheaded, even dizzy, but the song took over without his having to think about it. He sank down further, until his ears were underwater and his voice sounded very deep and echoey. The tub of water was an enormous ear, picking up sounds and voices through the pipes that branched all over the building, maybe all over the world. Michael stopped singing so he could listen to the world. Dishes were being knocked about in a sink. A toilet was flushed. A man and woman argued over how to bathe a baby. Michael could hear everything. When he was finished, he would *know* everything.

Already his mind was making connections he hadn't known before. He was lightheaded with wisdom. Losing blood made you wise, put you in touch with the oneness of things, or nothingness of things. There had been a particular reason why he did this, but Michael could not remember it. Nevertheless, he was glad he was doing this, relieved he had done it. Soon he could go under, into a warm ocean where he breathed water instead of air and would never need to come to the surface again. Weightless and naked, he could swim among the dead, watching for—who? Clarence. He groped around with his legs and back, trying to find the underwater door that opened into that ocean. All he found was the smooth, watertight surface of a bathtub.

The singing wore down to a mumbled hum, and stopped.

"Where are you going dancing tonight?" Jack called out, just to check on the boy.

Something thrashed in the tub and water splashed on the floor, then there was a long silence.

"Michael?" Jack stepped toward the closed door. "Are you okay, Michael?"

No answer.

The arrogant little bastard. He was doing this deliberately, trying to spook Jack, wanting to make Jack think he was crazy and had drowned himself in a bathtub. Or maybe it was Jack who was having the nervous breakdown.

He knocked on the door. "I have to come in, Michael. I need to get something." He reached for the doorknob, deciding to play the voyeur when he found Michael sitting naked and indignant in there. He preferred to be read as a dirty old man than as a nervous nelly panicked by worry. He turned the knob. The door was locked.

"Michael." He pounded on the door. "*Michael!* Say something, dammit!" His mind raced with everything he had feared that afternoon, racing back against itself in an attempt not to believe any of it. "This isn't funny! If you don't say something, I have to break down my own fucking door, you ass!"

Nothing. Not a damn sound.

"You self-centered little prick! You self-important little

shit!" Jack turned the knob and pressed against the door. Anger replaced fear, and he threw his weight against the door. Once, then again, and the old wood around the template cracked and the door flew open. The door swung against the tub, blocking the tub from view so all Jack saw at first was an empty bathroom, clothes piled in the corner and his own absurdly bug-eyed, furious face in the mirror above the sink.

In a corner of his left eye he caught a bit of bright color. He glanced.

There was a roar from deep in his body, diaphragm, and lungs driving up a groan louder than any cry.

The bathtub was full of blood. White legs lay folded in blood. Behind the door, Michael's face was slumped against the side of the tub.

His cry still rushing from his chest, Jack plunged both arms into the blood to pull Michael from it, as if it were the blood that hurt Michael. He swung the long body around and the head banged against the open door.

"Sorry! I'm sorry!" Jack cried and held the head to lift it around the door, wanting to rush the body into another room. The body felt hot and soaking against him. Then Jack saw a bleeding wrist and understood where the blood was from. He swept the weightless body down to the bathroom floor. The head hung over the threshold, stretching a pale throat over an enormous Adam's apple.

Jack grabbed the boy's jaw and shook the head. Nothing. But his white ribs rose and fell. He was breathing through his open mouth. "Help me!" Jack shouted into the apartment. "Somebody!" But he was alone with this. There was nobody here to help or to tell him what to do.

Dark blood crept through the net of seams between the

tiles. The wrists still bled, slowly, steadily. Jack grabbed a wrist in each hand, pressing the wounds into his palms to stop the bleeding. Direct pressure, he remembered. But that was for arteries and these had to be veins. There had to be more water than blood in the bathtub. It was brighter than the fresh blood on the floor and nobody had that much blood in them. Jack saw a tiny silver blade set neatly on the white enamel, like a spot rubbed there.

He gripped the wrists more tightly, afraid to let go of them, yet horrified to think he was doing the wrong thing and Michael would bleed to death no matter how tightly Jack held him. He gripped so hard he could feel no pulse, but he looked and saw Michael still breathing. The boy's face was relaxed, even content, mauve lips pulled back from his teeth like a smile.

Elisabeth Vogler appeared, and primly stepped around Michael's head to sniff at the tiled floor, where there was blood.

"No, Elisabeth! Don't!" Jack couldn't let go to push her back. He brought his leg around and kicked at her.

She leaped through the door again, coldly looked on, then stretched her back and strolled toward the kitchen.

Do cats drink blood? Was Jack hurting Michael? He half sat, half knelt over the boy and changed his position to give Michael more room. He lifted the boy's arms so the blood would have to climb before it could bleed out. He felt the blood only as a hotness in his palms. How long did it take for a person to bleed to death? How much time had passed? Jack's heart was pounding, but time seemed to stand still. Could he let go long enough to call the police or an ambulance? Or to tear a sheet in strips for bandages or something? Afraid to let go, Jack was trapped with a bleeding boy. If he shouted, was there anyone in the building who could hear him through the airshaft?

Then he heard somebody at the front door of the building.

"Somebody!" he shouted. "Somebody help me!" Would they hear him back here?

They did, because there was a knock at Jack's door. "Jack? Is that you, Jack?" It sounded like Margaret, the stocky old lady who lived on the third floor. Her voice was frightened and croaky.

"Margaret! Whoever it is! Get in here! It's life or death."

The door clicked then rattled in its jamb. "Jack! Jack, dear! It's locked!"

"Just a minute!" Of course it was locked. What should he do? Jack let go and jumped up, ran through the bedroom and opened the door, racing back to Michael without seeing who was there. "Call an ambulance!" he shouted. "911! 911!" He straddled the body again and tried to remember how he had done this. He crossed his arms and grabbed the wrists. The blood in his palms stuck to the blood of the wounds.

"Oh, Lord!"

Jack looked up and saw Margaret standing in the kitchen with her white hair and house dress, staring through the bedroom.

"Call the damn ambulance! Somebody's bleeding to death!"

She snapped out of her trance. "Oh! Where's your—? I see it." And she stepped off to the side, where Jack heard her pick up his phone and dial. "This is an emergency. We have somebody bleeding to death." Margaret instantly sounded very tough and no-nonsense. She gave the address and insisted they hurry. "Jack, they want to know if it's an accident or a crime?"

"A suicide," Jack shouted back. "A suicide attempt, I mean." He hoped. He leaned down and whispered, "Help is coming, Michael. Things'll be fine. Things'll be okay." Talking to the boy, he wanted to lightly slap his face to bring him to. Wanting to slap his face, he suddenly wanted to slap him hard, hit him across the face, grab him by the throat, and bang the bastard's head against the floor. He could not let go of Michael's arms, but he was suddenly furious with him. It was as if Jack had been knocked unconscious and only now came to and began to understand what had happened. He was breathing hard, choking up, sobbing. He was crying over this little idiot who wanted to kill himself. The pale face and bony body with bleeding wrists: "You phony bleeding Jesus," Jack muttered. "You cheap imitation Christ. I'm going to make you live, you twit. You're not getting out of this so damn easy."

"Jack?"

Margaret again stood in the kitchen where Jack could see her. Her arms were folded across her breasts as if she were freezing. She had not heard what Jack said, only his sobbing.

"They're on their way," she announced, shook her head and sighed, "Oh Lord. The world we live in."

The police arrived first, two uniformed patrolmen whom Margaret waved into the apartment. One cop put his hand on his holster the instant he saw Jack on the floor with Michael. The other cop said, "Oh shit," lifting a hand to his eyes as if he thought they'd walked in on something else. When they understood, the second cop, who was Jack's age, stuck his head into the bathroom and said, "Uh oh. Looks like somebody's been playing with Daddy's razor." There was nothing they would do before the ambulance arrived except take a blanket off Jack's bed and wrap it around Michael while Jack continued to hold the boy's wrists. "For trauma," they explained.

Then there were paramedics in the kitchen. A man in white waded into the bathroom. A young woman crowded in, taking over from Jack and ordering him out. His apartment seemed packed with people. Stumbling out to the kitchen, Jack passed a black man who yanked a white latex glove over one hand as he hurried back. Jack realized all the paramedics wore white plastic gloves. "These faggots can't do anything right," somebody said, but Jack couldn't tell who. Everyone he looked at seemed furiously busy, irritable yet intent on saving Michael.

A collapsed stretcher was brought in and carried back. The young woman came out, looking mildly uncomfortable as she handed Jack a torn sheet of paper. "This was in there. I think it's for you."

It was a note. Jack quickly read it. The note was terse, the way Michael was terse, afraid to go too deeply into anything for fear of what he might find. But Michael had gone deep tonight, hadn't he? "You never understood before." No, Michael hadn't done this solely for himself, but to them, to Jack.

They were carrying the stretcher on its side through his

bedroom, Michael strapped in and covered with blankets, one paramedic holding a plasma bag above the boy. Jack hurried out into the hall in front of them, before they blocked the door. The older cop was out there, getting Margaret's name and address. "He left this." Jack gave the cop the note. "Where're they taking him? I have to go with him."

The cop told Jack to ride over in the ambulance and he'd meet Jack at the hospital. "Some questions and forms we have to take care of."

They maneuvered the vertical stretcher around the corner and through the door as if it were a long table with folded legs. Once they were past, Jack hurried back into the apartment to close up the bathroom so Elisabeth Vogler wouldn't get in there. Already the apartment felt intensely deserted, empty. Medical wrappers were strewn on the bathroom floor; the tub was still full of bloody water.

Outside in the ambulance, Michael lay on his back, snugly bundled in blankets and straps, his face chalky in the bright white light inside the ambulance. "The Mets," said the black paramedic, apparently part of an earlier conversation. But nobody seemed willing to continue that conversation, embarrassed or annoyed there was a layman present.

They pulled up outside St. Vincent's, although it felt like they had driven further than the few blocks separating Jack's apartment from the hospital. They parked on Seventh Avenue outside the emergency waiting room. The night was chilly and Jack wore no coat; his shirt felt damp. The stretcher was wheeled up a ramp and through the waiting room, then disappeared behind a pair of swinging doors. Jack was told to wait.

He stood beneath the humming fluorescent lights, suddenly alone. Feeling people glance at him, he looked down and saw the front of his shirt and the knees of his trousers stained with different shades of rust or red clay. His hands were brown with dried blood. He thought he should wash them, then felt he should keep them like this until he knew the state of things. He stepped over to a row of scoop chairs and sat in one. He was exhausted.

The adrenaline was gone and he felt weak, slowly regaining consciousness, still waking up. Why did it suddenly feel so unreal to him? After all, this was exactly what he had been fearing all day. Which made it more unreal. How had he known? He did not believe in God or even ESP. He had imagined it. Such imaginative sympathy was disturbing, frightening. "You never understood before." But Jack had understood, without sympathy for such false drama, without love.

The intercom called, a voice talking to itself inside a seashell. Jack had been here before, not this hospital but *a* hospital. He thought about phoning Laurie or Ben. He did not have to wait here alone. But not yet. He was not ready to dilute his frightening bond with Michael by sharing it with the others.

Why had Michael chosen *him*? Jack knew it was hubris to think Michael had done this to Jack and Jack alone— Jack was too unimportant. Was it only by accident he had chosen Jack's home? He could've done it at Laurie and Carla's, where he lived, or at Ben and Danny's. And yet, perversely, Jack was glad Michael had done it to him. It was almost as if Jack would feel jealous if Michael had done it to someone else. He was angry with Michael for doing it at all, but relieved Michael had done it to him.

Oh God, he thought. He was closer to Michael than he ever imagined, bound more deeply to the boy than he ever wanted to be. If Michael lived—and Jack felt so weighed down by obligation he knew Michael would live—this was only the beginning.

12

"WHERE am I?" thought Clarence after he died. "Is this death?"

There was the sensation of floating and a feeling of resolution like the change of key from minor into major. Then a man and woman began to sing.

No, it wasn't death. It was Mozart. The sixth side of *The Magic Flute* still played on the stereo while tired bones and aching muscles reappeared and reassembled on the living room sofa. He had fallen asleep, and sometime between Tamino's reunion with Pamina and Papageno's reunion with Papagena, he dreamed again he had died. Death was never an event in this dream, only a sudden realization, like the realization by a cartoon character who has run off the edge of a cliff and just then notices he stands in midair. Clarence had learned not to panic. So long as you didn't panic you could continue to stand aloft in your own nonexistence, at least in dreams. Clarence was sometimes relieved and sometimes disappointed when he woke from these dreams to find himself still alive.

Dishes and pans banged in the sink in the kitchen. But it wasn't Michael. It was what's-his-name, the volunteer, Guy Temple—what a name—who had fed Clarence something macrobiotic tonight. Earnest, well-intentioned, admirable, obnoxious Guy. He was cleaning up, which meant he would be leaving soon. Michael had gone out, for a walk he said.

The window was open and it was a summer evening outside, footsteps and voices and car radios occasionally audible through the Mozart. He wore a bathrobe over his clothes, pulling the robe shut when he felt chilled, throwing the robe open when he felt feverish. Mozart sounded joyful, then threatening. Clarence had slept through the "Pa-Pa" song. Of course he wasn't dead yet. He was only in the M's. When he came home from the hospital and found himself stranded day after day on the living room sofa, he had decided to listen to his entire record collection, alphabetically by composer. It took longer than he had imagined. Summer was almost over and he was only to Mozart. He owned a lot of Stravinsky, and, more dauntingly, he had all his Wagner to get through. When he committed himself to this program, he superstitiously believed he would be well again by the time he finished listening to every record he owned. Now, he believed only that he would not die until he finished. Nights broken up by wakefulness and days broken up by sleep, his condition seemed to go on for years. He had been ill for so long he could not remember being well. Death was the only alternative he could imagine to this long, tedious dream of sickness.

Clarence had almost enjoyed being sick, at first. It was good to do nothing again and nice to be waited on by friends and strangers. And it was interesting to be abstracted from your own body. He became a connoisseur of aches and pains, an aesthete of illness, imagining the sunburst pattern of a headache in his skull, distinguishing the cakey textures of congestion in his chest, the bad tastes in his mouth. More interesting, it put him in touch with past illnesses. Healthy, he had never remembered being sick; he seemed to have lived two parallel lives, one in sickness and one in health, each unconscious of the other, and only now could he remember illness, most of it in childhood. He remembered little from college or after, years when he'd been well. Childhood seemed to have been all sickbeds, which couldn't be right, sweetly boring hours spent among picture books and toy soldiers and a jet of mentholated steam from a vaporizer. There had been days home from school, whole weeks in fact, although he could not remember being in pain. All he remembered were morning movies and Art Linkletter on television, pads of paper filled with drawing after drawing, and Asia, their maid, who alternately tolerated or indulged him on mornings his mother worked with his father at their hardware store.

Childhood was full of the presence of his parents, if not beside him then in the next room or just down the street, two gentle, private, hardworking people. They married late and died early, when Clarence and his brother were still in high school. His mother was in and out of hospitals for two years before she died of white lung—she had worked many years in a cotton mill before she met Joshua Laird. His father died six months later of a heart attack that relatives called a broken heart. There had been a numb, empty time afterward, a despondency like a dark sleep. He came out of that sleep when he went away to college, where he found a fresh, furious delight in the world around him, music and movies and even people seeming glorious things to him, new objects that had nothing to do with his past.

Illness was a kind of drunkenness in which he could wander among new thoughts and impressions. For a time he had looked forward to getting well, when he would have the soberness needed to put these new or recovered pieces together. But soberness never came to him. Life remained all content and no form, memories accumulating into mere clutter, like the music he heard where an occasional, familiar phrase peeked into his fog without ever building into anything, the passages between melting away into meaningless background noise. Already, *The Magic Flute* was over, without his having heard the jubilant chorus at the finale that he remembered loving so much.

"That was pretty," said Guy, coming in from the kitchen and drying his hands, looking very moral because he had done the dishes. "Would you like me to turn it over?"

Clarence shook his head and studied Guy. The fellow was Michael's age but seemed both older and younger than Michael. He wore a T-shirt today, and his plump thighs were encased in bright yellow gym shorts. When he sat on the chair opposite the sofa, the shorts pulled tight and there was a lump like genitals in his crotch, but he still looked terribly solemn and sexless.

"Your friend is being quite irresponsible this evening," he said, looking at his watch. "He told me he'd be back by now."

Clarence shrugged. "Maybe he stopped off in Central Park for a quick blowjob." He enjoyed needling Guy, who hated any mention of sex.

Guy lowered his eyes and crossed his legs, like an old lady. "I have an MCC meeting at nine, you see."

"Oh. That gay church thing," said Clarence. It continued to amaze him that gay men no longer *had* to have sex with each other in order to be gay. They could attend gay churches, gay political caucuses, or gay invalids. It seemed like such a strange use of sexuality. When he was Guy's age he was high on sex, the thing itself, not just the idea and identity. Ben assured him men were still getting laid, less frequently and more carefully maybe, but things had changed. Clarence had changed too, but then he was sick. "You go on to your meeting. I'll be fine until Michael gets back."

"He hasn't given you a bath today, has he?" Guy sternly sniffed the air. "When was your last bath?"

Clarence inhaled the rich sourness of his clothes, the tangy smell like iron under his arms. He smiled and said, "Your washcloth? My skin? Is that a proposition, Guy?"

Guy opened his mouth, closed it again, and blushed.

Clarence said it only for effect. The truth of the matter was, despite all his abstract thoughts about sex, he rarely had sexual feelings anymore. An erection was a special occasion. His memories of sex were not nearly as round and real as his memories of childhood illnesses, but distant and hypothetical, like his memories of health. Guy's sexlessness might only be in Clarence's mind. After all, he could not think of Michael sexually either.

"Thanks for the offer, Guy. But baths are Michael's department. And you wouldn't want me to cheat on Michael, would you?"

Baths were the closest he and Michael came nowadays to sex. Clarence was quite capable of bathing himself, but Michael insisted on being present, as if afraid Clarence might stay in too long and melt like sugar. He was embarrassed to have Michael watching him—he gave male nudity a bad name. Afterward, Michael wrapped a towel around him and rubbed him dry, which was nice.

"Perhaps I should be going," said Guy. "See you next Wednesday?"

"If I'm still among the living."

Guy frowned. Nobody wanted Clarence to talk about dying. "I'll see you next week. With a vegetarian meatloaf I think you should try."

"Yum," said Clarence as Guy kissed him on a whiskered cheek.

When the front door bumped shut in the distance, Clarence felt a sudden gust of energy. He was alone now. It was the presence of the healthy that exhausted him. Without their tiresome energy to compare himself to, he did not feel as sick. He sat up, then stood up and padded over to the stereo to play the last side of *The Magic Flute* again. He returned to the sofa and sat with his slippered feet on the floor, determined not to sleep through the "Pa-pa" song this time. To keep himself occupied through the churchy passage, he took up the copy of *Film Comment* Jack had dropped off yesterday. The magazine automatically fell open to Jack's article. And Clarence saw himself again, in black and white, his face screwed up around the eyepiece of a beautiful Arriflex camera, a movie director.

He took great, goofy pleasure in the image. Good old Jack. He really should thank him better, although what Clarence loved was his photograph. Here he was, just as he had pictured himself in fantasies since college: an eye, a camera, a hand directing an action. It didn't matter the pose was only a minor part of making a movie. There was something magical about it, simultaneously active and passive, the spectator who was also a man of action. And it was real. Finally, at thirty-eight, he had transformed a wish of himself into a fact, proved to himself he wasn't the sweet, ineffectual daydreamer everyone wanted him to be. He had made a feature film. It didn't matter the film was something as awful as *Disco of the Damned*—although he had certainly done it to poor Mozart under the credits. He had made a real movie, which somehow made it easier for Clarence to die.

It was a ridiculous thing to feel, but he felt it. He had made a movie, a bad movie, but he couldn't imagine the experience of making a good movie to be very different. An experience was more important to him than any results. "When you're dead you're dead." He remembered Ben saying that to Jack back in college, during a bull session about "transcendence"—Jack was still semi-

Catholic back then. Thinking of his mother and father, Clarence had laughed and wanted to hug Ben. It sounded so simple and obvious he had hoped it were true. He loved art and sex and filmmaking because he could lose himself in them. Soon he would lose himself for good and it didn't seem such a bad thing. He had experienced everything life had to offer him. He could be perfectly content if he died this very minute—or maybe not until after the "Pa-pa" song.

His attitude toward death changed from day to day, but always for the best it seemed. The few times death alarmed or frightened him, Clarence sincerely believed he'd live. When he was sure he would die, death felt perfectly acceptable. Lately, he'd been tending more toward death. It had nothing to do with the name of his condition, which the newspapers treated as an automatic death certificate—Clarence read only the arts pages. No, he was tired and bored and life had become one long sleepless night, a weary matter of duration with nothing to gain by living another year or even another ten. Was it cowardice? He sometimes wondered if he wanted to die just so he wouldn't have to go through the exhausting ordeal of making another damn movie. He wondered tonight if he were really as comfortable with dying as he seemed. He thought he had touched bottom, without a trace of panic, without any terror of death. Maybe it was only a false bottom and terror would come later. Maybe he was too shallow to be terrified by death. Or maybe he was just too damned tired to care.

Death could be a very natural, private event. But there were other people. It was the presence of other people that complicated dying. They all kept looking at Clarence, as if saying, "Live, live, live," like a pack of Auntie Mames. Or they looked at him guiltily, pleadingly, as if expecting something from him, a blessing or word of wisdom or judgment. They behaved as if their actions should be the most important thing in the world to Clarence right now. Couldn't they understand he was in no shape to judge or care? He felt benignly, tenderly indifferent toward all of them, and guiltily indifferent toward Michael.

He was glad Michael had gone out tonight, but he wondered where he was. He had been joking about the Central Park blowjob, but wondered now if Michael were actually up to something like that. Maybe. Michael had become strange this week, nervous and uncomfortable, and he had said goodbye to Clarence when Guy arrived tonight as if he were guilty about where he was going. He *hoped* Michael was seeing someone else. He did. He should. It might make it easier for him to live with what he had inflicted on this kid, this stranger.

Who was Michael anyway? What was he doing here? Clarence felt he'd spent the last three years in an exhilarating tumult of schemes and work, then came home sick to find he had a new guest in his life. He barely knew this guest, at least compared to his family in Danville or his old circle of friends or even the people from *Disco of the Damned.* And yet, he was now completely dependent on this visitor.

No, it wasn't quite like that. Michael was his lover. They had enjoyed each other's company for three years. But Clarence never took his lovers very seriously. Sex was fun and romance a lark, and nothing was permanent but change. And yet here was this kid, this "chicken" Clarence had pursued simply to amuse himself, and circumstances had turned him into Clarence's mother and father and keeper and prisoner. It was too absurd. If he were Jack, he would feel nothing but guilt over that. Clarence felt guilty, now and then, but he also felt grateful, resentful, and bitterly amused. If he had known things would end like this, he would never have taken the boy to the movies.

Papageno was playing his bells; soon he and Papagena would start "Pa-pa-pa-ing" at each other.

A key ring jingled outside the door down the hall. The door opened and Michael's footsteps approached, somber or timid or guilty.

And Clarence's next thought was that Michael should stay out until his song was over. It was a selfish thought. All his thoughts about Michael were selfish. But he had a perfect right to be selfish if he were dying. Didn't he? Didn't he? And when he died, he told himself, he could set Michael free.

13

"It was more luck than anything I did," said Laurie. "But when the stock market finally settled down again, none of my clients were hurt too badly."

"I got to introduce one of the speakers, and it was beautiful up there," said Ben. "The entire Mall, sun sinking by the Washington Monument, looked like a red and gold turkish carpet of gay people."

"Another season of *Nutcrackers* and *Messiahs*," said Livy. "An oboe is always on call at Christmas."

They sat together again in Livy and Peter's loft in SoHo. The place felt as big as a basketball court, half of it occupied by the worktables, light boxes, and canvases Peter used for his commercial art, the other half by the twin, alligator-long sofas, wing-backed chairs, and great oak table Livy had inherited from a great aunt. It was a

High-Tech Victorian space. A conventional double bed off to one side was piled with overcoats and parkas. There were smells of lamb, bayleaves, and turpentine tonight. Everyone chatted and caught up with each other, drank wine spritzers or beer and smeared cheese on whole wheat bread, complained about the snow outside and laughed about the messiness of their lives, pretending everything was what it had always been.

It wasn't until after New Year's that Livy and Peter had the old crowd over for dinner. Livy wanted to do everyone at once, but too much had been happening in the past months to get them all together. There had been Laurie's stock market crash and Ben's march in Washington and Livy's seasonal work as a musician and Danny's *Seagull*. And Michael, of course. His deed cast a shadow similar to the shadow cast a year ago by Clarence's death.

Livy and Peter had been more involved back then. This time, Livy kept herself and Peter outside the crisis. Michael wasn't Clarence, whom Livy respected as a perfectionist like herself and who had been a friend of Peter's. She could not bear another round of hospitals and hand-holding, sympathy and strained advice. She wasn't cold-hearted about it, simply practical. And she and Peter had drifted away from their gay friends over the past year. Livy tried to stay in touch with Laurie and Carla but had no reason to talk with the men. Peter tended to see only the people Livy was seeing. He preferred work to people anyway and was perfectly content to let Livy arrange their social life. Peter was terribly flexible. It was a joke among the others that if the right man instead of the right woman had come along, Peter would be gay instead of straight. He still thought about Clarence now and then, especially when he drank too much and wanted to feel sad.

Livy bustled about the apartment, happily dealing with everyone from safe inside her role as hostess. A stocky woman with little feet and salt-and-pepper hair, she was ten years older than her husband. She wore a long English country skirt tonight and blunt truths kept popping out of her mouth, as they were wont to do when Livy's attention was elsewhere. "You know what Fitzgerald said," she told them after describing her break with her old chamber group. "In your thirties you want friends, in your forties you know friends won't save you any more than love did," not noticing what a slap that was to Peter as well as her guests. Laurie glanced over at Peter, who smiled at her sheepishly. Everybody knew not to take Livy's bluntnesses too seriously.

Ben and Danny sat on one of the sofas, Danny's legs hooked over Ben's knees to make up for the fight they had had on the way over. Carla sat opposite them with Laurie. Exhausted after a day of too many sessions, Carla was very quiet tonight. Laurie, Ben, and Livy did most of the talking, leaping from one subject to the next as if there were nothing else on their minds, although Laurie kept glancing at her watch.

Then they arrived.

"Michael!"

"Mikey, hello!"

"It's good to see you, Michael!"

Like an insistent chorus of bells, they sang out his

name when he came through the door with Jack. Ben and Danny rose to their feet, Livy leaned in from the kitchen, Laurie and Carla turned to look.

Michael's cheeks and nose were bright red; snow still melted on his shoulders and in his curly hair. He directed a smile around the room, a faintly bashful smile that suggested a child sneaking into a cocktail party.

Jack was the one who looked uncomfortable, worried and ashamed as his eyes picked out this and that person without really looking at them. One would've thought *he* was the failed suicide.

Peter gave Michael a warm, intense look—full of concern, dinners past, and his and Livy's failure to visit him in the hospital—while he took his coat.

Except for Peter and Livy, they had all seen Michael since the suicide attempt, but never all at once like this and always briefly, like visits to an invalid. They had not yet seen him "well." One by one, they stepped forward to kiss Michael hello as he made his way toward a vacant stretch of the sofa. All attention was focused on Michael, with no clear purpose, like the moment in a production of a play or opera when a real horse is brought out on stage.

"Wine, Michael? Or beer? There's bread and cheese, Michael. Great bread."

And then, as if embarrassed by the absurdity of the attention they gave him, they suddenly pretended the horse wasn't there.

"But Danny and I will be staying with his relatives outside San Juan."

"That should be interesting," said Livy. "Do they approve of you and Danny?"

"Are you kidding?" said Danny. "They adore my Puppy."

Laurie watched Jack sit beside Michael on the sofa. They looked like a couple. Jack touched Michael on the knee and, without looking at him, Michael patted Jack's arm, confiding something to each other in the private manner of a real couple. Yet Jack told Laurie they weren't, not sexually anyway, although Michael had lived with Jack for almost three months now.

Ben thought it was proof of how, on a personal level, things always work out for the best. Danny gave it until spring. Carla found it a delicate situation but one that *might*—she was afraid to commit herself anymore—be good therapy for both of them. Livy and Peter found it curious. Only Laurie felt it was wrong, possibly dangerous that Jack and Michael were a couple, platonic or otherwise.

For one thing, she hated Michael for what he had done to Jack. His suicide attempt might have been more than a selfish plea for sympathy—Carla said the depths of the cuts proved he meant to succeed—but to have done it to Jack, where Jack would be alone when he found him, seemed a gratuitous act of cruelty. If he had succeeded, it would've destroyed Jack. She had talked around that with Jack, and he already understood perfectly. Yet he did not hate Michael. Once when she went with him to visit Michael in the hospital, she heard Michael insult him, call him a fat pig and old fart, simply because he brought Michael the wrong brand of toothpaste. "He's testing me," Jack claimed afterward. "And it's got to be difficult being around someone who's made you look like a fool by screwing up your tragic gesture."

Carla sat quietly beside Laurie, but it was a different kind of quiet now that Michael was here. Carla felt she had failed with Michael, failed to recognize an emotional breakdown that had taken place under her very nose. It shook her confidence in her own abilities. She blamed herself, which hurt Laurie and gave Laurie another reason to be angry with Michael, a more selfish one. She lightly touched Carla on the shoulder now, although she knew Carla wanted no sympathy for her failure and didn't really need it. Even in failure Carla could be strong. She calmly watched Michael, as if trying to understand her error.

Laurie watched Jack. He lost some of his self-conscious-ness when conversation shifted to the new French film whose poster Peter had done. Jack caught Laurie watching him and threw more effort into an analysis of the decline of French cinema she had heard many times from him. Michael listened, as if genuinely interested in what Jack was saying.

Reaching for the bread and cheese on the coffee table, a hand stretched from the sleeve of Michael's bulky blue sweater; there was a glimpse of wrist.

"The new Louis Malle film—was good." Peter's sentence struck a bump and he finished it but couldn't continue.

The entire room was centered around the purplish T-shaped welt on Michael's wrist, while Michael placidly loaded a slab of bread with brie then passed the bread to Jack.

"It was okay," Jack said to deaf ears. "But nothing compared to *Murmur of the Heart* or *The Fire Within*."

"Dinner should be ready shortly," Livy said, too loudly to sound natural.

Michael glanced up, then glanced down at his wrist, but continued to prepare a piece of bread for himself. He finished, shook his sleeve over the scar, sat back, and ate.

"I understand you're going back to school?" said Peter.

Michael nodded, swallowed what was in his mouth, and said, "Next week, in fact. It's only one more semester, so I might as well do it." He shrugged over it, like any undergraduate.

"You're still thinking about med school?" said Livy.

"No. It never really appealed to me. That was just what my family wanted me to do. Quite frankly, I've seen the insides of too many hospitals to want to be a doctor." He rolled his eyes and took another bite of bread.

He spoke with the same faintly affected phrasing he always spoke with, but he acknowledged what had happened in a matter-of-fact manner that sounded adult, even sane.

Jack looked at everyone as if to say, "See?"—even at Laurie.

"I'm sure you'll do fine whatever you end up doing," said Livy, and conversation resumed, including Michael without being dominated by his presence, all fear of saying the wrong thing momentarily dispelled.

"Right back," Laurie whispered as she gave Carla's hand a squeeze. She stepped quietly over to the window with her drink, as if wanting only to look at the snow crowding down through the streetlight below. She was uncomfortable with the cheerfulness that seemed a gloss over what had happened. The bright room behind her was reflected in the cold glass that looked out on a dark building.

Jack and Michael. Michael and Jack. Her sympathy

could not follow Jack into such a strange place. Even if Michael were sane now, and she didn't think he was, the dynamics were all wrong. Two mourners, two ex-Catholics, two masochists, with Jack the biggest masochist of the pair. It was all too stupid, sick, and Dostoyevskian for her to trust. A psychiatrist had treated Michael at the hospital and he was now seeing a good therapist recommended by Carla. But Laurie knew through Carla the limits there. They could unpack the misunderstandings, examine the guilt and soften the self-hatred that had been hidden behind Michael's pride, air his emotions and teach him how to live with them. But there was something else there, or not there, that prevented her from feeling Michael was quite human. Jack, for all his faults, was very human. She feared she was losing Jack to something she was too selfish or sane to understand.

"Hi there."

Jack's voice startled her. She had not seen him come up behind her in the window. He stood beside her, looking as uncomfortable as he had when he arrived with Michael. She was the one he was embarrassed to be seen by tonight.

"Oh, just feeling thoughtful," she told him, snorted and added, "and I'm only on my second drink."

Behind them, everybody laughed at something Danny had said.

"See? It's not so awful or creepy," Jack whispered.

"No. But it's strange," she admitted. "I'm only on the outside looking in, but Michael worries me. You and Michael disturb me. I still think you're playing with fire."

Jack sighed, attempted a smile, and said, "I'm glad you're

on the outside looking in. Seriously. I need to know there's somebody out there I can trust. Who can throw me a line if I need it. Because it is strange, isn't it?"

She was pleased to hear him talk this way, relieved to be told her distance could be useful. "Maybe I've just turned into a little capitalist. But I don't feel comfortable with sacrifice. Maybe it's my feminist perspective. It's funny, but I'd feel better if I thought you were *using* each other sexually. You're telling the truth when you say there's nothing physical between you?"

"There isn't. Not yet."

"You want there to be?"

"Sometimes, yes. But it's not a high priority."

She wondered if there ever could be, if Jack could hold Michael's body without remembering how he lifted that body from the bathtub. Without having seen it, however, with only her own imagining of it to go by, the image sometimes felt intensely erotic to her.

"That's good to hear," she said. "That you can still consider it, I mean. Because I don't want to think you've renounced everything for Michael."

"No," said Jack, "I don't *want* to use him as my hair shirt," as if still afraid he did just that. "It's no picnic living with Michael. He loses his temper with me, but I've learned to lose my temper with him, nicely. It's too small an apartment for two people, which is good, because he has to get out and do things. He's going back to school, which I look forward to." Jack laughed lightly. "Sometimes he's like living with a bigger, more difficult version of Elisabeth Vogler, one who talks back. But beneath all the irritation, I don't feel bad about it, Laurie. I don't know why, but he's made my life simpler, even easier. I don't feel guilty any-more, which is a nice change."

Laurie was relieved he still doubted he was doing the right thing. A Jack who could be righteous about anything besides books and movies was more than she could bear. But there was a peaceful note to him that was new, an undertow of quiet that might be fatigue or resignation or contentment, she wasn't sure which.

Without noticing themselves doing it, they had gradu-ally turned their backs to the window so they could steal looks at Michael while they spoke, reminding themselves to keep their voices low.

He seemed very calm, healthy, and unexceptional out there, sitting on the sofa in a starburst of elbows and knees, brushing crumbs off his sweater, then leaning for-ward to listen to Ben, who was holding forth on his hopes and fears for an AIDS activist group currently in the news. The others apparently felt comfortable enough to talk about AIDS-related things in Michael's presence. Michael asked Ben where and when this group met.

"He *looks* okay," said Laurie. "Is it real or is it an act?"

"Both," Jack told her. "He's still confused and he gets depressed. Sometimes. He's ashamed of what he did. Sometimes. But he can live with it now. *We* live with it."

"Fess up, Puppy!" Danny was poking Ben in the stom-ach. "The real reason you're so hung up on ACT UP is because it's full of cute boys who won't give you the time of day. It's in their bylaws!" Danny told everyone. "'We will have no elected officials. We will be completely democratic. We will not sleep with Ben Slover.'"

And Michael laughed.

It was a loud, irrational, natural laugh, more for Danny's delivery than the joke, a laugh that caught Michael by surprise. Only when he recovered from it did he ask himself why he had laughed, and why he should feel so happy to be here.

He took another swallow of wine, but his pleasure was more than wine. This light, this shiny blond floor, these people who kept forgetting and remembering his presence. All of it pleased him, but in a different way than it had in that other life when Clarence first brought him here.

He felt Jack and Laurie conspiring at the window and knew they talked about him, but Michael didn't mind. He trusted Jack to defend him and Laurie to doubt gently. He didn't even mind that Jack was no longer beside him and he had to face the others alone. He was pleased he could hold his own with them. He had come to this dinner tonight expecting it to be a challenge, a trial, and he was pleased he could meet it, surprised and pleased his feeling of shame could also be a source of strength.

When he arrived tonight, when he came through the door with Jack, Michael sensed each of the couples drawing a little closer together, not literally but with brief glances and subtle adjustments of posture—as if Michael were the Spirit of Loneliness, the End of Love, even the Angel of Death. He had not felt bad about that. It gave him a feeling of power, and having power, Michael could be comfortable. He was embarrassed by what gave him that power, but it was another person who had done that, someone capable of emotions so black and intense Michael found it hard to believe he had been that person.

He liked to think he was separated from that person by the raised seams on his wrists. Whenever Michael was nervous or depressed, he absentmindedly stroked his wrists through his cuffs, following each scar to its end, reminding himself where he had been.

He would die. Everyone in this room would die. It was one thing to know that, and something else to feel it. Mortality made most of their failings seem minor, tender, and bearable.

Michael knew he would continue to feel shame, guilt, and irritation. He would continue to think guiltily he had become Jack's burden, on days he didn't irritably think Jack had become his. He would continue to humor Jack's clumsy concern for his shifting states of mind, humor him out of shame, duty, respect, and affection. They would probably go to bed with each other, which would spoil what peace they had, forcing Michael to choose between the cruelty of refusing to be Jack's lover and the cowardice of consenting. He would finish school and choose to do something with his life, which he would later regret.

And yet, Michael felt he could live with all that, just as he lived with Jack, just as he lived among the foolish, well-meaning men and women chattering around him, just as he lived with himself.

Immortal, he thought with a sudden grin that caused everyone to look at him, people would be unbearable.